RELEASED

IN SEARCH OF A KING

RELEASED

IN SEARCH OF A KING

SURRENDERED*Pen*

SurrenderedPen LLC
www.surrenderedpen.com

All SurrenderedPen Titles, Imprints, and Distributed Lines are available at special quantity discounts for bulk purchases for sales promotions, premiums, fund-raising, and educational or institutional use. Special book excerpts or customized printings can also be created to fit specific needs. For details, write the office of SurrenderedPen special sales manager at the address above or visit their website at www.surrenderedpen.com.

Orders by individuals, U.S. trade bookstores, and wholesalers please visit SurrenderedPen at www.surrenderedpen.com.

Publisher's Note: This novel is a work of fiction. Names, characters, places, and incidents are either products of the author's imagination or used factiously. All characters are fictional, and any similarity to people living or dead is purely coincidental.

SurrenderedPen and the SurrenderedPen logo are trademarks of SurrenderedPen LLC.

ISBN 978-0-9898301-2-6
Library of Congress Control Number: 2015905630

Printed in the United States of America

First trade paperback printing: April 2015

Scripture is taken from the Holy Bible, New International Version®, NIV® Copyright ©1973, 1978, 1984, 2011 by Biblica, Inc.® Used by permission. All rights reserved worldwide.

Cover designed by Sam Barton.
Book layout by Derik Gadson.

To My Husband
You gave my voice time to get out. May the unfailing way you encouraged
me, be the same way I encourage others.

To My God
The first step in healing was to give my brokenness to you.
Thank you.

Prologue

Are people ever really beautiful? Forget about eye of the beholder and all that crap that mothers tell their children so they'll feel better about themselves. Is there real beauty, and if it truly existed, would ugly things ever happen? A required philosophy class essay fueled these musings from a college student. The questions sparked as she watched light reflect off the magazine cover. It gleamed and shined, begging the eyes to take in the photo of a woman. A long, bare leg poured through a slit in a diamond-sequined silver dress. Light shimmered down the leg and into an open toe stiletto. The leg was flawless, free of dark spots and wrinkles, cellulite and stretch marks. This lady, a supposed representation of beauty, made the female student meditate about the truthfulness of beauty.

She imagined her own leg protruding through the slit of the dress, the height-challenged, thick limb hanging like a pork leg in a butcher shop. The web of veins on the inside of her right knee resembled an ugly, dark and violent kaleidoscope. The sight made her shudder. A small, black mole on the top of the knee attempted to give her hope. If she believed what children in her neighborhood said, then she thought a mole was a beauty mark, a sign of uniqueness and one of quality. Back then she was only eight, and many of them, like her brother, were five years older.

But at nineteen, Mimi Combs had sense and did not believe those neighborhood kids. At present, their wisdom had landed more than half of them with at least one more mouth to feed. She shuddered again, this time knowing the answer to the question. She was not beautiful. Those children were liars like the mothers. There was no beauty. And yes, ugly things happened all the time.

Her eyes shifted to the next magazine. She moved her fingers slowly back and forth in a swirly line across the front cover. The touch tickled her fingertips, and she let them rest near the title of an article.

"Not in my house. Not my child." The voice came from behind her, just over her left shoulder. Its tone was clear but a little shaky, breaking the unwritten protocol of personal privacy, even in a grocery store checkout line. Mimi pulled her fingers away from the title's bold, white letters. The tickle in her fingertips ceased.

The voice belonged to a short, wide woman. Everything on her was round, from her bright cheeks to her full breasts to her thighs that were tightly wrapped in bright red velour pants. A child, with a thick hand wrapped around an open chocolate bar, was riding the woman's hip.

When Mimi first entered the checkout line, the woman's head had been buried in her shopping cart. She was fishing items out of the cart and placing them on the sliding counter one at a time. Mimi had to bite the urge to grab a few of the twelve million TV dinners and stack them on the counter. At the time, the little girl wearing snug jeans and a tight blue and white striped pullover sweater sat in the cart's seat talking to the candy bar in her plump little hand.

"Open it," she said, but the command was for the candy bar rather than the mother.

The woman had so much in her cart and was moving so methodically, that Mimi thought she would be waiting a long while. The magazines, some with their glossy covers and screaming titles, presented, as they normally did, a good way to pass the time.

But this cover, the one with the title that made the woman's words intrude on her thoughts, almost made Mimi vomit. The title, *Man Found Guilty in Child Rape Case*, begged her to turn to page 27 for more of the story. Just like any wave of nausea she had when something reminded her of her own tragic life, the desire to throw up this morning's bowl of Kellogg's Corn Flakes quickly passed. The wide, thick woman's words took their place in her senses.

Mimi blinked once, then twice. The woman spoke again in a louder voice, the kind you use when you believe your audience may be just a little deaf.

"Not in my house. Not my child. No way. No man is going to touch my child that way." The woman pulled the small version of herself closer, and the little girl squealed while dark, brown spittle oozed out the corner of her mouth. The child took another bite of the candy bar.

Mimi shook her head slowly to convey some agreement with the statement. Then she turned back to her own cart. She could hear the woman sigh loudly, then say, "Shoot! I forgot to pick up bread." The cashier kindly asked an employee to bring a loaf of bread to the front. Mimi slipped into her own mental conversation.

Where had she heard those lines before? Was it a movie? A TV show? A book? The question tapped on her mind like JoJo did when they were younger, and he wanted to irritate his baby sister. He would poke her forehead with his index finger until she acknowledged his presence. The question presented itself in this annoying way, while she watched the woman place the child back in the cart, and then her groceries. A loaf of bread protruded from the top of one of the bags. The woman paid for her purchases and left while the question continued to plague Mimi.

"Paper or a plastic?" the giddy cashier asked Mimi. The question tapped as she walked back to her dorm carrying two plastic bags filled with milk, Ramen noodles in every flavor, bread, lunchmeat, peanut butter and jelly. All of this was the hallmark of great sustenance for a college student.

Halfway to her dorm, and walking in step with the rhythm of the question, she found it—the location of a memory buried beneath images of laughter, tears, anger, and fear. She found the place and the time where she had heard those words spoken before.

Mimi stopped in the middle of the sidewalk, the two plastic bags hanging on each side. She spoke to the wind and said, "Not in my house. Not my child."

She toyed with the memory, turning it around several times and replaying it. As Mimi tripped over other memories and paused to watch them unwind, she knew it had been only a minute or two. Still, she stood there like some talking statue. If anyone had been walking by, they would have thought she was a bit crazy, but the street was empty.

Then she saw him. He was not a memory of a time she had forgotten, floating by like scenes on a movie screen. He was real. And he was now and today, not a past she had been hiding. Wearing khakis, a tan turtleneck, and a Parka coat usually found on those battling Alaskan-like temperatures, he moved quickly toward her. His face was set with a confident smile, but his eyes betrayed him and yelled his uncertainty. His stride was long, and in seconds he stood in front of her, still wearing that smile and those conflicting eyes.

Once his smile widened, he parted his lips to speak, but Mimi blurted, "What are you doing here?"

Part 1

In the Beginning, There was a King

Chapter 1

Innocence

June 9, 1978

Dear Daddy

I luv you. I hav a gud time at the park. Thank you for takin me. I luv you so mush Daddy.

Luv

Mimi

"*Stink, stink, stink, stink, stink, stink, stink*," Mimi muttered the closest she could get to a curse word without getting in trouble with her mother. "S-T-E-N-K," she said again. In her mind, she began to spell the word she was really thinking. *S-H-I* . . . She stopped there, feeling someone could hear inside her head. Her mother would spank her for even spelling the word.

She hurled her brown crayon at her bedroom wall. It smacked against the drawing of Grandma Eunice at the beach in a red one-piece swimsuit, leaving a small dark spot in the yellow sun. *Ugh! The picture is messed up now.* She inspected the remaining pictures. Next to the drawing of Grandma was her brother JoJo, sitting on his bike in front of the apartment building. And next to this was her drawing of her mother Faye, sitting on the hood of their black Dodge

Charger, waving back at her. Lastly, was the drawing of her father, Joe. In this picture, he was sitting on the couch smiling at her with a glass of vodka in one hand. In his other hand, he held a piece of paper. This had been her hardest drawing yet. She had to draw a picture inside another picture. Her father was holding the picture she had drawn of her mother.

Each drawing was a bit better than the one before it. By the time she made the picture of her father, she was able to at least color inside the lines. And when she showed the picture to JoJo, he guessed right away it was their father instead of something strange like a monkey. In the beginning, all her pictures of people looked like monkeys to JoJo. Her brother, her biggest critic, insisted she was making everyone's arms too long.

But this latest drawing was her hardest project yet. She picked up another crayon; maybe drawing with her favorite orange crayon would help. Biting the inside of her lower lip, she struggled to draw the arms that were hugging the air. She wanted to put a picture of a hug at the end of Daddy's letter. Sometimes, when she saw people write letters on TV, the writer ended the letter with X's and O's, or with tiny red hearts or big red lips. She wanted to do something different. Under the word "luv," she was trying to add these hugging arms. Unfortunately, she discovered it was hard to draw them, even though it looked easy when she saw it in one of her father's newspapers. Two arms coming from the white background of the newspaper, circling each other to grab nothing but invisible air. It should have been easy, but it was not. Her second attempt looked like a snake biting a stick.

Arrph! The second crayon splat against the wall. A fatter dark spot decorated the white wall between the drawing of Daddy and the drawing of Mommy. Mimi picked up the letter. It was taking too long to finish because of the problems.

The first problem happened on Saturday. She wanted to add the word "expectation" to the letter, but she was not sure how to spell it. Whenever she tried to say the word, it came out as "echspeckshun." She knew what it meant. Mommy used the word whenever she wanted JoJo and Mimi to be good when the family went somewhere. Her mother would say, "I have an expectation that you both won't need a whack on your behind." Then she would add, "Don't disappoint me." Mimi surmised when someone met your expectation it made you happy. Mommy was always in a good mood if they behaved well during a family outing. She wanted her father to know her expectation was to go the zoo again, and this would make her happy.

To make sure she spelled the word right, Mimi marched into the kitchen where her mother was writing down a grocery list for Sunday dinner.

"Mommy, spell echspeckshun."

"What?" said her mother, eyes still focused on the list.

"Echspeckshun. Echspeckshun. I wanna put it in my letter to Daddy."

Five minutes later, her mother rolled her eyes and put a hand in the air like a crossing guard halting traffic, "You're done," she announced. "That letter has all it needs. I'm sure your daddy will love it."

With her head down and lips poked out, Mimi walked back to her bedroom. She did not have the precious word added to the letter. At just six years old, she had trouble with some of the letters of the alphabet. Sometimes when she heard the letters, she did not write them down correctly. But Mommy didn't have patience for every request to repeat a letter or to slow down.

The second problem came on Sunday. JoJo bumped into her while she lay on the rug pondering the spelling of the word "expectation" and whether it was worth it to ask her mother for help again. A cup of red fruit juice, which she promised not to spill on the hardwood floor, sloshed onto the letter, helping her keep the promise but ruining the letter at the same time.

"JoJo!" she screamed.

"Sorry!" he screamed back.

"You did that on purpose. You pee-pee head."

"I said I was sorry. Why you laying in the middle of the floor anyway, dummy?"

Her mother's voice asking what they were shouting about stopped her from flying into her brother's stomach with both her fists. Because of her stupid brother, she had to re-write the letter.

Today was Monday, and the new problem was drawing the hugging arms. Looking over the remaining crayons, she selected the blue one and thought about the day as she fought again with the picture. It was going to be an exciting day. She would be visiting a museum with her class. Mrs. Hunter, her teacher, said this museum had special science stuff that students could touch, and they could also have fun there. Mimi had never been to a museum where she could touch the stuff and have fun at the same time.

She smiled and held up the paper with her third attempt at the hugging arms. Her smile faded quickly. The arms looked like the letter "O." Where had she gone wrong?

Setting the drawing and the crayons aside, she sat up in bed and stretched. Then she reached for Monica and Matt, the Barbie and Ken dolls her mother had bought her last Christmas. The minute she unwrapped the gift and saw them behind the plastic window of their boxes, she renamed them. They looked more like a Monica and a Matt to her. And she was doing well with keeping them, too. They had all their limbs, and Monica's hair was still straight and long, although she was itching to give Monica bangs like her own, just so she could see how the doll would look with them. But her mother had said the doll's hair would not grow back if Mimi cut it. *Stink!*

"Good morning, Monica and Matt." She kissed each doll and put them back on the table next to her bed. Then, she waved to the white, furry, stuffed cat that sat at the foot of her bed. She always slept in one place, so she never knocked him off.

"Good morning, Mr. Puff Tail." He was a gift from Daddy with a warning that this was the closest she was going to get to a real cat. When she heard this, she cried and left Mr. Puff Tail sitting on the living room floor for the rest of the day. But he looked lonely, and she actually thought she heard him meow. She later learned he had a switch on the outside of one paw. When turned to the "on" position, it made him meow and purr.

Lastly, she looked up to the ceiling and said, "Good morning, God," like Grandma taught her to do. As soon as Mimi could speak, Grandma started teaching her to say "God." While Mommy was coaxing her to say "Mama," and Daddy was pushing her to say "Dada," and even JoJo, who was five years older, was making silly faces and chanting, "Say JoJo. Say JoJo," Grandma insisted on saying, "Remember, God loves you. Can you say 'God' for Grandma, Mimi? Try it, sweetie. Say 'God.'"

In the end, her first words were "Mama" and "God."

When Daddy heard her first words he said, "What? I can't get any kind of support. Not even from my own daughter."

As she grew older, her grandmother taught her that it was good to say good morning to God because it let him know you were grateful for waking up.

Mimi was ready to start her day now. Her mother had already laid out her museum outfit. Of course, this was done after careful consideration from Mimi. She would be wearing her pink khaki skirt and her button up shirt with the pink polka dots all over it. She loved this shirt because the sleeves were short and puffy and came down to her elbows. The sleeves reminded Mimi of the dresses the princesses wore in the storybooks. She felt like a princess whenever she wore the shirt. Her outfit included pink socks whose tops folded over to show frilly white lace on the edges. Mommy even said she could wear her black patent leather shoes instead of her stupid old sandals.

She jumped from bed and began putting on her outfit. Pink was not her favorite color. Orange was. But this outfit was so pretty that she wore it every time she got a chance to do so.

Her door flew open. Mommy rushed in and the smell of Ivory soap mingled with flowers filled the room. Her mother was already dressed for her job as a secretary. She wore a pale green pantsuit with a vine of pink roses around the hem of the jacket. It was one of her mother's favorite outfits. In her hand she held a white washcloth.

"I knew it, Mimi. I knew you'd be in here getting dressed. Did you forget something, young lady?"

Mimi had the shirt on, but the buttons were still undone. "Sorry, Mommy."

"It's okay. I know you're excited, sweetie, but you don't just want to look good. You want to smell good, too. I got you a new washcloth. Wash up first. Brush your teeth. And Daddy will make sure your outfit looks all right and that your hair is done."

Mimi twisted her face, eyebrows up, nose twitching, lips poked out. "Why? Daddy can't do my hair. He doesn't know how. Boys don't know how to do hair," she said.

"I showed him how you like your hair," her mother said. "I just have to go in early today, sweetie. I'm so sorry. How about if I ask Miss Merle to double-check Daddy's work? Would that be okay?"

She slowly took off the shirt and began considering the facts. Miss Merle, the neighbor, was old, but she was a girl. She could fix anything a boy like Daddy messed up.

"Okay," she said.

"Great." Her mother dropped the washcloth on the bed and hugged her. "Have a good time at the museum, my Mimi-girl."

Mommy liked to add extra little words like "girl," "bean," and "bear" at the end of Mimi's name, especially when she could not do something the way Mimi wanted her to do it. She kissed Mimi's forehead and ran out the bedroom door shouting orders to Daddy and JoJo. Her mother did not like being late, and since she needed to catch the train from their home in North Philadelphia to downtown Center City, she spent her mornings moving around like the Tasmanian Devil in one of those Bugs Bunny cartoons.

Removing her nightgown and underwear, Mimi left a trail of clothes on her bedroom floor as she headed to the bathroom. She liked playing with water. Bathtub water. Shower water. Pool water. Fire hydrant water. She turned on the faucet to fill the sink with water, and her smile broadened. The sink was not an exception. No matter where the water was, she could pretend all sorts of water stories. The princess who was rescued from the big ugly shark by the merman. The famous swimmer who leaped from the cliff into the deep, dark water. She popped up from the water unharmed and won a gold medal. Sometimes, she pretended she was on the beach with her friends, Kayla and Bizzy, and they were talking about school and their other friends and going to the museum. Then stupid Bobby Benson would come over to talk to them. He was so stupid. Then Gregory Michaels would come over to talk to them, and they would let him sit on the beach with them because he was really nice.

Daddy knocked on the door. "Mimi, you have to hurry up. You don't want to be late to school today."

"Okay," she shouted back.

"Do you need anything?"

"No, Daddy. I'm coming out now."

She ended her "make believe" time by running into the water to swim with Kayla, Bizzy, and Gregory while sticking out her tongue at Bobby Benson. She quickly filled her wet washcloth with soap to begin washing up. As she was wiping soap from her stomach, she turned toward the bathroom door and jumped.

"Daddy, you scared me," she said.

"You gotta move faster, Nugget." Daddy wasn't into adding extra words to her name. He just liked calling her "Nugget" every now and then. When she asked why, he just shrugged and said, "'Cause you're a little, itty bitty person."

She liked when he called her Nugget. He was the only one who called her that, and it made her feel special. Nobody else in the world was called Nugget.

Her father handed her the towel, but he did not leave the bathroom. He watched her dry her body. He watched as she lathered soap on her face, and then splashed water to rinse it away. She dried her face with the towel and dropped it on the floor.

"Mommy said you going to do my hair today. Do you know what you doing, Daddy?"

"I sure do."

"Maybe you should go get the hair stuff so we can work on it after I get dressed."

"Okay," he said. But still he didn't move. He kept staring at her.

What was he staring at? Was it her belly button? She looked down at her stomach and touched her belly button.

"Did I forget to clean something, Daddy?"

"No, Nugget." He scrambled to grab the towel from the floor, and he quickly left the bathroom.

Chapter 2
A Typical Family?

JoJo ran around the bases. His feet barely touched the mats. First, second, third. He was headed home, long legs pumping, cleats kicking up dirt. His cap flew off his head, and his neatly trimmed hair glistened with sweat. A knowing grin was glued to his face. He kept running.

"Go, JoJo. Go!" Daddy cheered with the rest of the people in the stands. He jumped up and down and waved his hands like a crazy man as JoJo slid into home base—a move Mimi felt was truly unnecessary. The catcher didn't have the ball. It disappeared into a patch of tall weeds at the back end of the field. Two kids had gone into the patch to look for it while some woman, probably the mother of one or both of them, hollered about the possibility of poison ivy.

Sometimes JoJo just liked to slide. He said all the pros did it. Yet, on the rare times when Mimi watched a game with her big brother, she did not see many people sliding into home. It also looked as if it might hurt. One time she noticed a large purple welt on JoJo's thigh and winced. "Ouch!" she said out loud.

"It comes with the game," he said, using his fake announcer's voice, which was actually good.

At twelve years of age, baseball had become JoJo's major goal in life. Mimi couldn't figure out when this happened. In her mind, JoJo went to sleep one night talking about the adventures of his G.I. Joe action figure doll and woke up the next morning with his baseball mitt attached to his hand and rendering unrequested tales about the "greats" like Reggie Jackson and Lou Brock. Dinner conversations were sometimes consumed with talk of baseball plays and baseball games. She was often fighting and losing the right to watch her favorite television show when certain games were on.

JoJo was cocky, too. He spent what she estimated to be hours in front of the mirror in his bedroom with his shirt off and his arms flexed to reveal small peaks for muscles. He puffed out his chest and raved about being strong and how such strength would help hit baseballs into outer space. Modeling one running pose after another, he reported their effectiveness in propelling him around the baseball diamond. One morning he found a hair in his armpit and spent the rest of the day spouting about becoming a man who would be the greatest baseball player in the world.

No matter how hard she held her hands over her ears, JoJo's self-appraisals made their way in. Most often this was because he wrestled her to the ground and shouted such information into her ears, especially when he saw she did not want to hear it. If he did not wrestle her down, he would tap on her forehead with his pointy index finger until she had to let go of her ears to cover her forehead. The moment that happened, he began stating a list of qualities about his baseball skills. Her annoying brother had become even more annoying. She didn't think it was possible, but he had done it.

Her thoughts were interrupted by her father's shouts. "That's my boy!" He pounded his chest with each word in the sentence. "Go, JoJo. Go!"

Tiny drops of sweat ran down the sides of Daddy's slender, square face and shined against his chestnut-colored skin. Their journey slowed at his high cheekbones, but continued at a fast pace once they cleared the area. Her father wiped sweat from his heavily lashed eyes with both hands. He opened his big, round hazel-colored eyes with their slight downward slant, glanced at her and winked. Sweat collected on the bridge of his long, broad nose, just above his flesh-colored full lips and in the hair stubble on his chin. He wiped these areas with his hands and then wiped his hands on his pants.

Joe Combs was tall and well built, and when he stood he blocked the view of about two to three rows of baseball families in the bleachers. Her mother tapped his leg and pointed at the bleacher seat. He folded himself back onto the bench while her mother glared at him.

JoJo had been playing baseball for two years. Mimi had to break down and admit he was good, but her father treated every game as if it was the first time he had ever seen JoJo play. His shouts could be heard a block away. He stomped his feet so hard the metal bleacher rumbled.

When JoJo first started playing baseball and her father acted this way, her mother would say, "Sit down, Joe. You're embarrassing him." But he ignored the command. Soon, she stopped trying to get him to sit down and chose to glare at him or turn her head and pretend she was not with him, which was hard to do since he made them all wear matching T-shirts to nearly every game. The shirts carried JoJo's name, or a favorite baseball team of his on their fronts.

Mimi's butt hurt from sitting on the hard bleacher. She twisted her body so that she could sit on one cheek, but it did not help. She had to keep shifting between butt cheeks every minute and that made her legs hurt. She was dying to ask the question that always made Mommy smile while it made Daddy frown.

To no one in particular, she asked, "What inning is it anyway?" From watching JoJo's games, she learned one important piece of information about baseball. The last inning was the best. It meant her misery was almost over.

"I think it's almost the last." Her mother smiled at her. Her father quickly flashed a frown, and then he was back to rooting for his son.

She shifted to the other butt cheek and thought about what they would do afterward. They always went to a fast food place after one of JoJo's games. It did not matter which one, as long as she could get a cheeseburger. Angels must have created cheeseburgers because they tasted so good. Nothing else explained it. She licked her lips and thought she actually smelled a cheeseburger.

"Whoa!" the people in the stands shouted in unison just then and stood. When they sat down, she saw JoJo's team moving out of their wooden dugout and onto the field. She had missed something. She also realized it was not the last inning.

"Do you believe that?" Joe asked, talking more to the crowd than to Mimi or Faye.

As the game droned on, Mimi began thinking about what clothes to put on Monica and Matt for next week's doll meeting with Kayla and Bizzy. Once a month, they brought their favorite dolls to school to meet each other.

Bizzy had Barbie and Ken dolls just like Mimi. She opted to leave their names the same and pretend they were rich white people who travelled all over the world. She actually knew about the places the dolls visited because her dad had to travel sometimes for his job. Every now and then he would bring a doll outfit back for Bizzy's Barbie and Ken. Once, he even went to China, but neither Bizzy, Mimi, nor

Kayla knew where China was. Mrs. Hunter showed it to them on the big globe in their classroom. It looked all bumpy and green with red lines going through it. It was an ugly looking place to Mimi.

Kayla also had dolls, but her family was more into their ethnic culture than Mimi's family. Kayla's father had marched with Dr. King, which she knew must be important because her own parents talked about a Dr. King. She didn't know what it meant to march with him, but she knew it was the reason every doll in Kayla's house had a shade of dark skin. Some of them were too old to be touched, according to Kayla's father. The dolls they could touch were called Friends of Barbie, whose original names were Christie and Brad. But Kayla's father helped her choose new names, which were Maalik and Zahabu. Kayla told Bizzy and Mimi that Zahabu meant "golden child," which was interesting since the doll's skin was not at all golden. There was a boy in their classroom named Maalik. This made it easy to remember Kayla's boy doll, but they kept confusing the girl's name, and eventually called her "Z" whenever Kayla brought her to school.

Behind Mimi, two ladies whispered to each other, and her attention moved to them. Her ears perked as she strained to hear what they were saying. She put both butt cheeks on the bleacher seat and leaned back just a little. She was small, and when you were her size, adults, other than your parents, sometimes forgot you were in the room with them. You could sit right next to them at a table, and they would have an adult conversation with plenty of details for about a full five minutes before they noticed you and quickly changed the subject. Adult conversations were how Mimi learned about people's secret lives, such as how the youngest child of the neighbor upstairs may have a different daddy from the rest of the kids, and that when Miss Merle died last year, they found a lot of stuff in her apartment that she had gotten without using money.

After hearing an adult conversation, she would ask Mommy about some specific detail. Her mother's face would scrunch up like she had just eaten something sour, and she would say, "Where did you hear that?" Then she would remind Mimi about her expectations when listening to adult conversations. Somehow Mimi forgot those expectations when it came time to hear another adult conversation.

The ladies behind her had their heads close together. She did the same thing with Kayla and Bizzy when they did not want anyone to know what they were talking about. But the ladies spoke louder than a whisper because occasionally something would happen in the game, and people would wildly cheer.

"It's a darn shame," said the first lady. Her hairstyle was big, and it made her face small, too small for her head.

"I know. I know," said the second. "My heart goes out to that mother." She had painted her face a dull color that did not match her gold eye shadow, red lips, or the hand she used to pat her cheeks. The color of her hand was darker than her face.

"Well, I don't get how she didn't know. You'd think if a thing like that was happening in your own house you'd know, ya know?" said Big Hair Lady. "And you know what? A mother always knows."

"Yes, but sometimes they just don't. Like I was watching one of those television movies about a family that had the same problem. The mother didn't know because there were no signs. The child never said a thing until they asked her."

"There *are* signs," growled Big Hair Lady. "You just have to look for them. Kids say things without opening their mouths."

"I know," said Dull Painted Lady, touching her cheek with her mismatched hand, "but I think sometimes you just can't tell because everything looks okay."

"You gotta be kidding me. If she watched her kids, knew her kids, she would have known." Big Hair Lady shook a finger at Dull Painted Lady.

"Well—" Dull Painted Lady's eyes fluttered, reminding Mimi of traffic lights that warned drivers to slow down in school zones.

"Dirty, disgusting dog!" Big Hair Lady said. "They should put him *under* the jail. How old was the kid anyway?"

"I think six."

"*Pervert!* Sick *pervert.* What kind of man thinks it's okay to touch a kid? And his own at that." Big Hair Lady snarled and her eyes bulged.

"I know . . . Takes a sick and crazy person." Dull Painted Lady touched her cheek again and left the small imprint of her fingers there.

"And I'll tell you what. Man touch my child, I would know. And when I'm done with him, his next of kin won't be able to identify the body."

"I know. I guess it's something you would know."

"Sure would," said Big Hair Lady, clapping her hands together. "Something like that going on . . ." She stabbed the air and snapped her head with every word in her next sentences. "Not in my house. Not my child."

Mimi's butt was aching. She glanced at Mommy who was staring back at her. Her mother leaned toward Mimi and whispered, "Mimi-bean, it's not nice to eavesdrop on other people's conversation."

For once Mimi remembered to whisper back like Mommy taught her. She leaned toward Mommy's ear and cupped it with her hands. "What's eavesdropping?" she asked.

Mommy sat back. She could be real pretty sometimes, and this was one of those times. Her hair was pulled into a ponytail that hung down her back. She had used oil to smooth the hair at her temples. It looked curly, like baby's hair. Her light brown eyes glowed against her brown skin that reminded Mimi of caramel candy. She had mascara on her eyelashes but a clear gloss on her lips. Quarter-sized hoop earrings hung from each ear, making her look sophisticated.

"You know what eavesdropping is. We've talked about it before."

She did know, but in that moment she had forgotten. Mommy's serious eyes bearing down on her like a monster in a story brought the definition to her mind. Mimi looked down at her hands which rested in her lap. She hated disappointing her parents, especially her daddy. Her mommy, yes, she hated it then, too, but with Daddy, she felt terrible.

"It means when you listen to someone else's conversation when they are not talking to you," Mimi said.

"That's right." Mommy's serious eyes bore into her. "And my expectation is that you will remember that." As some sort of last minute thought, she patted Mimi's hand.

Mimi looked back at the game and shifted her buttocks again. "What inning is it?" she asked, but neither her mother nor her father answered. Mommy was looking back at the ladies. Then she glanced at Daddy. For some reason he was no longer shouting for JoJo. He sat up straight with his lips pressed tightly together. He looked a bit sad and she wondered if he had been eavesdropping too. Had he heard Mommy and was now feeling bad about disappointing Mommy? Mommy shifted her gaze to Mimi, and noticed Mimi was watching her. Suddenly her mother shook her head quickly as if saying no to something and waved her hand in the air as if swatting a fly.

Chapter 3
Those Sad Clown Lips

June 15, 1980

Dear Daddy,

I love you. You are the best Daddy in the whole wide world. You are the king of Daddys. Thank you for evrything you do for us. Like wen you got to work and wen you buy us cheese burgers at McDonalds. You are a good faver. I love you. Happy favers day,

Love,

Mimi

P.S. Yur gif is in the box.

Writing letters, yes! It was a good way to gather all the words in her head into one place. When those words did not want to come out of her mouth, or if they sounded stupid when they did, she picked up paper and pencil and wrote a letter. When she wrote letters, she got the words just right. And if she made a mistake, all she had to do was get another piece of paper and write the letter again, only without the part she messed up.

Mimi wrote letters to just about everybody she knew. She wrote letters to her mother, who was too busy to read them. Mommy would fold the letter and stuff it into a purse or a pocket with a promise to read it later. She wrote letters to JoJo, which usually said something about him not being a very good big brother. In one year, he had grown two inches-taller, and his head was full of big ideas about himself. Mimi wrote letters to her grandmother, who treated each one like it was an award from a contest. Grandma Eunice kept each letter in a bright yellow box with Mimi's name written on the sides. Once in a while, Mimi wrote a letter to her grandfather. Years ago, he had gone to sleep one night and did not wake up the next morning. Grandma had said that Grandpa was in heaven, so Mimi wrote "HEVEN" in big letters on the front of the envelopes and gave them to her mother to mail.

She wrote letters to Bizzy and Kayla because she could only talk to them during recess. They had been put in separate classes for third grade, so recess was the only time she saw them. She wrote letters to Monica and Matt, her Barbie and Ken dolls, and even Mr. Puff Tail, her furry, white stuffed cat. After all those letters, the only fair thing to do was write letters to Barbie, Ken, Maalik, and Z (Kayla and Bizzy's dolls). To keep all those letters safe, she put them into a folder her mother had given her.

Now that she was in third grade, she still liked the dolls, but she was more interested in a singing group called the Jackson Five. Their cute lead singer was singing by himself in what people called a solo career. She was in love with his smile and even considered writing him a letter. Sometimes, he came on TV, and you could buy a T-shirt with his name and face on it. She begged her father for one. He bought one for everyone in the family and made them wear the shirts to one of JoJo's baseball games. That was exciting and embarrassing at the same time.

She also wrote letters to God and thanked him for her family and her belongings. And she asked him to watch over her grandmother because she had a funny feeling Grandma was going to go to sleep one day and not wake up just like Grandpa had done.

But the letters she wrote to Daddy were the most special. She wanted him to know how much she loved him, so she wrote letters to tell him. His eyes would fill with water when he read her letters. Then he would hug her and give her a big kiss on the cheek and say, "I love you too, Nugget."

One day she wrote him a very special letter. It was almost a whole page long. She printed the words carefully and had seven full sentences on the page. She counted each one. Her teacher would have been proud of her.

She wrote the letter just after her parents had a terrible argument. Lately, they had been arguing more and more. Like JoJo, Mimi had also grown in the last year and was no longer small enough to hide and eavesdrop on adult conversations. But hiding wasn't necessary. The arguments were loud; her parents were mean and nasty toward each other.

Their last one was about money. While she was leaving the kitchen, as she had been ordered to, she heard Mommy say, "Can't you just ask for more money? You've been there long enough."

"It don't work like that, Faye. Hon, I don't have the seniority."

"It's a supervisor job. You could run the place yourself. You don't need seniority. You need experience and intelligence. You have both, but you don't want to do any better. You—Mimi, get your butt in that room before I put it in there for you."

Mimi raced to her room, but she could still hear parts of the argument.

"I don't get this. Why don't you want to take care of your family?" Mimi heard the refrigerator door open and slam shut. "Be a damn man and take care of your family."

"Faye, I'm trying. You don't understand."

"Understand what? What don't I understand? Tell me."

"Well, sometimes . . . I get so sad. I remember this stuff I guess . . . Stuff I don't want to remember. And . . . things are changing ... And I . . . I don't know . . . you know what I'm saying?"

Mimi heard a pot slam on the stove. "Joe, I have no idea what you're talking about. But here's what I do know. The Joe Combs I married made a promise to me. The Joe Combs I'm looking at ain't that promise."

It was quiet. No more slamming of things. Just quiet. A few minutes later, she heard her father's footsteps as he walked down the hallway to the bedroom and closed the door. She decided then and there to write him a letter.

Usually, after a fight with her mother, he looked like he had lost. Mommy would come into Mimi's room and say something cheery about her dolls, her bed, or school, but Daddy would sit in the living room and look at the TV with his eyes partly closed and his lips turned down like a sad clown.

Chapter 4
A Child's Love, A King's Choice

July 10, 1980

Dear Daddy,

I wish you wasn't so sad. Sum times people fite. I fite with Kayla and Bizzy a lot. But we still love each other. I know Mommy loves you. She don't want you to be sad. So plese smile for Mommy and me and JoJo.

I love you,

Mimi

Shopping with JoJo was a nightmare. He spent hours looking at sneakers and somehow still picked ones that were just like the white pair of Keds he had on his feet already. After the last shopping trip, Mimi came home with tears in her eyes. Her mother wore a scowl, and JoJo, carrying a bag that contained a white pair of Keds sneakers, grinned from ear to ear. With the memory of the trip fresh in Mimi's mind, she decided to stay home with Daddy while JoJo and her mother went shopping this time.

Her father was in the living room studying the TV with his eyes half-closed and those sad clown lips. His right arm dangled over the arm of the chair. In his right hand, he loosely held a can of beer, which slowly dripped tiny beads of water onto the floor. The fingers of his left hand drummed against the other arm of the chair to a tune only he could hear.

To a stranger, her father appeared unapproachable, but she marched up to him, surveyed the slits in his eyes and the beer can for a few seconds, and then moved past his extended arm to his side.

"Daddy," she said.

"Yeah, Nugget." He did not look at her.

"Read this." She thrust the letter in his face. It brushed his nose, and he jerked his head back a little. He took it from her and read the words. She thought he was a slow reader because he kept looking at the paper, but he did not speak.

"Daddy, did you read it?" she finally asked, impatience lacing her voice.

He looked at her. A tear rolled down his cheek. She had never seen him cry.

"Daddy, are you okay?" She hated to see anyone cry. It always brought tears to her own eyes. She could feel the sting of hot liquid at their corners.

"I'm fine, Nugget. You just made Daddy so happy he has to cry. I know if no one else loves me, you do." He reached for her arm as she shook her head in agreement with his words. "You love your daddy very much, don't you?" He pulled her onto his lap and pressed his face against hers.

"I do, Daddy. I love you so much. Didn't you read that in the letter?" It was obvious to her that she did love him, and for a moment she wondered about the quality of her letter. It must not have been as good as she believed. He should have known she loved him just by reading the letter.

Her father ignored her question and asked his own. "You love me so much, don't you, Nugget? And you're proud of me, aren't you, Nugget?" He was crying harder. She could feel several tears roll into her eyelash as he pressed her face closer to his.

"Daddy," she said, pulling her face away from his, but he continued to squeeze her.

"I love you, too, Nugget."

Mimi's body tightened. Every muscle was playing its own game of Freeze Tag, but there was no one waiting to tap her on the back if she decided to unfreeze her body. Her father's hand was no longer wrapped around her waist. It rested on her private part. He moved his fingers between her legs like he was gripping a ball. He snuggled his face into her hair and took a deep breath.

"Thanks, Nugget. Thanks a lot." Then he let her go. Her muscles began to move again. She wanted to ask him about what just happened. *But what did happen?* She didn't know. She didn't understand it. Leaving the letter with him, she walked slowly back to her bedroom, stopping only once to look back.

Chapter 5
Something's Wrong

October 3, 1980

Dear Grandma,

Sumthing is rong. I'm not suposed to tell you, so plese don't tell nobody else. Plese promiss me you won't tell. Daddy and Mommy fite a lot. They screm at each other and they knock stuff over and brek things. You should see the mirra in the bed room. I'm scared. I just want them to stop. Can you make them stop? I try to pray like you sed when sumthing bother me. But they fite. Please help, Grandma.

We can talk about them wen I see you this week end.

Love,

Mimi

"Just dropping them off, Eunice. Faye will pick 'em up on Sunday."

"I wish you wouldn't call me that," she said, turning toward her grandchildren. "How are my grandbabies today?"

Mimi watched as her father pulled their suitcase from the trunk of his car, which appeared to double as his personal trash can. A couple of empty beer bottles lay next to a full six pack. The work shirts he wore for his factory job as a machine operator were balled up and thrown near the back.

Empty wrappers from McDonald's and Blimpie's were crumpled and tossed everywhere. Her grandmother also noticed the trunk and slowly shook her head as she grabbed the handle of their suitcase.

"I'm not a baby," JoJo said, crossing him arms.

To Mimi he looked just like a baby about to carry out a tantrum. Her brother was getting grouchier and grouchier the older he got. Yet, she watched as he wrapped both arms around his grandmother's waist and gave her a tight squeeze. He was such a confusing boy.

"That's my grandbaby," Grandma said, squeezing him back just as tightly.

Mimi couldn't take it. She needed to get some of this good loving too. "Hi Grandma! Hi Grandma!" She jumped up and down with her arms outstretched toward her grandmother.

"And that's my other grandbaby." She released JoJo and scooped up Mimi with her free arm, while still holding on to the suitcase with the other hand.

"That's your name, Eunice. That's why I call you that," said her father. Mimi had forgotten he was standing there.

Her grandmother kissed the top of Mimi's head. "Grandbabies, I got the best weekend planned for us." She ignored their father, who glared at her and slammed the trunk with such force that the car shook a little. Her grandmother looked up at him and spoke slowly.

"It may be my name, but you don't have to use it. There is something else you can call me. And you know it's Mom. I am your mother, you know."

"Yep. I know. And you know you really don't deserve to be called that," said their father.

"Let the past go, Joe,"

"I ain't finding it so easy to forget. You want me to forget, Eunice. Like you, huh?" He moved one step closer to their grandmother.

"Dad?" said JoJo.

"Daddy?" added Mimi, squinting at him. There was enough arguing at home for her to recognize the beginning of one.

Their father paused. He seemed to consider what to say next. Then he went over to JoJo and shook his hand. "Be a good man, son." He picked Mimi up and buried his mouth in her neck. He blew hard, and she burst into laughter.

"That's nasty, Daddy," she said, laughing, her entire body relaxing into the moment.

"Have a good time, Nugget." He put her back on the ground and kissed her forehead.

As he got into the car, Mimi ran to the open window of the passenger side. "Daddy, two things," she said as she stuck two fingers up. "I'm going to miss you sooooo much. And you didn't say good-bye to Grandma."

Her father yelled, "Good-bye, Eunice." In a gentler voice, he said, "I'm going to miss you soooooo much, too. Step back, Nugget."

As he pulled away, her grandmother came up behind. While Mimi waved an excited good-bye to him, Grandma said, "Lord, you know I'm trying."

"Trying what, Grandma?" Mimi asked.

"Nothing for you, baby. I'm talking to God." She turned toward the house and announced, "Now, let's get the weekend started."

As they started up the walkway, Mimi surveyed the house. It was beautiful. Their grandfather had worked on it until the day he died. The garden boxes he built for every window on the front of the house still sported their bright pink color. The front door still had a darker shade of pink paint on the bottom where JoJo had accidentally thrown his baseball while practicing a curve pitch. Unlike the washed away red bricks of their apartment building, the planks of the house, occasionally covered with dots of green algae, still possessed the bright whiteness Mimi enjoyed,.

Her grandmother's house was in Chester, Pennsylvania, and what Mimi loved best about it was that it was not attached to the neighbors' houses. All around the house there was enough space to make ten circles, one inside the other. She had tried it one day, running around the house in a circle and each time making the circle wider. It had taken her up until ten times before she touched the neighbor's fence on the left of the house and the bushes of the neighbor on the right.

As they entered the house, she saw three wicker baskets waiting by the door.

"Grandma," she said, "are we picking apples tomorrow?" She could not contain her joy, hopping from one foot to the other.

"Yep, we are."

JoJo groaned. "Didn't we just pick stupid apples at Linvilla?" he asked.

Mimi stopped hopping, balled her fists, and glowered at her big brother, daring him to say another word. She did not want him ruining her good time. She liked picking apples at the nearby orchid.

"That was a year ago." Her grandmother smiled and rubbed the top of JoJo's head.

Mimi beamed as she studied her grandmother. In her eight-year-old eyes, her grandmother was a perfect person because she was not normal. Normal grandmothers moved slowly, could barely see or hear, and spit a little when they spoke. Not Grandma. Her grandmother moved quickly. Sometimes, when she skated with them, she beat them back to the starting point. Her grandmother could hear and see clearly and often spoke about having eyes in the back of her head, which reassured JoJo and Mimi that she saw everything they did, both good and bad. And her grandmother did not spit when she spoke. Mimi knew this because sometimes she watched her grandmother's lips carefully. She never saw spit fly from them.

Her grandmother was as tall as her father, with a hint of muscular tone in her thin arms and legs. Her pale face possessed hard and soft features that blended together. Grandma's square chin combined with full lips that shifted shape from circle to triangle as she talked. Mimi liked to watch her lips move and guess what shape they were making. Her long, pointy nose combined with the warmness of her heavily lashed light-brown eyes that slanted slightly. Mimi longed for those eyelashes because her own were short stubs. Soft tendrils of salt and pepper curls fell onto Grandma's high forehead in six or seven places, giving her an elegant look. No, her grandmother was not normal at all in her eyes.

JoJo gave Mimi one of his fake smiles, and then gave his grandmother a real one. "Okay, Grandma. Anything you say."

"Afterwards, we can watch a baseball game on TV. Aren't the Phillies playing tonight?" Grandma Eunice asked.

JoJo perked, straightening his slouching shoulders and put on his baseball cap. Just like that, his grandmother had made him happy. She had a way of doing that.

Grandma removed the cap from his head and said, "Not in the house, baby." And she kissed him again on his head. She turned toward Mimi, who was on to another topic, now that JoJo had been dealt with.

"Grandma," she began, "will we get a chance to talk this weekend?" JoJo was already heading upstairs, but Mimi winked at her grandmother anyway.

"Sure will." Her grandmother winked back.

That evening, Mimi handed the letter to her grandmother. JoJo had gone to his bedroom. She suspected he had the radio turned to the loudest setting that allowed him to block their voices out, but not cause his grandmother to shout a "turn that thing down" warning up the stairwell.

Grandma sat at the spotless kitchen table. Mimi wondered if her grandmother ate food when she and JoJo were not visiting. The kitchen always looked too clean to eat in. It was not like their kitchen at home, which always had a fresh set of dirty dishes in the sink.

Mimi had been anxious all week. She wanted to give Grandma this letter so badly. She once thought of calling her and telling her to come get the letter, but that didn't seem fair since Grandma lived a half hour drive away.

As Grandma read the letter, Mimi studied her face. At that moment, everything looked wrinkled on her "not normal" grandmother. From the corners of her eyes to the corners of her lips. Even the corners of her nose had wrinkles crawling from it in a small spider-like pattern. Her large, mahogany-rimmed glasses slipped down her nose a bit. She took them off and rubbed her eyes. A long, wavy, white and black lock of hair fell from the top of her head and landed on her hand. She pushed it back in place behind her ear.

"Grandma, what should we do?" Mimi asked.

"We're going to pray."

Without asking, Grandma pulled her to the floor so that they were both on their knees praying. Mimi kept one eye open and on her grandmother. Tears and sweat mixed together on her grandmother's face. She prayed for a long time, telling God everything on her mind. There were things Mimi was sure she should not know about her grandmother. Grandma was asking God for forgiveness as if she had done something wrong. She was asking him to show her how to help Mimi's parents. When she was done and had said "Amen," Mimi stood up. She also said "Amen" and began rubbing her knees.

"Your floor is hard, Grandma," she said, still rubbing her knees. When her grandmother did not answer, Mimi looked at her.

"Grandma, I thought prayer was supposed to make you feel better."

"Yes. It does," she said.

"Then why are you crying?"

"You stink," Mimi said, sitting on the couch with her legs crossed underneath her. Mr. Puff Tail sat with his white head nestled against her leg. His fur felt a little stiff. She probably shouldn't have used the soap powder to clean an ink spot from his ear.

"And you got a big, big forehead," said JoJo. He lay on the floor on his stomach with his feet raised behind him. He wore sweat socks that were dingy from a failed washing. As he swung his feet up and down, the breeze of musty sweat rose up into Mimi's nose.

"Wash your feet," she said, pinching her nose shut. "Peeeewwwww."

"You wanna smell my feet, Mimi?" JoJo stood and towered over her. Sometimes he looked like a giant. He pulled the sock from one of his feet and dangled it in front of her nose. "Smell my feet, Mimi. Smell my feet."

"Ugh, you're so nasty. Mommy!"

JoJo fell back on the floor and laughed one of his belly laughs. He had to hold his stomach when he did this. It was times like this that Mimi thought he acted more like a three year old than a thirteen year old. She wiped the smell from her face.

"You are so stupid!" she screamed.

"I know you are but what am I?" he asked.

Pausing, she cocked her head. Sometimes she had to think hard about what he said to her. It never made sense, but she wanted to make sure she wasn't missing something.

"Mimi and JoJo—stop making so much noise. If I have to come in there . . ." Mommy was lying on the bed in her bedroom. Lately, she had to lie down often. She excused this as having a headache, but if Mimi listened with an ear next to the closed bedroom door, she could hear crying. The headaches usually came after an argument with Daddy.

The front lock jiggled. When it opened, their father entered holding a grocery bag and dripping with rain. The bag was soggy, and so were its contents. Mimi knew this was likely to cause her mother to have a hissy fit. Joe Combs was a tall man, but today, as he walked past his children with his feet dragging and his shoulders slumped, he appeared to have shrunk.

He placed the grocery bag on the floor and pulled off his jacket to hang in the closet. When he retrieved the bag, it left a faint, wet square on the carpet. He moved to the kitchen. Their mother appeared in the living room doorway. She glanced at her children. JoJo was back on his belly with his feet up in the air. The sockless foot was white with dry skin. His eyes darted from the TV to their mother and back. Mimi did the same. When their mother and father were near each other, things just exploded.

Her mother wore a long, yellow terry cloth robe. The belt at her waist was pulled tight. She looked like Big Bird as she walked past JoJo and Mimi and stopped near the wet square on the carpet floor.

"Joe," she shouted. "Look what you did!" She burst into the kitchen.

As their parents' voices escalated, Mimi uncrossed her legs and hugged Mr. Puff Tail. Hot tears formed at the corner of her eyes. Their fights were getting worse, and Mimi waited to see if her father would hit her mother. That's what Sierra told Kim, who told Kirsten, who told Rhonda, who told Bizzy, had happened to her mother. Sierra said one minute her parents were screaming at each other, and the next minute she heard a tumbling sound like when someone falls down the steps. Then she heard a slap, followed by her mother crying. Mimi waited to hear if her mother cried from the sting of a slap across her face.

JoJo, who had sat up and faced the kitchen, looked over at her. He got up and sat next to her on the couch. He put one long arm around her shoulders and started rocking her. For once, she did not mind the smell of perspiration from his armpits. He rocked her the same way he did when she was younger and could not or would not go to sleep. Back then he seemed to be the only one who could soothe her.

"Mimi, did I ever tell you about the time I bet Herman Grimes he wouldn't eat a roach?"

She shook her head.

"First off, who would name their kid Herman? That's like saying I'm a ghetto nerd, so beat me up." He laughed. "Naw, but Herman was cool though. He used to eat all kinds of insects just to show you he could eat them and not die."

The voices in the next room escalated to a soprano level, but Mimi only heard JoJo's voice as he talked about Herman and the roach. Her ear was pressed against his chest, and the story sounded muffled coming from inside his body.

When he finished the story, he wiped her tears. Then he took Mr. Puff Tail from her and smoothed his fur.

"This cat needs to comb his hair." JoJo stood. "Let's go comb his hair."

As they trudged from the living room, he squeezed her hand and said, "Don't worry. I'll take care of you and Mr. Puff Tail, Mimi-cake. Okay?"

Mimi nodded and followed JoJo. She wanted to forget about the possibility of hearing a slap. She wanted to forget the feeling that something was all wrong between her parents.

Chapter 6
Daddy Has Something to Tell You

When Daddy arrived to pick them up from their grandmother's house during one of their visits, he looked messy. His clothes were wrinkled. His shirt was not tucked into his pants, which was something he constantly told JoJo to do. His hair needed to be brushed. And a small smudge of dirt was on his chin.

"Rough day?" said Grandma as she handed him two plates wrapped in foil. "This is their dinner. Faye told me she had to work late, Joe."

"Thanks, Eunice," he mumbled as he took the plates from her hands without looking at her. Grandma shook her head slowly, studied him for a moment, then gave JoJo and Mimi a kiss and a hug before they piled into the backseat of their father's car.

When they arrived at their apartment, she and JoJo crashed through the front door as they each pursued something to take with them to the nearby park. JoJo was getting his baseball, and Mimi was hunting desperately for her jump rope.

"Come on. Whatcha looking for?" JoJo yelled as he stood at the apartment door. "Let's go!"

"I can't find my jump rope."

"I'm not waiting."

"Please wait, JoJo."

Daddy came to her bedroom door and watched her as she bent low to look under the bed. He watched her as she pulled toys from her toy box. He watched her as she opened her closet door, glanced inside and shut it.

"Where is my rope?"

"Mimi!" JoJo called.

"I'll bring her over," said Daddy. "Go on, son." That was all JoJo needed. The door slammed before the words "Go on, son" came out of their father's mouth.

She was looking in her sock drawer for the rope now.

"Nugget, I've got something to tell you," he said. "Sit down."

"But Daddy . . ." she started.

"It will only take a sec, then we can both look for your rope."

Mimi sat on her bed, crossed her feet, and started swinging her legs. One of her white socks with the frilly laces was smudged and the lace a little ripped.

She bent down to wipe the smudge and said, "Daddy, it's hot in here."

"Sorry, Nugget. I'll open a window."

He opened the window, but Mimi scowled. "There's no wind, Daddy. It's too hot. I want to go outside to the park with JoJo."

"Okay, baby. But first, Daddy has to tell you something." He seemed to glide onto the bed next to her and place an arm around her shoulder. "Daddy loves you."

He sounded so sad that she made herself look at him and not complain about how hot his body felt next to her.

"Sometimes parents fight," he said, gently rubbing the bare leg that showed from underneath her shorts. "Sometimes they say bad things to hurt each other."

She looked at his eyes and ignored the heat from his hand on her leg. She could feel sweat forming on her forehead.

"It's okay, Daddy, right? Because you can fix it, right? You'll make it better."

Her father moved his face closer to hers, looking as if he was about to kiss her. The front door slamming startled him.

"Mimi, JoJo. I know I don't see your things lying on this living room floor. Come and get this stuff."

Daddy touched her chin and kissed her softly on the forehead. "If I can, Nugget. I will. Just for you and me. I will fix it. Your jump rope's in the bathroom."

"Ah . . . that's where I left it. Thanks, Daddy." She kissed him on the cheek, ran to the bathroom, grabbed the rope and headed toward the apartment door. She was ignoring all the rules about walking to the park without someone else.

"Stop it right there. Where do you think you're going?" asked her mother. "Come in this kitchen right now."

"Hi, Mommy," she said as she slowly moved through the kitchen doorway. Her mother did not sound happy.

"Hi, young lady. What did I tell you about the things that happen in this house?"

Mimi was confused. Her mother had told her so much, she was not 100 percent sure what she was supposed to say.

Faye Combs wore a pink skirt and blouse with a pink plaid jacket with tassels on the sleeve ends. Her stockings clung to her legs. Mimi felt hot just looking at them.

"I said, 'What goes on in this house . . .'" Her mother waited.

"Stays in this house," Mimi finished.

"So why did your grandmother call to pray with me today? I told you not to talk about the private things that happen in our home. Didn't I?"

"Yes, Mommy."

"So, you're on punishment for breaking a house rule."

"Mommy!" Mimi screamed out like she did when she stubbed her toe hard. It hurt that bad to be on punishment.

"Don't dare ask me a question about it." Her mother shoved things into the cabinets and then ran water to clean the dishes. She stopped and took a deep breath. "Mimi-bean, I really don't want you telling your grandmother, or anyone else what happens in this house between your father and me. Okay?"

"Okay, Mommy."

She stroked Mimi's cheek. "But you're still on punishment."

Her father came into the kitchen. "What's one of them on punishment for now, Faye?"

"Mimi, go to your room."

Mimi groaned loudly then quickly stopped when she saw her mother's face. She didn't want to go to her room, but she knew she had no choice.

As she left the kitchen, she heard her mother say, "Did you ask them?"

"Faye, stop it already," said her father.

"Oh, no you don't. Not this time. You don't get to stop talking about what you can do to be a better man for your family."

"Faye . . ."

"You know what! Forget it, I got my own promotion today, buddy."

Chapter 7
Praying Don't Seem to be Working

November 30, 1980

Dear God,

My Mommy and Daddy keep fiteing. Cents you didn't get my prayers, I thot you mite get my letters. I asked Grandma, and she sed you did get it, but to write a letter if it made me feel better. So I'm writing a letter.

Plese help my parents stop fiteing. Plese help them love each other agin. Like they used to. They used to laf with JoJo and me. They used to take us places. Now all they do is fite. Plese make them stop.

Love,

Mimi

The gray aroma of winter permeated the air. It was everywhere. In the white-streaked salt marks that covered Grandma's car and the car she drove behind. In the huddle of people who waited to cross the street with their scarves tied tightly around their necks. In the shudder of the stray dog who hugged the wall of the store to protect itself from the wind.

Grandma Eunice was driving Mimi and JoJo from church back to her house. Gospel music blared on the radio, and the driver's side window was ajar.

"Grandma, it's cold," Mimi and JoJo almost said this at the same time, so they turned to each other and shouted, "Jinx!"

"Stop that," said Grandma. "No superstitious crap in this car."

"That's a bad word, Grandma," Mimi said.

"Oh my Lord. You're right, baby. Please forgive me. Old habits die with you. Let me roll the window up some. I'm just boiling hot."

"It's November, Grandma," JoJo said as if she were oblivious to the time of year and required additional education.

"Still don't mean it can't feel like July in my bones." She turned to quickly smile and wink at Mimi. At times, Grandma seemed to get some joy out of annoying JoJo.

Mimi laughed at the response. She loved her grandmother, and moments like this made it so easy to just open her mouth and start telling her the biggest problems.

"I had a good time in church today."

"I'm glad you did."

"But I'm still confused about something."

"What's that?"

"What do you do when God doesn't answer your prayer?"

"You have a prayer that he ain't answered yet?"

"Yes."

"Well, what is it?"

She glanced at her brother, who was sitting in the front seat while she sat in the back. Slumped down with his eyes closed, she thought he had drifted into sleep.

She whispered, "I still been asking God to stop Mommy and Daddy from arguing. I even wrote him a letter. But they still arguing, Grandma."

"What did Mom tell you?" JoJo sat up and turned toward Mimi. "Shut your mouth up!"

"JoJo." Grandma reached over and patted his hand. "It's okay. I won't say a word this time."

Mimi was relieved. She knew she had already said too much.

"And JoJo, don't you say anything. It's our secret . . . Mimi, God hears your prayers, and I'm sure he saw your letter. I'm not sure why he hasn't answered this prayer, but I can tell you this much. A lot is up to your parents."

"What do you mean?" She leaned over the back of the front seat to hear better.

"I mean, all God can do is provide opportunities for people to do better. It's up to them to take advantage of those opportunities. Not sure if your parents want to do that."

JoJo slammed his fist against the door. "Mom said not to talk about this. Stop it!"

"Okay, JoJo." Grandma patted his hand again. Then she reached for Mimi's hand to pat it, which was awkward because she was driving. Her elbow was bent back like a chicken wing. "Let's just keep praying for him to send them opportunities."

The month was December. The day was Christmas Day. Only one of these two events was a favorite of Mimi's. While she hated the coldness of December, she loved the promise of gifts on Christmas Day. She ran into the living room and saw tall piles of neatly wrapped Christmas gifts. Metallic green, red, silver, and gold covered gifts glowed beneath their fake Christmas tree.

She had begged for a real tree like Bizzy's family had. Bizzy came to school and described every inch of the tree, from how it smelled to the little pine needles it left on the rug. A real tree seemed to make Christmas feel like that of the Waltons. Their Christmas story had just played on TV last night.

She wanted a Walton-like family, one where everyone was kind and no one argued. One where even brothers did not make fun of their sisters or boss them around. The Walton family talked through their problems, and the mother and father always loved and cared for each other. In the Walton family, people said "good night" to each other, and looked forward to seeing each other in the morning.

A real Christmas tree might have some magic to it. *Look at what it did in the Walton family*, Mimi thought. She imagined herself saying, "Good night, Mommy. Good night, Daddy. Good night, JoJo"—while the tree gleamed and glowed in their living room.

But her mother complained about the maintenance and cleanup of a real tree and had brought out their fake one with silver plastic needles for leaves. She let JoJo and Mimi decorate it. And since Mimi thought every single ornament and decoration they owned belonged on the tree, it looked like a flashy dressed, saggy, gray-haired man whose body was leaning toward the ground.

This didn't matter to Mimi at the moment. She was more interested in what was under the overdressed tree. She was about to burst from happiness. Colorful boxes formed a wide semi-circle around the tree. Her broad grin showed she had just lost another tooth. She stuck her tongue through the huge space between her teeth.

The tooth came out around Thanksgiving break when JoJo flipped her over to demonstrate a wrestling move. She went soaring through the air and into his bedroom wall. It took her about five minutes to realize the tooth was gone, and ten minutes to realize they had put a long, black scratch on the wall. They both agreed to wait until asked about the scratch, but their mother never said a word. She was busy conducting daily arguments with their father.

"It's Christmas morning!" Mimi shouted, hoping to awaken the entire apartment building. She guessed she was not the only child who was up. Her assessment was confirmed when she heard the footsteps of the upstairs neighbor's five children running across the floor. Sometimes they could get real loud. But even their foot stomps and thumps had been no match for one of her parent's shouting matches.

Daddy was first to appear in the living room, still wearing his clothes from yesterday. His face was unshaven, and his eyes were red and puffy. Again, and more often lately, he needed to brush his hair. He smiled at Mimi, showing yellow stains on his two front teeth. He walked to the big chair and fell into it.

"Don't shout, Nugget. Daddy had a rough night."

Leaning closer toward him, she whispered, "It's Christmas Day, Daddy!" He answered with a smile.

A bare foot JoJo walked in wearing an old T-shirt and pajama bottoms. He gave them both a wide, loud yawn and fell across the couch. "Let's get this Santa Claus thing started," he said, snapping his fingers.

Looking fresh and clean, Mommy came in wearing fitted jeans and a silk blouse. Her hair was pulled back into a ponytail. Her skin shone and her face had been scrubbed free of makeup.

"Morning, my loves. Let's see what Santa brought you." She made a wide path around Daddy sitting in the big arm chair and sat on the floor next to the tree.

Mimi did not need another invitation. She started going through boxes and handing them out like a drill sergeant. When she was done, she and JoJo had ten boxes each, while her mother had five, and her father had two small boxes. She felt sad for him, but she noticed JoJo already had two of his boxes open and was admiring his gifts. One box contained a new pair of cleats and the other a new glove. He was turning them over and over to inspect every part.

"I like them," he said.

"There's more. Keep going. Both of you," said Mommy with flushed cheeks. A bright smile Mimi had not seen in a long time danced on her mother's face.

Daddy was on the floor now, between JoJo and Mimi's boxes. As they opened each one, he moved wrapping paper out of the way and gave helpful information about what the gift could do and what other related items might be found in other boxes.

Mommy's smile left suddenly, and she scowled at their father.

Mimi and JoJo were on their last box each and decided to race to see who could open the gift fastest. JoJo's fingers swept over the wrapping paper. Before Mimi was done pulling back the tape from one side of her gift, JoJo had the contents of the box in his hands. Tickets to a football game sat on top of a forest green wool blanket. Pretending to faint, he fell off the couch and onto the floor.

"Oh man! Oh man! Oh man! The Eagles . . . Really . . . I've never been to a football game. Oh man. Wait until I tell my friends." He hugged his father so hard that they both fell backward onto the floor.

Mimi's box contained a dress up kit with two dresses and clear plastic slippers.

Daddy said, "You're always dressing up. This will give you something nice to wear instead of your mommy's clothes."

She grinned and leaped into her father's lap. "Thank you. Thank you. Thank you, Daddy."

Standing next to the tree, her mother had unwrapped a glass vase. It was a gift from JoJo. He begged their father to take him to the store to pick it up after saving all his birthday money to purchase it. The vase rolled from their mother's hand and fell to the floor breaking into three large pieces.

"Mom!" shouted JoJo. "You broke it!"

She ignored him. "Thank you, Daddy," she said the sentence in Mimi's tone of voice. "Thank you, Daddy." This time she used a poor imitation of JoJo's voice, which had been cracking a lot lately. "Joe, do you care to tell your children who purchased their Christmas gifts?"

Daddy climbed back into the big chair and rested his uncombed head in his hands. "Faye . . ."

"Never mind. You two go to your rooms for one minute. I need to say something to your father, and then I'm taking you both to Grandma's for breakfast."

Standing over the broken vase with her fists balled, their mother's breathing quickened. She looked down at the pieces and added, "I love the vase, JoJo. I really do. So sorry I dropped it."

They both went to JoJo's bedroom but left the door open. Their parents tried to argue in low tones, but pieces of it kept rising to the surface. JoJo and Mimi heard phrases like "nothing good from you;" "always picking;" "taking credit for what you did not do;" and "three months to find a new place."

At the last phrase, both Mimi and JoJo stared at the opened doorway waiting for one of their parents to appear. A half hour later, they heard the front door slam, and their mother came to JoJo's door.

"How 'bout you two get dressed? Grandma promised to make waffles."

JoJo and Mimi looked at her. Then Mimi asked what she was waiting for her big brother to ask, "What about Daddy? Is he coming?"

Using her index finger, Mommy dabbed at the corner of her eyes. Her eyelids fluttered. "No, your daddy won't be coming b—" She exhaled loudly.

"Just get dressed, please." She left the room.

Truly, Mimi knew something was terribly wrong with her parents. Would things get worse?

Part 2

The King Becomes a Monster

Chapter 8
A New Place for Daddy

April 24, 1981

Dear Daddy,

I am so sorry you had to move agin. I mis you. Mommy is giving me a birthday party. Can you come? And can you get me a bike for my birthday? JoJo says he will teach me to ride it. Plese come to my party. Hdo you like your new apartmint? Is it nice? Can we come over? Can we spend the nite?

Love,

Mimi

The first of their father's many places had been an efficiency. JoJo and Mimi had to walk into a house and pass a woman who slept while two children used her chair as home base for a game of hide-and-seek. But the trip didn't end there as they ascended two sets of stairs, went through a door, and finally stood in a room. This was their father's home.

His small room played the role of kitchen, living room, and bedroom, all at the same time. However, conversion to a bedroom required Daddy to pull a bed from the depths of a worn couch. A much smaller room in the back of the efficiency served as his bathroom. Mimi did not know how he kept himself clean in this space, as every turn included crashing into the wall, the sink, the toilet, or the shower. Strangely, when he first stood to give them the grand tour, which lasted thirty seconds, his shaggy appearance matched the shabbiness of the room, and the two blended together as one.

Their mother refused to let them spend the night. She told them it was not safe. So JoJo and Mimi had day visits that always ended with their father promising to look for a new place so they could stay overnight.

Mimi was not sure he was looking hard enough. He seemed comfortable in his one room, and he called it "making the best of the situation." JoJo called it "living like a poor man." She simply felt a great sadness for her father.

She expressed her feelings to her grandmother, who put Mimi in her lap and rocked her back and forth before answering. Mimi felt like a baby, and images of her own infancy filled her head as she saw herself as the center of her family's world at one time. She knew she was too big to be sitting in her grandmother's lap, but the rocking wiped away some of her sadness, and eventually, she fell asleep.

When she awoke, she was on Grandma's couch. Through the open curtains of the window she could see a streetlight had come on. It provided the only light source to the darkened room.

Her grandmother entered and flipped on a lamp. Mimi winced at the bright light.

"So you're up, grandbaby. Let's get something to drink."

In the kitchen she listened to Grandma's favorite song while sipping iced tea. Her grandmother had been experimenting with adding different pieces of fruit to the tea to change its taste. She had added raspberries and mint leaves, which sweetened the tea and cooled Mimi's tongue for hours after the drink was consumed. The singer was singing the words, "A change . . . a change . . . has come over me."

Mimi had heard the song so many times before, and she found herself automatically joining the singer, whose lyrics she occasionally butchered by adding her own words. Grandma was also singing. She embraced Mimi's editorial mishaps and strains to reach high-pitched keys. With spoons in hand, they pretended to be on a stage giving a concert.

Five songs later, they fell into the chairs at the kitchen table and commended themselves on their performance. Suddenly Grandma became still and quiet. She placed a hand on Mimi's shoulder. "Your daddy will be just fine. If I know Joe Combs, and I want to believe I do, then he will be fine. Don't worry."

"Okay, Grandma," Mimi said. And with her world at peace, she asked for more tea.

But after that conversation, five more efficiencies and a brief stay on a co-worker's couch had been part of their father's search for a final place he could call home.

As their car pulled up to his new apartment, Mimi and JoJo exchanged doubtful looks then glanced at the back of their mother's head. She continued to look straight ahead.

The building was one of two dingy-looking giants that faced each other, as if ready to begin boxing. Colorful graffiti letters greeted them on the walls. Discarded bottles littered a cracked and broken concrete path to the door. The last efficiency, at least, had been nestled in a quiet area of the city. This new apartment was in a noise infested, busy housing project in the northern section. Their father apologized to his children, and using a weary voice, explained that given child support and other problems, it was the best he could afford.

Mimi knew her father was trying to find a place that allowed his children to have overnight stays, but she did not like the new location at all. Everything was bad looking and awful smelling. She had stepped in spit when she got out of the car. The decaying aroma of garbage invaded her nose instantly.

Daddy was waiting for them at the building's entrance and held the door open.

As their mother stepped from the car to help them unload, she muttered the words, "Court ordered visitation, my . . ."

"Hurry up, kids," he called. "I left my keys upstairs."

"I'll be back on Sunday," she said, hugging each of them harder than she had ever done before. Mimi felt like her mother was acting as if she might never see them again.

"Okay," Mimi and JoJo responded in unison. They carried their sleeping bags and backpacks to their father. He grabbed both sleeping bags and let them walk into the building.

"I miss you guys. You look so good. Mimi, you must be an inch taller. Did you get my birthday gift? I'm sorry I couldn't come to the party, Nugget, but it didn't seem like a good idea. How's school? You ready for the summer? How's the team, JoJo? Here we are. We'll take the elevator to the fourth floor. That's where I live."

He was talking fast and not waiting for an answer. Mimi and JoJo followed him. Their eyes darted to the worn, tattered carpet, to the cracked walls, to the elevator with the poor excuse for a lightbulb.

Their father said, "Umma get something better one day." He spoke more to himself than to his children.

The apartment was a one-bedroom unit at the end of a darkened hallway. Most of the apartment was taken up by the living room. Fading yellow paint covered the walls. Globs of dried paint stuck to the floor. Sheer curtains decorated two windows, which faced the alley behind the building. To the left of the living room was a small kitchen with a stove, sink and fridge tightly wedged next to each other. A bedroom and the bathroom were on the opposite side. As Mimi stood in the doorway of the bedroom she assessed it was no bigger than the nurse's office at her school. Even cluttered, the office contained more space than her father's small bedroom.

"Here we go," he said as he settled their sleeping bags on the floor. "You won't really need these. JoJo can sleep on the couch, and Mimi will sleep with me. You kids hungry?"

"Mommy made us eat before we came," Mimi responded.

"Of course she did." He gave a quick smile. "Well, I got this little TV. Wanna watch some TV?" He turned it on.

The television was half the size of the one they had at home. The picture was fuzzy.

"Dad, when are you coming home?" JoJo sat heavily on the couch.

"Yeah, when are you coming home?" Mimi sat next to JoJo. Her shoulder was pressed against his arm.

"You know I can't come home. Mommy and I are getting divorced."

The day after her mother first mentioned the word divorce, Mimi went to school and asked her teacher what it meant and how to spell it. The third grade teacher's name was Miss Allabet. She was a short woman, who was about the same height as some of the boys in her class. But her voice was gruff. When she spoke, she sounded like a man.

Miss Allabet asked, "Why do you want to know?"

"My mother said that she is going to divorce my daddy. She was crying too hard to tell me what it meant when I asked her."

"Oh." Miss Allabet took off her glasses and wiped them clean on her sweater. Mimi noticed she did this before she said something that was hard to understand.

"Well, it means your father and mother won't live together anymore."

"Why? Is he going somewhere?"

"I guess he will go to his new place?"

"Why? What's wrong with our place?"

"I don't know, Mimi."

"Doesn't he like us anymore?"

"I'm sure he does."

"Then he should live with us. Why would he want to live anywhere else?"

"I don't know, Mimi, but this is something you and your mommy should talk about. You can ask her the same questions."

Miss Allabet turned to go to a student who was calling her name.

"Well," said Mimi. "Can you at least tell me how to spell it?" Miss Allabet spoke slowly while Mimi wrote each letter on a piece of paper.

That night the phone rang. When her mother answered it, she took the phone to the bedroom and shut the door. Later, she explained what divorce meant. Mimi tried to recall the letters of the word while her mother spoke.

The divorce seemed to be treating their father badly, while it treated their mother well. She had bought a new car, got promoted again at her job, and moved them to a new home in what she called a better school district. Mimi missed Bizzy and Kayla. She even missed Bobby Benson a little.

"You know," her father began, "we have two days together. Let's not spend it talking about divorce and coming home. Let's do some fun things." He tickled her stomach and hugged JoJo by the head.

Mimi and JoJo exchanged another look. In her brother's eyes, she saw the same sadness she felt. Divorce stank.

Chapter 9
Grandma Was Hiding in the Closet

"Seven . . . eight . . . nine . . . ten. Ready or not, here I come."

Mimi jerked away from the corner in which she had been counting. Her eyes darted up and down and left and right as she scanned the room. Grandma was not the best hide-and-seek player. First, she was too big; second, she was too slow. This had happened overnight. Her once 'not-normal' grandmother had been moving slower and having a hard time seeing things. She tried to keep up with her grandchildren, and playing hide-and-seek was a game she loved but just happened to be awful at playing. Mimi knew she would find her grandmother's hiding place soon enough.

She peeked behind the green tweed couch. No Grandma. She looked under the massive dining room table and behind the squeaky kitchen door. These were places her grandmother had hidden before and had been found. This time both places were empty. No Grandma. Mimi scratched her scalp.

"I'm coming to get you, Grandma," she called as she headed into her mother's bedroom.

She peeked under the bed. No Grandma. She looked behind the open bedroom door. No Grandma. She stood in the middle of the room with her hands on her hips and put a finger on her chin.

"Hmmm . . ." she said loudly. "I wonder where my grandma could be."

At the closet door, she saw a purple piece of fabric sticking out from under the bottom of the door. She tiptoed to the door. Mimi couldn't just burst into the closet. She had to make a performance first.

"My grandma is so smart. My grandma is so kind. My grandma is so found. Gotcha!"

She flung open the door and expected to see her grandmother smiling down at her with wisps of hair falling into her face and her mouth wide open in laughter. Instead, her grandmother was kneeling on the floor with her forehead pressed against the door frame. She was taking large, deep chunks of breath like Mimi had to do after chasing someone faster than her through the schoolyard.

"Grandma?"

"Go . . . get help . . . Go . . . get help . . ." she said between deep inhales.

"Grandma, are you okay?"

"Go . . . get . . . help . . . hurry . . . baby."

Grandma was responsible for watching Mimi in her new house, while Mommy went shopping with JoJo for yet another pair of sneakers. He had insisted that a certain pair he saw advertised in a commercial would improve his baseball game beyond belief. After much begging and a few negotiations around extra chores, her mother had broken down and agreed to take him. JoJo's face had flashed anger, stoniness, and finally defeat as he realized his mother was going shopping with him. He wanted to go alone, but there was nothing he could do to change her mind. They went to a mall whose location Mimi was sure he selected because none of his friends would be there. They had just left and would not return for hours, knowing JoJo.

Mimi ran over to the neighbor's house, ignoring all her mother's rules about running on their grass. Her fists pounded on the front door like small hammers. Mr. Avery came to the door dressed in his robe and a pair of black socks and sandals. His thick, hairy legs were visible also. It was not time for bed, but Mr. Avery appeared to be headed that way.

"Mee-mee," he said. Mr. Avery had a way of holding on to the sound of her name. "What brings you over? Mommy needs to borrow something?" He also spoke to her like she was two years old. "Let me get my wife for you."

"Something's wrong with Grandma," she blurted as he turned away from the door.

"Say what?" he asked, turning back to her.

"Something's wrong with Grandma," she repeated, pulling Mr. Avery's arm. "She won't get up off the floor in the closet. Something's wrong with her."

Before she got out the last sentence, Mr. Avery was down his front steps and running across the grass with his robe flying open. Striped shorts and a white undershirt were unveiled for the entire neighborhood. Mimi wondered how he could break his own rule about the grass. Well, he had not told her it was a rule; her mother had.

He called back at her, "Tell my wife to call 911, Mimi."

The ambulance arrived twenty minutes later with its lights flashing and siren blaring. Mimi covered her ears as she watched two men in white uniforms emerge from the back of the ambulance carrying a small bed between them.

"What's that for?" she asked Mrs. Avery, who tightly held Mimi's hand and insisted she wait beside her instead of going into the house. Mrs. Avery did not answer the question.

One of the men appeared at the doorway of her home. "Mimi," he called out. "She wants to talk to Mimi."

Mimi tore away from Mrs. Avery's hold and ran toward the man. Mrs. Avery was not far behind, but the bulk of being pregnant slowed her. She brushed past the man as he said, "Whoa there," while flailing his arms to reach for her.

Her grandmother was lying on the little bed the two men had brought with them. A clear, plastic mask covered her mouth and nose, and she was breathing better. Grandma saw Mimi and tried to speak, but the plastic mask muffled her words. She pulled it away from her face, but a rubber band held it in place, so she was not able to pull it too far. Her voice sounded like one of Mimi's classmates at school when he was having an asthma attack. It was like water running through her words. The other man worked on her grandmother's free arm, pumping up a black bag wrapped around her arm.

"Stay with Mr. and Mrs. Avery, Mimi-cake." For the first time, she noticed that Grandma and her mother both liked to add other words behind a person's name.

"I want to go with you, Grandma." She put a hand on her grandmother's arm. "Please, can I go with you?"

Her grandmother smiled. "The best way you can help me, sweetie, is to pray like we always talk about. Do you remember . . ." The mask flew back into place over her mouth and nose, and her grandmother took a deep breath. She pulled the mask away again.

"Do you remember how I said you could always help Grandma?" Mimi's head felt weird. What had her grandmother said? Hot tears burned the corner of eyes before rolling down her cheeks. Oh, there it was; she remembered.

"You said to always pray for you. Grandma, I'm scared."

"And . . . when we're scared we should . . ."

"Pray."

"And when we're worried, we . . . should . . ."

"Pray."

"Good girl. Okay, you pray and stay with Mr. and Mrs. Avery until your mommy comes home."

The plastic mask fell back into place, and her grandmother's hand fell on top of the little bed sheet. The men got busy and pushed Mimi aside as Mr. Avery wrapped an arm around her shoulder. Mimi knew she would pray and write God a letter.

November 14, 1981

Dear God,

Grandma went to sleep but she didn't wake up. Maybe you alreddie knew that. I miss her. I miss her stories. I miss dancing with her. I miss going places with her. I miss talking to her. I know she is in Heaven with Grandpa. I wunder what Heaven is like. I wunder if they are having fun. I think they are.

Any way, please take care of them for me. Please take care of Grandma.

Love

Mimi

The cuff of JoJo's shirt peeked out from under his jacket sleeves. Most of his black socks showed beneath his pant legs. He had buttoned the jacket, but it still pulled apart at some of the buttonholes, and the white shirt he wore gleamed through. Every few minutes, he tugged at the tie around his neck, which seemed to be squeezing his throat. Her mother paid no attention to JoJo's discomfort. Dressed in a black two-piece skirt suit with black sheer stockings and black pumps, she used a cream colored handkerchief to dab at the corners of her eyes.

Mimi sat between her mother and brother on the red cushioned seat of the wooden pew. She wore a gray dress with a white ribbon that went around her torso just beneath her armpits. The dress had a white collar that formed a "V" shape down the front of her dress. She cried at home, but now she was too fascinated by the funeral proceedings to cry. Mimi wondered what her grandmother would think of all the people weeping, the lavish presentations, and the many songs. Grandma might have liked all of this.

The other interesting thing was her father. He wore a black T-shirt beneath a black jacket and faded khakis. The knees of his pants were thin and worn. He closed the jacket, but some of the white logo on the T-shirt could still be seen. His eyes were red rimmed. He sat straight and stiff in his seat in the back of the church, and he did not look to the right or left.

The minister was talking about how her grandmother had been the best "asset" (whatever that meant), to the church. He raved about her cooking, her kindness, and her generosity. Then he mentioned that what she loved most were her grandchildren. He started with JoJo and talked about how his grandmother liked to watch him play baseball. He said she believed he was very good. Next, the man talked about Mimi. He said she loved to talk to Mimi because sometimes it was like talking with a friend.

Mimi shifted under his gaze and turned to look at her father. The minister had gone through a whole list of family members who her grandmother loved. But for some reason he had not said anything about her father. She wanted to raise her hand and remind the minister that he forgot to say something about her father.

Then the minister added the words "and her son, Joseph . . ." But he did not use a bunch of fancy words. And he ended by saying, "She loved you, son."

The organ music filled her ears, and people were now praying. Was the funeral over? She watched her grandmother in the casket. All her favorite colors were used. Grandma loved orange and pink, and sometimes on a good day she liked a spot of light blue. Her casket was white with pink inside. She wore the light blue dress she sometimes wore to church. Grandma had complained that it was too heavy, even in the winter, but because it looked so good on her, she was willing to suffer a little.

Everyone stood, and people began to walk by the casket, then over to her family. People she did not know bent to hug her and whispered how sorry they were, or said, "God bless you," or something about praying for her family. The ribbon on her dress came undone with all the hugging. She wanted to tie it, but the people kept coming. Eventually, she saw her father in the line. He stopped at the casket and studied his mother's ashen face. The face of the person in the casket didn't match Grandma's at all.

As her father approached, Mimi put on her best smile for him.

"Dad-dy," she said.

He bent down to swoop her into his arms.

"You okay, Nugget?"

"Yes, Daddy. Are you okay?"

"Yes, I am." He set her back on the floor and placed a hand on JoJo's shoulder.

"How you doing, son?" JoJo hugged him.

When they pulled apart, her father turned to her mother. "I'll take them home with me after the funeral."

She snapped her head away from her drenched handkerchief and blinked. "What?"

"I'll take them with me after the funeral. That way you don't have to bring them."

"Joe, they're not going with you." The line began to back up as people waited to greet her mother. Some people walked around her father and moved on to other family members.

"Yes, they are. It's my weekend with them. Faye, don't make this hard. We'll stop by your place, grab some clothes, and I'll take them with me. Heck, they have stuff at my place, so they may—"

"They are not going with you, Joe. Their grandmother just died. They have to go to the gravesite then back to the house."

"Do you think that's a good idea? Especially for Mimi. She might get nightmares."

Mimi could not figure out what would give her nightmares, but she felt happy her father was extra concerned about her.

A woman waiting behind her father coughed loudly.

"Faye, you want to argue, go ahead, but then I'll just have information that you wouldn't work with me to see my kids. You want that at your next little court date?"

Her mother rubbed her forehead. "Go to the back of the room, Joe. I think you're wrong, and you know you're wrong. Your kids . . . your kids' grandmother died. Joe, your mother died." The word "died" was harsh and louder than all her other words.

Her father caressed Mimi's cheek and kissed JoJo on the forehead. Then, while looking at Mimi, he said, "I know *my* mother died."

As people left the church and piled into their cars, her mother led JoJo and Mimi to the long, black limousine they had arrived in. Their father approached the vehicle.

"Faye." His voice was shrill.

"I'll drop them off after the cemetery. At least let me have that with my kids." She slammed the car door. Tears rolled down her mother's cheeks.

Mimi wiped them away and put her head on her mother's shoulder. Why couldn't both her parents be happy?

Chapter 10
Bad Dream

"Daddy, I had a bad dream. Grandma came to read me a story, but she couldn't get the book open because her fingers were all dirty and muddy. Then she started to cry, and her tears were black like dirt."

He sat up in the bed and pulled her onto his lap. He massaged her back while she spoke.

"Daddy, is Grandma in heaven?"

"I guess so, Nugget." He buried his nose in her hair and took a deep breath. "Your hair smells good."

"Mommy's using a new shampoo. She says it will give my hair moisture." He played with her braid now, rolling it and unrolling it between his fingers.

"Really!" he said.

"Yes. Now, Daddy, about heaven. Will Grandma get to do the things she likes in heaven? She liked to go to the park with me. Once she went down the slide. But she skinned her knee, so she decided not to do that again."

He rubbed her arms and her legs. Up and down. Up and down. Pressing a little too hard.

"That hurts, Daddy."

He eased the pressure but kept rubbing.

Mimi continued, "I hope she gets to do everything she likes to do. I think she would be sad if she couldn't do what she wanted to do. Right, Daddy?"

His hand went up her nightgown, and he was rubbing her stomach.

"Mimi, you love Daddy, right?"

"Yes, I do, Daddy. I love you so much. Aw shoot. I wrote you another letter, but I left it at home. In the letter I said I hope you don't fall asleep and not wake up like Grandma. I don't want that to happen to Mommy or to JoJo either."

"If you love Daddy, you'll do anything Daddy asks you to do, right?"

"Yes, Daddy. You and Mommy said I have to be a good girl and good girls do what their parents tell them. What's the word for it, Daddy?"

"Obey."

"Obey."

His hand eased down between her legs. Her body stiffened. She remembered when she brought him a letter after he argued with her mother. The way he touched her then was just as weird and uncomfortable as it was now.

"Good girls do the things that will make their daddies happy. If you just let Daddy touch you here and don't tell anyone, that will make Daddy very happy."

Mimi tried to look into his face, but the lights were still out and the moonlight that fell through the small window in his bedroom only showed the contents on his bureau. He had a bottle of cologne, underarm deodorant, and lotion. Lotion was something her mother made all of them keep on their bureaus. She warned that dry skin would lead to wrinkles.

Mimi remembered her grandmother's wrinkles. They did not seem so bad now.

Her father kissed her cheek. First the left, then the right. His voice became raspy as his breathing increased.

"You love Daddy, so you'll do this for him."

"Okay, Daddy." She felt something hard beneath her buttocks. She thought he had gone to bed with the flashlight he sometimes used when the power in his apartment went out. He picked her up and pulled her under the covers.

"Daddy loves his baby. He'll always take care of her."

Mimi swallowed. In her head, she saw her grandmother standing in their kitchen. She was talking about something that happened to her when she was a child. Grandma smiled and scratched her nose. She always scratched her nose whenever she was about to end a story.

She said, "I just knew then God was with me. He's been with me ever since."

Mimi wondered if God was with her right now.

Chapter 11
"Loving in a Special Way"

When JoJo was not with her, the weekends at her father's place were difficult.

Sometimes JoJo had to go on weekend trips with the activity club their mother had enrolled him in. Mommy was all about preparing them for college, and that meant they had to have extracurricular activities for their college applications. She enrolled JoJo in a science club that went to museums after school and did weekend field trips to museums in other cities. JoJo, who hated science, went with the flow and eventually started enjoying it when he met a pretty girl with long black hair and big, heavily lashed eyes. Her name was Sharita, but he called her Rita for short.

If there was a weekend outing, it meant JoJo could not visit their father. At fifteen, he did not mind it at all.

"Dad's apartment is smelly. I don't know any kids in his neighborhood. There's nothing to do when we go over there but watch TV and eat," JoJo complained.

He was right. It was boring. And all that eating had turned Mimi into a plump ten year old, who occasionally found herself at the end of a fat joke at school. Her mother had enrolled Mimi in a dance class, hoping the exercise would help take off some of her extra pounds. But it had not helped. She was eating more than she was exercising. As jeans refused to cooperate by buttoning closed and shirts threatened to rip at seams, her mother shopped for larger clothing.

At least when JoJo went, her father was careful not to touch her. On one visit, he was in the middle of "loving her in a special way" when he heard the toilet flush. He practically threw her out of bed, put a finger to his lips, and frantically said, "Shh, shh, shh."

JoJo heard him quieting her on his way back to the couch and opened the door a crack. In the darkened room, he barely made out the image of Mimi on her side and his father sitting up in bed. His undershirt lay on the floor.

Her father whispered, "Be quiet. Mimi's still asleep. You hot too, huh? Can't sleep either?"

"Naw." JoJo stretched out his yawn. "Just had to pee. Night, Dad."

"Night, son."

Her father's heart was pounding so loud she could hear it. She swore JoJo heard it as well. That "near catch" scared her father so badly that he stopped touching her if JoJo came with her. When she came alone, he was much freer, leaving his bedroom door open, and, at times, not waiting until bed time to "love her in a special way."

Mimi could not concentrate on anything but fear of a weekend when JoJo was not going with her. She began to orchestrate activities where she had to do something on the same weekend. But dance class did not have as many weekend events as the science club did.

One day she worked up enough courage to ask her father about what they were doing. He sat at a table in his normal faded white undershirt and boxer shorts. He had made her a generous breakfast of her favorites: frozen waffles with chocolate sauce, sausage, and lemonade. For some reason, she could not get enough of lemonade, especially when he made it, because he loaded it with sugar. All the food made her fatter, but he looked thin, like the stray dog in the empty lot across the street with its eyes bulging out of its head.

She sat across from him, already fully dressed, because she found that her father got more worked up if she was wearing her nightgown. Over the past year, she had learned several ways to manage his urges. Some were successful. Some were not.

"Daddy, what are we doing today?" she asked.

"I thought we'd go see that movie you been bugging me about. How's that sound?"

"It sounds good." She put a piece of waffle in her mouth and swallowed without chewing. "Can I ask you something?"

"Sure, Nugget, you can ask me anything."

"Why do you have to keep touching me in a special way?"

He stopped chewing. For a moment, he looked the way the kids looked when they played Freeze Tag at school. It was a game she stopped playing because somebody always caught her. He laid his fork on the table and went into the bedroom. She watched the opened door and heard him rummaging through his closet for something. He had become a pack rat, keeping everything he found on his job as a trash man. Her father was careful to shower and wash his clothes to guard against the smell of work in his home, but he could not stop himself from keeping some of the things people threw away. It was how he furnished his sparse apartment. The unmatched chairs for his kitchen table, the stained clay lampstand, the crooked coat rack that sat next to his front door, and the white wooden table he used as an end table next to his couch. All of these came from the garbage.

He had scrubbed them, sanded them, and painted anything he brought home to make it look almost new.

She heard him bump his head and curse. The closet rack was too low for his height, and if he looked on the bottom for something, he often forgot about the rack when he stood up and would crack his head against the bar.

He emerged from the room with a folded piece of paper in his hand. He opened her hand and placed the paper in it.

"Read," he said. His voice was barely audible.

The paper looked familiar. The creased lines. The uneven tear like it had been ripped from a notebook. She used this paper to write her letters. There was a time when she just tore pages from the notebook her mother gave her. Now she was a bit more careful. She unfolded it. She had written the letter the night her parents argued, and he looked beaten, sitting in his chair in the living room. He had been wearing the sad clown lips then.

"You said you loved me." He sounded like he was accusing her of something. "You said you loved me and that I shouldn't be sad. You make me happy. Touching you makes me happy. When I'm sad and I have bad memories, like you have nightmares sometimes, touching you makes me happy." The slant in eyes deepened. "Did you lie? You don't love me, do you?"

This was spinning out of control. Mimi loved her dad so much. She needed to take care of him since her mother did not care about him. Her mother often referred to him as "that dirty dog." When Mimi came home and explained how his apartment was not as nice as their home and what things he needed to make it a better place, her mother responded, "That dirty dog did it to himself. He cared more about himself than his family. I don't care what he needs. The dirty dog."

Her father's eyes were moist. He asked again, "Don't you love, me? Don't I deserve to be loved instead of hurt? I shouldn't be hurt all the time, right?"

She shook her head up and down. Mimi had been clutching the fork the whole time, and chocolate sauce ran down the handle and onto her hand.

"I love you." She lowered her head. "I'm sorry."

He was suddenly the happiest man in the world. "Thank you, Nugget."

She didn't ask him again about what they were doing. To her, he was not far from being like the men they passed whenever they went shopping in the city. The men who lay on the sidewalk or slept on top of manhole covers, often begged for a dollar. One time, after one of them had requested a dollar from her mother, Mimi stopped to ask him a question. Her mother, who hated shopping in the city, had already moved on and was racing down the street carrying bags with JoJo trailing behind her.

"Why do you need a dollar?" she asked.

"To eat," he said without blinking his eyes, changing his facial expression, or lowering his outstretched hand.

"Can't you get a job?"

He dropped his hand and gave an irritated exhale. "Look, little sis, my wife left me, my kids don't call, I lost my job, I lost my home, I lost my car. I lost everything."

By then her mother realized Mimi was not as close as she needed to be. She called to her, "Mimi, come on and leave that man alone." She turned to him and said the only thing she could think of.

"I'll pray for you because I don't have a dollar." She ran to catch up with her mother. Telling him she would pray for him reminded her of Grandma. She knew it would be what her grandmother thought was best. But lately, Mimi wondered if God could hear her, or were his ears full of wax?

Chapter 12
People Are Different in Middle School

January 18, 1984

Dear Daddy,

I got an A on my math test today. It's the fourth A I got so far this year. I really like math and I like the teacher. I'll be taking my school pictures next month, so I'll send you one in the mail, or I can bring it over to your house.

I thought about what you asked me the last time I was over. You keep asking me the same question, Daddy. Like you don't believe me. I do everything you ask, and I keep our secret, but you still keep asking me the question. Yes, Daddy, I do. I do love you. And I do want to make you happy. I'm just not happy when you touch me. I wish there was another way I could make you happy.

But if this makes you feel better, then okay, Daddy. I know that the divorce was not a good thing for you. I just want to help you, Daddy.

I love you,

Mimi

Talking to her dad was easier this way. She could say what she wanted without looking into those eyes—those sorrowful eyes that pulled her in like the wind gales of a tornado. When she met those eyes she forgot which words to use and the tone in which to say them. Writing letters saved her from those eyes.

The clang of a tray and its contents spilling onto the floor, followed by the wail that the owner had to get another lunch, brought Mimi back to her present reality. To other students passing by, she was another nerd doing her schoolwork during lunch break and not a girl whose father's touches birthed letters of verification of her love for him. She was harmless, insignificant, and almost not there.

Mimi folded the letter in half and pushed it between the sheets of a notebook. She would not have brought it to school normally, but she was in the middle of crafting it this morning when her mother informed her it was time to leave. Quickly, she stuffed the letter in the notebook while thoughts of protecting it flooded her mind. Her mother stood in the doorway motioning Mimi to join her in the walk to the car. She could not put the letter in her normal private place in her closet without her mother questioning why she was delaying their leaving. The only thing she could do was put the notebook with the cherished letter in her book bag and follow her mother out the door.

She placed her lunch tray on top of the notebook, a comforting action to hide it from other students. Mimi picked at her half-eaten hot dog and beans. She was going to finish it definitely, and she pulled a forkful combination of beans and hot dog to her mouth as her eyes roamed the depths of the cafeteria.

Seventh grade was not what Mimi expected. People were older, and their concerns were a bit different from when they were in sixth grade. For some, clothes, friends, and appearance became ultra-important. She had an acquaintance or two at school, but they were not like Kayla or Bizzy. Since her mother moved them away from their home in Philadelphia to the Delaware County area, she only saw her friends when she begged her mother to take her to their old neighborhood for a weekend visit. She talked on the phone with them, but ended up being placed on punishment for using the phone after bedtime. Eventually, different schedules and conflicting plans diminished these calls to every now and then, instead of the daily forays she had when they first moved.

Mimi missed the girls so much, but even they were changing. Kayla was taller with model-like features. She looked like a real life Barbie with mocha-colored skin, a heart shaped face, and large, round eyes. She decorated those eyes with eyeliner and blue eye shadow, which she could only apply in school, away from the sight of her parents. Bizzy was still the shortest of their trio, but she had become more athletic with muscular definition in her legs and arms. Light complexion, amber-colored eyes, and an inviting voice had made her popular in almost every circle at her school. Both girls were beginning to attract the attention of boys.

The only one whose change had not drawn a boy's eye was Mimi's. She was a few pounds heavier than she wanted or needed to be. Although she was not dramatically overweight, she was hefty with thick, jelly-like legs that rubbed when she walked. Her stomach stuck out a little, making sit-ups a nightmare during gym class. When she looked in the mirror, Mimi did not see the model or the "girl next door" looks that Kayla and Bizzy possessed.

Her hair, a constant nemesis, waved back at her in a mirror. She couldn't talk her mother into a perm to calm her tangled mess. The concession had been a weekly wash and press with a hot comb. In the mirror, Mimi saw the square shape of her father's face, his big round eyes, and his long, broad nose. His full lips were also on her face, but they now carried a small scar above the left side. It made her look as if God made a mistake when he drew her lips; the scar was a reward from another wrestling match with JoJo. He had flipped her right into the edge of the table. The feat would have won applause at a wrestling competition, but it only produced uncontrollable bleeding, a trip to the emergency room, a row of five neat stitches, and a month long punishment for JoJo. Mimi smiled as it dawned on her that this event was the last time JoJo played wrestling with her.

Her father had come to the hospital on that day. He had to get a friend to drive him to their suburban town. Wearing an old overcoat and a shoe with a tiny hole on the front, he cried. He screamed at JoJo. And he threatened their mother with a court date to sue for custody if she could not take care of them. In the end, it all turned out to be minor, but it made her parents even better enemies. She could not say anything about her mother without a snort, laugh, or outright tirade from her father. The same happened when she mentioned him to her mother. Their constant battles made JoJo sink into sports, and it made Mimi eat.

The eating produced a girl most students called nice when they got to know her, but some refused to go that far and picked on her weight instead. As a result, she distanced herself from some of the kids and did not put too much effort into making new friends. She longed for the end of a school day when she could just go home.

Mimi was still surveying the lunchroom. Shoving another forkful of beans and hot dog into her mouth, she noticed a girl staring at her. The girl wore round, black-rimmed glasses that were probably a must for all her activities. Her pale skin brightened her green eyes, reminding Mimi of Christmas lights in a window. A set of stubborn freckles spotted her cheeks, the corners of her mouth, and her chin. Her dark, blonde hair was tied in a ponytail behind her head and seemed to disappear until she turned her head to the left or right. A set of diamond tear drop earrings dangled from the girl's pierced ears. Mimi had never seen her before, which was strange, since silent observations made her aware of almost everyone at the school.

The mystery girl picked up a bag and walked over to where Mimi sat. She moved quickly, causing the previously hidden ponytail to bounce from side to side. Other students were also at the table, but since they were engaged in their own conversations, it was as if Mimi was alone. The girl sat down with a thud, and the table rumbled. The students looked over with an air of irritation followed by dismissal.

"Hi," she said.

"Hi." Mimi knew her one word response was full of doubt, surprise, and a bit of fear. What the heck was going on? A forkful of hot dog and beans was suspended in the air, waiting to enter her mouth.

"My name is Ava. What's yours?"

"Mimi . . . Mimi . . . Combs." The fork was still in the air.

"Do you have a brother who plays baseball?"

"Yes."

"Wow. He's good." Mimi noticed Ava's face was a little crooked. Like one side started to slip down and caught itself. You had to stare really hard to notice it, and right now Ava had her face just a few inches from Mimi.

"You don't look like him," she said.

Mimi returned the fork to her tray and picked up a napkin to wipe her mouth and hands. "He's my brother."

"I'm sure he is, but you don't look like him. Who do you look like? Your mother or your father?"

Mimi had heard this question before. The older she got, the more she saw bits and pieces of Joe Combs creeping over her. But JoJo seemed to have gotten a mixture of their parents' best parts, which made him look handsome. He was well on his way into their father's height and build. He had their father's wavy hair and his hazel eyes, their mother's round nose and thin lips. While JoJo looked like an Adonis, Mimi looked like the female version of Joe Combs.

"My father," she answered, feeling torn. Mimi wanted this girl to go away, and she wanted her to stay. This was the longest conversation she'd had with anyone in school, and the topic wasn't even project related.

"Mmm." Ava plopped the bag on the table and retrieved a plastic baggie with a multi-seeded sandwich. "Whole grain. My mother wants me to be healthy. Want to taste it?"

"Do you like it?" Mimi asked.

"No, but you might." This girl was strange. Through bright red lips, she asked the next question. "Are you in Miss Becker's math class?"

There it was. Nobody sat next to Mimi like this and talked. This girl wanted something, and Mimi was about to find out what.

"Yeah. Why?"

"I just saw you in her class when I passed by the other day. I also have her, but in the morning."

"Okay." Mimi was determined not to help Ava get to her point. The bell rang, signaling the end of the lunch period.

"Okay, gotta run." Ava had not eaten any of her sandwich. She stood. Her slim frame hovered over Mimi. "Maybe I'll see you for lunch tomorrow."

Ava hadn't asked for anything, and she had assumed she would sit next to Mimi if she saw her again. Mimi was stunned. But her amazement turned to interest when the next day and the day after that and the day after that, Ava sat next to her at lunch. Before Mimi knew it, she was handing Ava her home phone number and true to her promise, Ava called. The phone calls morphed into overnight stays. Suddenly Mimi had a friend—a possible replacement for Kayla and Bizzy.

Mimi had not realized she had a friend until she and Ava had experienced nearly a half dozen overnight stays at each other's homes. She was still watching and waiting for Ava to ask her for something. She felt sure Ava wanted to take something from her, and she didn't understand why she couldn't let this feeling go.

They were in Mimi's bedroom when Mimi discovered Ava had become a friend. Sitting at Mimi's desk, Ava screamed, "Mimi!" Ava was excited. The excited Ava spoke quickly. When she was mellow, she spoke slowly. She did both of these versions with too much animation. Mimi had to ask her to slow down or speed up, depending on which version of Ava she was speaking to.

Ava called her name again. "Mimi!"

"Yes, Ava."

"I want to ask you about Bertrand Campbell."

"I don't know him." Mimi was lying on her stomach and flipping through a magazine. The pages fluttered as Ava spoke again.

"Oh, that boy is sooo cute. I think he noticed me today in Farber's class."

"What makes you think he noticed you?"

"He looked at me and smiled."

"You sure that wasn't gas. Babies do that when they have gas."

Ava howled with laughter. "This is why I like you. You sound so serious and you make me laugh." The funny thing was Mimi was serious. But in the next moments she replayed the conversation while Ava rattled on about Bertrand Campbell. Ava had said, "I like you." The phone rang, and she heard her mother say, "Mimi, it's your father."

"Tell him I'll call back later."

Ava had paused long enough to let this exchange occur, and then she returned to ruminations about what it felt like to kiss Bertrand. Mimi sat up with her back against the bed and Ava's words dancing around a thought.

She mused about the fact that she had a friend. However, she could not shake the feeling that Ava wanted something. Was it because in Mimi's life somebody was already taking something from her? Didn't that mean that everyone wanted to take something?

Chapter 13
Uh Oh, That Period Thing

"What the—"

They were in the girls' locker room changing for the class she hated most. Physical Education was not Mimi's strong suit. They were doing gymnastics now, which included everything from the uneven bars to the ropes, her arch enemy. She could not get one foot over the other to get her hefty frame up the rope. So far she had made no progress. She could not make it more than a half foot away from the floor mat.

Mimi stared at the crotch of her underwear. They had seemed a little moist, so she checked to make sure she had not peed on herself. She was pee free, but a large, black smear blotted her underwear. She began to shake and leaned over to Ava.

"I think I'm sick," she whispered. "I might be dying."

"What?" Ava was already in her shorts and shirt and was tugging a thick sock onto her foot.

"I think I'm sick."

"Why? What's wrong?"

"I have a spot in my panties?"

"A spot?" Ava's head twisted to the side, a gesture she did when she did not understand something. She seemed to be pointing her ear in the direction to hear better. It also made her look like a chicken with a twisted neck. Mimi wanted to laugh but remembered she was dying.

"I got a black spot on my panties. See." She extended the elastic waistband on her underwear and tugged at the crotch, so Ava could see the spot.

Ava peered in. She put her hand against her chin and rubbed. Then she picked up her other sock and pulled it onto her bare foot. As if she were an expert who did not have to worry about ever being wrong, she said," You're not dying. You just got your period."

"My what?"

"Your period. I got mine last year."

"What do I do?" Mimi still wasn't convinced she was not dying.

"Your mother didn't talk to you about your period?"

"No."

"Well, let's talk to the teacher. They might want to let you go home." Ava put her hands over her heart. "Home sweet home."

They called Mimi's mother and sent her home with a white, thick pad wedged between her legs. She remembered seeing pads like this in her mother's bathroom. She asked what they were for, and her mother had said, "They're for when you become a woman."

At the time, she had looked at her mother's tired face. Her eyes had dark circles beneath them. A single strand of gray hair twisted itself from the rest of her head and blew in an imaginary wind. Mimi decided at that moment she was a long way from looking like her mother and being a woman, so she did not have anything to worry about.

Now she trudged the steps of the front door of her house wondering if she would be turning into a woman now with a single strand of gray hair. Her mother sat her down at the kitchen table with a glass of milk and a slice of chocolate cake.

"You might be craving chocolate," she said.

"Actually, I am." As Mimi started to eat her cake, her mother began an explanation of "the period" and what it meant for a young girl.

Mimi dropped an unfinished bite of cake back on the plate. She did not like the part about this happening every month, and she liked it less that she could get pregnant if she had sex with a boy. She had heard girls in school talk about pregnancy, sex, and boys, but all these words coming from her mother's mouth nauseated her.

Later, her mother took her to the store where she brought maxi pads and tampons, with instructions on giving each one a try and deciding which made her more comfortable. By the time they left the store, Mimi knew she was going to hate this period thing. It was already a nuisance.

The next day, she spoke with Ava about it.

"Why didn't you tell me you had your period?" Mimi asked.

"What do you want me to do? Go around telling everyone I got my period. Tacky," Ava said.

"I'm supposed to be your friend," Mimi said.

"You are, but I didn't think you wanted to know I was bleeding in my underwear. I'm sorry." She shuffled her paper into one neat stack, which was a sign she was a little irritated. "Anyway," she continued, "did your mom get pads?"

"Pads and tampons. I'm supposed to decide which I want to wear."

"Wow. I went with choice B. At least it sounds like your mother was pretty calm about it. My mom was so hysterical about the "next step" in her daughter's life, she almost threw a party." As she spoke, Ava raised her hands and extended the forefingers on each to draw quotes in the air around the words "next step." She rolled her eyes. "Can you imagine having a party to celebrate something like that happening to your body? Yuck."

Mimi smiled. Ava had a way of making her laugh at the most silly things. She leaned against the wall.

"Well, now you have to be careful with boys. You could get pregnant."

"What's all this talk about getting pregnant? I'm not going nowhere near a boy now."

The next month, Mimi came home and sat down at her kitchen table. She watched her mother wash and cut vegetables for a full fifteen minutes before she spoke.

"Mom?"

"Yes, honey." Her mother kept her back turned to Mimi. Her focus was on the chicken she was flouring for dinner.

"Can I talk to you?"

"Sure, honey. What's up?"

"I think I'm pregnant."

Chapter 14
I Might Be . . . Pregnant

May 7, 1984

Dear Daddy,

I'm sorry I didn't call. I have a lot of homework. I won't be able to come over again this weekend. I have karate class, and we're finally going to learn how to throw a punch instead of just blocking them all the time.

I'm so sorry, and I know you told me not to tell anyone, but I think I might be pregnant. I'm not sure what to do. I have to tell someone. Please tell me what to do, Daddy. I don't want to get in any trouble. Girls who get pregnant get into trouble and people talk about them. I don't want anybody talking about me, Daddy.

Please call me and tell me what to do.

Love,

Mimi

Years from now she would look back at this moment in her life and use the word "premonition" to describe it. A feeling in her gut told her something was coming, something unfamiliar and painful. It was heading her way, and if she could have seen it, she would have most likely ducked. But Mimi could not see it. She only sensed it; this invisible thing had a distinct presence of misery associated with it.

The moment occurred as she watched her mother clutching the phone. She squeezed so tightly that Mimi saw a vein pop out on the side of her face. The phone must have rung thirty times. Her mother paced heavily up and down the kitchen waiting for an answer on the other end. Although she wore sneakers, their sound against the linoleum was kin to the thud of hard boots on concrete.

"He'd better answer this phone." A tear trickled down her cheek. She sniffed and wiped it away. "Go get your coat, Mimi."

When Mimi returned to the room, her mother was already in her own coat. The receiver was back on its hook. It looked humungous, too big for the cradle it sat in.

"We're going to the police."

"The police!" Mimi backed against the wall. "Why do we have to go to the police?" Her voice trembled a little, and she thought it sounded like it belonged to someone else. Why was she so afraid?

Her mother's eyes were full of disbelief. "Your father raped you, and I want the dirty bastard killed!" Each word was laced with anger and hate.

Mimi's mind raced. She was trying to figure out how they got to this point. Why were they talking about a word she had learned in first grade from another student? At the time, she thought rape was a tool you used to clean your yard. Years later, she would find out that rape didn't have anything to do with a yard.

Her mind traced back to when she sat at the kitchen table and asked her mother if she could talk. In the mental checklist, she saw the step where she told her mother she might be pregnant. This thought had become a prevailing presence because her father had done something he never did before. This time he did not rub against her, or put his fingers in places they did not belong. This time he had done more than kiss her. This time he pushed himself inside her. It hurt so much, and when she screamed in pain he covered her mouth until he was done.

The whole time his voice was calm and husky. In between breaths, he talked about the time he took her to his friend's house to get her ears pierced (something her mother was not happy with). To help deal with the pain of having a heated needle pressed into the flesh of her earlobe, he had suggested biting on a book during the piercing process. The funny part was that it worked because she had something else to focus on. "Pretend you have the book now, Mimi. Bite on the book now, Nugget."

She did, but bit her tongue. That hurt too. Then it was over, and he was on his side of the bed. Her private part hurt so bad that she started to cry. He pulled her into his arms and cried with her.

"I'm sorry, Nugget. I'm sorry, Nugget. I don't know what happened. I'm sorry, Nugget." Then with agony he said, "Don't tell anyone. Please don't tell anyone."

She must have fallen asleep because when she awoke she was dressed in a different nightgown and had on clean underwear. And the bed sheets had been changed. Her father was gone. When she went to look for him, she found him on the couch balled up like a baby and snoring.

From that moment on, an image took over her mind. She would dream about what happened and wake up with her hands between her legs to protect herself. The voice of her father still in her ears as he pleaded with her to keep what he had done a secret.

It was during a conversation she had with Ava, which made Mimi believe she could be pregnant. Recalling the night made her cringe. Ava had been lying across Mimi's bed with her head buried in a fashion magazine. Her eyeglasses had slipped down her nose and were resting on the tip. This usually happened whenever Ava read deeply. Oblivious to the position of the glasses, she simply lifted her head higher so she could see through them. Her pointed chin was almost resting on the magazine.

"Can you believe people wear this stuff?" she asked, pointing to a picture of a woman in a long, black, shimmering dress with feathers all around the waist. "Where do you go that you can wear this stuff? I don't see anyone at the mall in an outfit like this."

Mimi was only half listening. Images of her father popped in and out of her head like the Barbara Eden character on the *I Dream of Jeannie* show. Jeannie magically popped in and out of her genie bottle. The television show had been one of Mimi's favorites.

"Ava, how does a boy get a girl pregnant?" She had been sitting at her desk, but moved to the bed and crossed one leg under her bottom. "I mean, I know they have sex, but how does she get pregnant?"

Ava closed her magazine. "This period thing has you freaked out, doesn't it?"

Mimi did not respond, afraid of what might fall from her own lips.

"Okay, listen," Ava continued, "a boy puts his thing inside the girl, and if it spits semen inside her, she could get pregnant. But why are you so worried? Ain't no boy spitting semen inside you. You're fine." She opened the magazine.

Mimi shook her head. She still had trouble understanding why Ava was such an expert on this subject, and why she spoke about it as if she was giving instructions on making a grilled cheese sandwich. "What if a man did it?" she asked.

"Did what?" Ava pushed her head closer to the magazine, as if looking through a magnifying class.

"Spit semen inside of you."

"Then I guess it would still work. He's still a boy, right? Just an older boy. Why are you so—" Ava turned toward Mimi and pushed her glasses up on her nose. She sat up and pushed her back against Mimi's pillow. She asked, "Why are you so worried about this?" Without waiting for the answer, she added, "Did something happen to you?"

"No." Mimi realized she had responded too quickly. She tried to get her thoughts together. She was not ready to tell Ava or anyone else about her father and the "loving in a special way." Ava's unwavering eyes were on her. "I mean, I-I-I I'm just thinking about it. I-I-I don't want to get pregnant."

Ava spoke slowly. "If you're not doing anything with a boy, you won't get pregnant." She sounded like an expert again. "What happened to you?" she demanded.

"Nothing, Ava. Darn it, can't I just ask you a question?" Mimi slapped the magazine from the bed.

"You're not telling me something, Mimi."

"Stop it. There ain't nothing to tell. I'm sorry I even asked you the question now. Drop it!"

Ava crossed her arms. "Naw. Something's wrong. My mother says when a person keeps asking you a lot of questions about something, they're hiding something from you." Ava had a habit of quoting her mother as if she too were an expert in all things. "You'd better tell me what's going on."

"Or what, Ava? What? Just drop it!" Mimi stood up. She wanted to run.

"No!" Ava said.

"Yes!" Mimi yelled. She didn't know if she had just begun yelling, or was already yelling.

"No!" Ava yelled back.

Before Mimi saw her fist, she had already punched Ava in the head. Then she was on top of her, punching and slapping and yelling, "Drop it! Drop it! Drop it!"

Her mother and JoJo rushed into the room and pulled them apart. Ava started packing her stuff while Mimi crumbled to the floor and bawled.

"I don't know what's wrong with you. What's wrong with you?" Ava screamed. "I'm getting out of here. Don't call me. Don't you call me. I tried to help you, you crazy, fat—" She stopped. Tears fell from her eyes. She threw her book bag over her shoulder and took a deep breath, which only released more tears. "I want to go home. I want to go home, now."

"I'll take you," Mimi's mother said, looking from one girl to the next and back. "Are you sure we can't work this out, Ava? Mimi-bean?" Mimi was still on the floor sniffling. Ava was breathing hard. Her glasses were nowhere in sight. A bruise on the side of her face was beginning to turn red with a jagged blue line running through it.

"I just want to go home," Ava said in a low voice. She left the room with Mimi's mother on her heels.

JoJo sat on the edge of Mimi's bed and handed her a tissue. "What was that about?"

"Nothing. I don't want to talk about it." She crawled onto her bed and covered her head with a pillow. "Can you just go away?" she asked in a muffled voice.

"Girls," JoJo said, slamming her bedroom door.

Nearly a month had gone by since she attacked Ava. She tried to apologize, but Ava tensed if Mimi just passed her in the hallway. Mimi was saddened by the loss of a good friend, but she was still worried about being pregnant. The dreams had taken on a life of their own as she saw herself with a swollen belly and kids at school pointing and laughing.

She had to do something, so she did what made her feel better. She wrote a letter to her father. Since her last visit, he had not called or begged a visit from his children. She mailed the letter to his house the next day, but that night she awoke with a terrible pain in her stomach. She tossed and turned and finally called her mother.

"What did you eat today?" asked her mother. Mimi went through her list while clutching her stomach and grunting. "None of that sounds healthy. Let me give you something for an upset stomach, and we'll see if it helps."

It did, but Mimi felt sure it was the first sign of pregnancy. After another restless night, she wrote another letter. This one was to her grandmother.

May 11, 1984

Dear Grandma,

I know it's been a long time since I wrote you, but let's face it, I'm not sure where Mommy was sending the letters I addressed to heaven when Grandpa died. No, this one I'm going to keep, but I think you can probably still see it from heaven.

Grandma, you may (or may not) know this, but I've got a secret that is eating at me. Daddy has been touching me in my private area for two years now. He started doing it more whenever I visited him and JoJo wasn't with me.

It wasn't so bad at first, because it seemed to make him happy. And afterwards, he was so nice to me. He would buy me things and take me places.

But now something happened, something that makes me think I'm pregnant. My ex-friend told me that after a girl gets her period . . . oh yeah, I forgot to tell you I got my period. Anyway, she told me if a boy puts his thing inside the girl and spits something called semen in her, then the girl could get pregnant. Well, that's what Daddy did. He put his thing inside me. He probably spit semen inside me, and now I'm worried I might be pregnant.

I guess the reason I'm writing you is because I don't know what to do. I beat my best friend up because I don't know what to do. Please don't be mad, but can you tell me what to do from heaven?

Love,

Mimi

She folded the letter into the smallest possible square and taped it to the underside of her nightstand. Her mother was not nosey, but just in case . . .

That night as she slept, she dreamed of her grandmother sitting in front of her at the kitchen table. Mimi was a baby, and she sat in her high chair smiling and laughing as her grandmother played choo-choo train with a spoonful of food. When Grandma was done, she wiped Mimi's face. Mimi then opened her mouth and in her own voice said, "What should I do, Grandma?" And her grandmother put her hands on both sides of Mimi's head and said, "Say God, Mimi."

The next day she walked into the kitchen and sat at the table. Her mind was turning over and over the idea of being pregnant. But she was even more petrified of the idea of telling her mother. Her grandmother had told her to ask God, or at least this was Mimi's interpretation of the dream. She had said a prayer as soon as she awoke, and she believed she heard God say, "Tell your mother." But as she sat at the table watching her mother's back as she moved around the kitchen, doubt followed by dread filled her body. She began chewing on a nail. As she gnawed, her mother suddenly spoke.

"Are you going to visit your father this weekend? Seems like it's been a few weeks since you saw him, which is a bit strange. You're daddy's little girl. I'm sure the d—" She stopped whatever word was in her mouth. "I'm sure he wants to see you."

In that moment, she found her own words, and they began with, "Mom, can I talk to you?"

"Sure, Mimi-bean."

Her mother had not called her "Mimi-bean" in a long time. It was another sign from God. So Mimi admitted, "When I go over Daddy's house, he sometimes . . . touches me."

Placing the wooden cutting board on the table, her mother walked back over to the kitchen counter to get a rinsed cucumber, "Touches you?" she asked. "What do you mean?"

"I mean, he . . . he . . . he touches me in my . . ." she struggled for the word she had heard her mother say when describing how to use maxi pads. "Kit kat. That's it. He touches me in my kit kat."

Telling her mother this long kept secret was exhilarating. Her conscience felt a release, like the fire hydrants they turned on during the hottest summer days. She continued the story without paying attention to the growing change in expression on her mother's face.

"When he touches me it makes him feel better, so I don't mind so much. Sometimes I just close my eyes and go somewhere else. But this helps Daddy. He ain't been the same since the divorce, Mom. And really I don't mind, but the last time . . ."

At some point her mother had left the cucumber in the sink and sat down at the table with Mimi. Mimi hadn't noticed until she heard her mother say, "What happened last time?"

"Last time, Daddy put his penis inside me." She wiggled in the kitchen chair because this part of the story wasn't so easy to repeat aloud. "And I think I might be pregnant because Ava said that was how a boy got a girl pregnant." Mimi rubbed her face. "There," she announced. It was good to tell it, and now they could take care of it and go on.

Mimi noticed the change in her mother's skin. It was darker. She slowly asked Mimi to repeat what she said.

Telling the story for the second time was easier because relief filled her with every sentence that left her mouth. She knew this was what she had to do. Grandma and God had been right. She just had to tell someone, and that someone was her mother. Her mother would help her address the pregnancy, and it would all be over.

She had no idea of the numerous questions that would follow the confession. Before she knew it, her mother knew everything Mimi promised her father she would not tell.

Her mother began to cry, then she let out a scream that was surely heard in the next county over.

JoJo came into the kitchen and watched while she rocked and moaned.

Tears began to well up in Mimi's own eyes. She was back to doubting the advice of her grandmother and God. She did not know news about her pregnancy would make her mother so upset. One minute Mimi had been free, and the next she was locked up again with a new kind of fear.

JoJo watched them both and wrung his hands. It was always his first reaction to something he did not understand.

"What's up?" he asked.

Her mother continued to cry, and Mimi said, "I might be pregnant. I'm so sorry. I'm sorry."

"What can I do?" he asked. "Is it that kid from school that I always see staring at you on the playground?" Mimi halted her tears. What boy from school? She never knew a boy at school was looking at her. She started to ask JoJo when her mother picked up the phone and started dialing.

"JoJo, go to your room until I call you," she ordered.

And now, here they were, she and her mother, eyes red and swollen, driving to a police station.

Chapter 15
We Got Him

It took Mimi a full hour to realize they were not asking questions about her pregnancy. They were asking questions about her father. What did he do to her? How had he touched her? Where did he touch her? How long had it been going on? At some point, it became embarrassing.

Although the woman who spoke to her had a gentle face and soothing voice, she could feel the men watching her as they stood outside the door. One man was talking to her mother, who was still dabbing her eyes with a tissue. Occasionally, she would say something while twisting her head and stabbing her finger in the air. This made the man pat her mother's arm.

"Miss," Mimi interrupted the woman's next question. "What's this got to do with me being pregnant?"

The woman put a hand on her shoulder. Through the fabric of her shirt, Mimi felt its warmth. "I don't think you're pregnant, hon, but your father, your daddy, touched you in a way he should not have touched you."

"What do you mean? It didn't hurt. I mean, except for the last time. At first it was scary, and then I just got used to it. Sometimes I just fell asleep while he touched me. Daddy wouldn't hurt me. He loves me."

"He probably does, hon, but some daddies show their love in a way that is inappropriate." *Inappropriate?* She knew what that word meant. She had used it correctly on her last English exam. The woman continued, "Your father shouldn't touch you in the places we just talked about. And he should never let his private part touch your private part. Do you understand what I'm saying, hon?"

Mimi looked into the woman's face and realized she was no longer just twelve years old. With that statement, her world had changed.

They brought her father into the police station in handcuffs. His eyes were puffy and red. The left side of his face was dark and swollen. A line of blood trickled from his nose and his lip. His hair was natty. Her mother saw him first. She raced toward him before anyone could stop her and clawed at his face, drawing blood from every scratch she put there. It took two officers to hold her back.

"You bastard!" she screamed. "I'm getting a good lawyer, and we're going to make sure you go to jail for the rest of your stinking, miserable life!" She stopped struggling and rested against the chest of one of the officers. "Why? Why?" she asked. "She loves you. Why hurt her?"

Her father exploded into the loud cry of a wounded animal. Mimi ran to him and wrapped her arms around his waist. "Daddy. Daddy. I'm sorry, Daddy. I'm sorry."

He continued a loud moan.

In the end, it was Mimi's last letter to him that helped to convict. That, and the awful examination of her vagina that revealed she was not a virgin anymore, though she thought she was. In fact, it was all her letters to her father that the attorney kept bringing up in court. She was not allowed to stay for most of the proceedings. But she knew he was talking about her letters because he had copies of them laid out on the table in front of him. They were letters she wrote to her father expressing how much she loved him, but there were also letters asking him why he kept touching her. One letter asked him about a funny shaped mole on the tip of his penis.

After reading the letter, her mother had said, "Oh my God! How could I not know this was going on?"

The attorney reached over and patted her hand. "She took the letters right to him. You wouldn't have known."

Mimi hated this attorney. His name was Peter J. Brown, Esquire, and he as a friend of a friend of her mother's. He was tall with pale brown skin and a flat, pointed nose. His eyes were dark brown, but he wore round rimless frames that hid them most of the time. His hair was curly and short, and when he smiled, his teeth were way too white. He seemed to be always smiling at her mother, or patting her mother's hand or rubbing her mother's shoulder. To Mimi, he was too friendly.

She hated Mr. Peter J. Brown, Esquire because he made her feel like it was all her fault. She already knew it was her fault. In the courtroom, her father sat wearing a worn, oversized gray suit because of her. He looked like a little boy. Because of Mimi, her mother cried late at night when she thought JoJo and Mimi were asleep. And JoJo barely said anything to Mimi anymore. If it did not involve passing him something at the kitchen table, he did not open his mouth to speak to her.

This was all her fault, and the attorney confirmed it.

The court case did not last long at all. Within a week, her mother was emerging from the courtroom with the attorney's arm wrapped around her shoulder. Smile after smile illuminated her face, and her eyes sparkled with water. She embraced Mimi so hard that she lost her breath.

"We got him!" she said. "We got him!"

They got him with fifteen years. At least it was not the rest of his life, and Mimi believed she could surely visit him during this time, just to let him know how sorry she was for telling the secret. When she voiced this to her mother, she heard the crash of glass hitting the floor. Her mother had dropped a pitcher of lemonade.

"Are you crazy!" she asked. "No, you can't visit him! As far as I'm concerned, you're never going to see him again. I hope he dies in jail."

Mimi was nearly thirteen the year her father went to jail. Her mother said, "Let's just move on with our lives." But Mimi did not feel like moving on. She had changed everybody's life forever, including her own. She made a decision, sort of a vow, on that day to never tell anyone else about what happened. She would not even talk to her grandmother or to God.

Part 3

The Search for a King's Love

Chapter 16
She Met a Boy; She Met a Girl

August 29, 1986

Dear Daddy, Grandma, JoJo, God —

My Daddy's in prison.

My Grandma is dead.

My brother hates me.

And God can't listen to a person like me.

Why would he? I got a lot of problems. I mean, a lot. I'm not pretty. I have no talent. And because I did not keep a promise, my father is in jail and my family is messed up.

I don't even have someone to send this stupid letter to.

Help me, somebody.

Love,

Mimi

High school was . . . high school. What else did she expect? Mimi had watched JoJo navigate it with so much success that she suspected she would fail at it. But she did not fail; she just became unimportant and invisible.

By December of ninth grade, and she had managed to go from class to class without making any true friends. People who knew she was related to JoJo asked how he was doing at college, but they never inquired about her own status.

Mimi convinced herself that being invisible was great. It was best to sit in your seat and answer only when called on, and make the answer short and sweet, so no one even knew you had answered. When you were invisible, people did not point out your faults like they did with poor Walter Riley and Nita Thomas. Walter's clothing, not ironed, too small, and musty-smelling, showed that nobody cared about him at home. People harassed him constantly. And Nita's mother refused to perm her daughter's hair, citing a natural look with corn rows or a small afro to be more preferable. In high school, permed hair had become an unwritten requirement. Her own mother had finally broken down and allowed an occasional perming to be done to Mimi's head. Nita looked miserable with her hair, and leave it to teenagers to spot misery.

Invisibility allowed Mimi to hide the secret. Who would want to be friends with a girl who did that nasty thing with her own daddy? No one did things like that with their own father? When she was visible, people could see what had happened written on her like words in a book. If they knew, she was certain they would gossip about her. They would judge her. She couldn't bear that.

So yes, invisible was just fine with her. She had messed up too many lives already. Why bring other people to her misery? Why create misery? In comparison to the other options known to her, invisibility was her savior. The only challenge with invisibility—loneliness.

But just as the first snowfall had made its way onto the doorstep of the house and Christmas break was only one week away, two things happened to modify her world of invisibility. She met a girl, and she met a boy.

Mimi met the girl while trying to get her locker unstuck. Since the first day of school, it had been threatening never to open again, but each time with just a little jiggle and a tug, it flew open, nearly caving in her nose. On the day she met the girl, she was struggling with it like a wrestler against a better opponent. She tried to do it discreetly because that was how she managed invisibility. Mimi waved small hellos and spoke very little. And she never did anything that might draw attention. The non-cooperating locker threatened her invisibility as she grunted to get it open.

The girl appeared next to her without warning. She banged on the locker next to the handle, and then said, "Pull up and pull out." Mimi dutifully followed her instructions, and the locker flew open, nearly caving in her nose once again. She was sure the locker was trying to kill her.

"Used to happen to me, too. Ya know you could ask for a new locker." This was how she met Alaska Yvonne Hart.

While checking out a book from the library, she met the boy. Mimi imagined she had to be the only teenager who planned to spend Christmas break reading the book, *Little Women*. Her English instructor mentioned it as an offhanded suggestion, but Mimi could tell by the teacher's weak smile that she was trying to cover a fanatical love of the book. Mimi decided she ought to see what was so great about it.

She had found a lone copy in the school library and was studying the back cover when the boy appeared next to her and said, "*Little Women*, huh? You got Miss Bane for English, don't you?" That was how she met Xavier Munroe Wright.

Since the beginning of the school year, her lunch routine included quickly eating her meal in the cafeteria and spending the remainder of the period in the library. She had learned a lot about the librarian's private life just by sitting at a desk and reading. The lady was a bit of a gossip and may have been a borderline alcoholic.

Alaska changed all that by inviting Mimi to eat lunch with her in the cafeteria. Initially, Mimi shunned the offer, fearing a mess up of any sort would threaten the invisible persona she easily had been able to create. Her refusal had no effect on how Alaska treated her whenever they met. The girl was kind and easy to talk with. Over time, Mimi noticed something interesting about Alaska. She did not seem to have a single group of people that she spent most of her time with. Depending on her roster for the day, Mimi might pass Alaska three or four times in the hallway. Each time Alaska would greet her brightly, while at the same time she might be engaged in a conversation with any one of the varying personalities in their high school. Mimi found herself wondering how Alaska could talk as openly and freely with the school basketball star as she could with the first violin of the orchestra. But she could and did. She appeared to be well liked by everyone.

Mimi had been standing outside her new locker when Alaska invited her to lunch for a second time. She had gone to the locker to grab a cupcake she had stolen from home. "Stolen" was the correct word since her mother had taken the cupcake out of the brown paper bag and replaced it with an apple. After warning and admonishing Mimi about her weight and what a cupcake would do to her butt, her mother made the mistake of leaving Mimi alone in the kitchen. When Mimi determined it was safe, she returned the cupcake to the bag and put the apple back in the crisper.

Alaska had a contagious smile resting upon an unblemished and inviting face. Her hair was a mound of curls. Her voice had a soft touch, which promised not to hurt. Before Mimi could find the words to decline again to safeguard invisibility, she was saying, "Sure."

As they entered the cafeteria, people spoke to Alaska, but very few acknowledged the presence of the brown-skinned, large-eyed girl next to her. One boy, whose name would not make its way to Mimi's frontal lobe, stopped Mimi and asked about JoJo. Upon hearing he was doing well, the unnamed boy sauntered away. The table at which Alaska sat for lunch was unoccupied when Mimi and she arrived. But within minutes, students from the well-dressed to the just-getting-by stopped by to chat, or sit and eat with them. The empty table was suddenly a busy bee hive, and invisible Mimi sat at the corner of it, watching and in-taking.

From the frenzy, Mimi made an important discovery—one she was ashamed of not knowing. Alaska was running for student government, and it actually looked as if she might win. Even the popular students wanted to vote for her. Mimi surmised it was because they simply believed she could do the job.

"Hey, I'm sorry," she said. "I didn't know you were running for student government." She felt like her next sentence needed to be said as some form of thank you for the lunch invitation. "I will be voting for you." She should have punched her own arm because until that moment she had no idea who the candidates were.

"Thanks," Alaska responded.

Mimi scanned the cafeteria. Her eyes rested upon a tall metal box with a glass window. Behind the window were some of the same snacks she had been bringing from home. Her favorite, the Peanut Chew bar, was on the third row from the bottom. When had the school placed vending machines in the cafeteria, or had they been here all along? And why did she not notice them? One challenge with invisibility became clear to her. Sometimes you went unseen, and sometimes you did not see.

She cleared her throat and turned toward Alaska. "Do you want to go into politics when you're older?" she asked.

"Nope." Alaska had been chewing slowly on a bite of a peanut butter and jelly sandwich. "You're wondering why I'm running for student government, aren't you?"

"Yes," Mimi answered.

"I think I can make a true difference." Mimi looked at her for a moment. Out of a politician's mouth, that would have sounded cheesy, but out of Alaska's mouth it sounded genuine. The girl believed she could make some type of impact on the school.

"So what do you want to be when you're older?" Mimi wanted to bite a hole in her own tongue. The question was juvenile.

Alaska did not notice or care about the quality of the question. She quickly answered, "A marine biologist."

And once again Mimi found herself staring at this girl, who had the physical attributes for the cheerleading squad, but she was not using them at all. "Of all the careers in the world, how did you get to that one?" she asked.

Alaska shrugged. "I saw a show on television about life in the ocean. It was so interesting to see what lives at the bottom of the sea. And tah-dah."

"Can you swim?"

"No."

"How long can you hold your breath?"

"I don't know."

"Well, what do you have to do to become one?"

"I don't know."

"Do you have to go to college?"

"S'pose so."

And this was the difference between Alaska and her. The difference that became endearing to Mimi. Mimi's life required careful planning. Every step had to be orchestrated around probable mishaps and definite pain. But Alaska could wake up deciding to wear her green shirt, and just as she was about to walk out the door, run back up the steps to change into her navy one. To Mimi, Alaska approached life like she happened to it and not like it happened to her. Alaska's personality countered Mimi's character so greatly that she calmed her. Also, Alaska said things that made Mimi feel better about herself.

Once, when she came to school wearing her last pair of clean jeans because she forgot to follow her mother's new "do your own laundry" rule, she felt self-conscious about the fact that she had worn similar looking jeans the day before. She swore someone would think she wore the same pants two days in a row.

No one noticed but Alaska, who asked "Didn't you have pants on like that yesterday?" Mimi shrunk inside at the question. She wished she could snap her fingers to bring back the invisibility. Alaska had no volume control, so Mimi thought the whole school heard the question. But Alaska's next words made the difference for Mimi.

"Well, I meant to tell you they look nice on you. Are you losing weight?"

She and Alaska grew into good friends, but Alaska was one of her only two friends. It pained her to see girls and boys in large crowds, laughing and joking with one another, and creating a bond that she knew she would never experience. She imagined JoJo once enjoyed this camaraderie since he had been popular in high school. Unfortunately, she had none of his talent, none of his gregariousness, none of his appeal. She only had her brain, which earned her a certificate in the nerd crowd as another kid who did not fit because she was "too smart." She kept to her books because they were easier to deal with than people. Books did not require you to look them in the eyes.

Secretly, Mimi envied Alaska. Her appearance and personality were ample reasons to do so, but these were not Mimi's reasons. Her jealousy's target was Alaska's confidence. Alaska was not fearful of nightmares that recorded themselves as dark circles under sleepless eyes. Her stride was not marked with timidity. Her voice was not shrouded in low tones to which people sometimes barked, "Please, speak up. I can't hear you."

Mimi enjoyed their friendship, but she never kidded herself that she might be Alaska's best friend. She treated the relationship as what she knew it to be—a blessing. It most likely spared her from being noticed and emotionally tortured.

Her friendship with Xavier was a little less overt. He talked to her, but never carried on a conversation for more than a minute. Xavier always appeared to be rushing to the next location. The brief pause to speak with Mimi was like something he did because it was along the way. He was in two classes with her, English and Algebra, but he sat in the back of the room and spoke only when spoken to.

He didn't have popularity, but he had respect. Something Mimi had watched him receive with her own eyes. It happened on the day the clocks were turned back, giving every thankful soul one more hour of rest. That additional hour should have placed everyone in a lighter mood, but it had an opposite effect on both students and teachers. The day had been filled with quick tempers and short fuses. Mimi had spent the entire day hiding in her own shadow.

On days when lunar teachings seemed truer than ever, the biggest and the meanest students should have remained at home, as a simple gesture of compassion for the rest of the world. But on the day the clocks went back, Mason Field came to school anyway, knowing, for some inexplicable reason, he was not in the best of his bad moods. He was angrier than normal.

High school rumors reported Mason was two grades behind. He should have already graduated. While his schooling slowed, his body had not. Mason had a wide head and a massive chest. He looked like a twenty-year-old man and behaved like a ten-year-old boy. On the day the clock went back one hour, Mason was already at the end of his lunch when Xavier walked into the cafeteria to eat his own. At that moment, Mason's mind informed him he should say something derogatory about Xavier's mother, and the something he chose was about the color of her skin. Mimi had finished her lunch and was executing her escape route to the library when she heard the comment and froze. She was not alone; the entire cafeteria hushed since Mason had basically shouted the comment at Xavier.

Xavier possessed a lanky frame. He had a thin, tight face with gentle eyes and a deep brow, which made it look like his mind was always preoccupied. Yet, when he spoke with people, he did so as if he paid attention to every word they said, even if they only said two words. He did not have the handsome looks that girls drooled over, or the body that even women lusted after, but he was handsome in an everyday way. Sometimes Mimi looked at him and thought he would grow into a strong and confident protector, like the lumberjack that sold paper towels on TV. Xavier's response to Mason was delicate, yet sharp. It ignited in Mason the need to sail across the cafeteria floor at Xavier.

And then it was over. Mason was on the floor holding both eyes. Xavier stood over him, fists balled and ready to land two more punches. The cafeteria was quiet for one more moment, and then erupted like stock market brokers on a trading floor. Mason was suspended. Xavier was exonerated as having defended himself. Respect oozed from battlers and peacemakers as the word spread that Xavier was not an instigator, but he also was not a wimp. At the time, Mimi had slunk from the cafeteria with her mind filled of images of Xavier defending himself and essentially his mother.

She dismissed those images until he spoke to her in the library. The interaction, small as it was, ignited thoughts of him that battled against images of her childhood and her father in her mind. Often, when she thought he was not looking, Mimi would stare at Xavier and try to memorize certain features of his face and body. She tried to imagine what it felt like to have his arm around her. She already knew what the star basketball player's arms felt like. At least in her mind she knew, since he had done no more than bump into her accidentally and say, "'Scuse me." After he walked away, she remained in the spot as his scent lingered. She had smelled cinnamon. Mimi fantasized enough to know his arms were solid and secure. That had been easy, but she could not quite get the feeling of Xavier's hold to fill her mind. He was a mystery. She didn't quite understand why he bothered to acknowledge her.

By the second year of high school, they had worked beyond "Hey, what's up?" to an in-depth conversation about a teacher who was being fired for inappropriate behavior with a student. The conversation, initiated by him, began simply when Mimi bent to pick up her Civics book. He appeared next to her like an apparition and bent down with her to grab the stray textbook. His arm slightly brushed against hers.

"Keep that up and another teacher will be in danger of being fired," he said.

"What?" she said, straightening up only to drop another book. He bent to pick it up.

"I said if you keep bending over and showing everyone your goodies, they'll be firing another teacher."

She twisted her face, eyes squinted, nose up, lips poked out. What the heck was he talking about?

He laughed. "I mean, you look nice. Have you lost some weight?"

She had, but not intentionally. Mimi was sick with worry about the second year of high school. The first had been so lonely, especially during the summer. She had lost touch with Bizzy and Kayla. In a moment of delirium, she had reached out to Ava, who still had the same phone number, but who answered her excitement by hanging up in Mimi's ear. Alaska hadn't engaged her beyond school. She hadn't extended an invitation to her party to Mimi. Instead, she said "I thought you didn't like things like that." Where Alaska ever got the idea that Mimi did not like parties was baffling. She did not know being invisible would work so well, and she did not know if she could take three more years of her own creation. Sure, she had Alaska's tailwind support, and occasionally, Xavier acknowledged her presence, but no one else paid her any attention.

Added to her personal drama was the fact that she had been having dreams about her father. Dreams of being ten years old again, and his long fingers stretching out toward her and pulling her to him. As a result of all this stress, she sometimes just forgot to eat.

She found a response to Xavier. "I did. Just a little, I did. Umm. Umm. Thanks." She felt like an idiot.

"Sad, isn't it?"

"What?"

"Teachers can't even be trusted." She knew the teacher, and she knew the accuser.

"What makes you think it's true?"

He tilted his head. For the first time, because she never dared stare directly into his eyes, she noticed their color—dark gray with flecks of white.

"That's true. I don't know if it's true. I just believed what everyone else said."

She dropped her eyes to his lips, a safer place.

"You can't believe what everyone says. I need some proof. Like everything you hear on TV. It's not always true. Give me proof. Besides, that boy who said it happened—" Mimi stopped. She had said too much. More than she wanted to say. She kept her eyes on his lips, but she could feel his eyes roaming her face.

"Never thought about it like that. That girl has been known to lie, cheat, and steal. Guess we better wait for the jury. Shoot, I gotta run. Don't want to be late to Mr. Jockstrap—I mean, Jocceyson's class."

Xavier was backing away and smiling, and then he turned to run to class.

Buzzzz!

That was the school buzzer announcing the start of the next class. Mimi was already late. She waited and inhaled the scent he left. Pine cones.

Chapter 17
You're the Reason

JoJo came home from college at least twice a year, and each time, Mimi sat huddled in her bedroom waiting for him to go back. His college was on the other side of the country, but she wished it were the other side of the world.

Whenever JoJo announced he was coming home, her mother would perform as if royalty were visiting them. She cleaned his room until it reeked of a mixture of Pine Sol and Pledge. It was ridiculous because the room remained untouched in his absence; neither she nor her mom bothered to open his bedroom door while he was away.

Her mother also cooked all his favorite meals and stocked the refrigerator with all his favorite snacks. JoJo played college baseball, and his appetite had not changed from his days of playing high school baseball. He was ravenous every hour of his stay. In addition, her mother took him shopping and inquired about everything that was happening in school, even though she called him every week to get the same details.

JoJo appeared to accept his mother's intrusion in his life as a necessary part of their existence. He answered her questions, and he picked up the phone when she called. He ate her meals. If he went to visit friends, he made sure she knew where he was and when to expect him home.

Along with his return, he would bring small gifts, which he purchased from the college bookstore. Trinkets really, because it was all he could afford. He brought their mother such treasures as a mug with bold, black letters that read "Best Mom" or a pen with the college's name on it. Their mother's response would have made anyone think she had won the lottery. She grinned and thanked him repeatedly for thinking of her. On the other hand, Mimi always got a T-shirt that was too small, a sign that he had grabbed it on his way to the register.

His routine when he arrived at the front door was always the same. A big hug for his mother made her squeal with happiness and say, "JoJo, baby, let me go. Let me go." Then she would lock her arms around his waist and tightly return the hug. With Mimi, he wrapped an arm around her shoulder and squeezed briefly, while grunting, "Hi, Mimi." That was it. No Mimi-bean. Mimi-nut. Mimi-pumpkin. Mimi-runt. Nothing. Just Mimi.

It had been this way since the day he found out what their father had been doing to her. His brotherly affection was replaced by a frigid reception. If she walked in a room, he walked out. At the breakfast table, he directed his conversations toward his mother or the thin air. When told to do something for Mimi like drive her to a store to get school supplies, he did so with nearly complete silence. Any dialogue consisted of monosyllabic responses such as "Where?"; "What?"; "Yes"; "No"; "Here" and "6:00 p.m."

She was carrying a disease that he wanted no part of. After their father went to prison, JoJo was home one more year before he was off to college. That year was probably the beginning of Mimi's loneliness and shame. Loneliness crept in because her once protective, once playful, big brother pretended she did not exist. Shame followed because her mother insisted on pretending her father had died, and nothing at all had happened to Mimi. They never discussed it. They never referenced it. They approached topics about other children being molested as if it were a new phenomenon.

JoJo's latest stay was during Christmas break. He would be home for two weeks. According to her mother, he planned to spend one of those weeks at the Florida vacation home of his latest girlfriend. Mimi let a cheer slip from her mouth when she heard this, and she had to pretend she was yawning when she saw her mother's irritated look.

JoJo's girlfriend was named Tomas. When she called their home, she whined his name into the phone. He had a picture of her on his bedroom mirror. Once, when his bedroom door was open and he was gone for the day, Mimi ventured into his room and surveyed the picture. The girl had long, fake hair, a face caked in makeup, and a long skinny neck. Mimi once heard JoJo tell their mother that Tomas "came from money." But as Mimi studied her picture, she believed that Tomas looked like she came from a celebrity magazine, and that was the closest she probably had been to money.

The week he spent with them included Christmas Day. Mimi sat on the couch with her legs crossed under her. JoJo and her mother sat on the floor chatting and opening a gift he had bought. Mimi already held her own gifts. JoJo had given her another T-shirt with his baseball team's mascot on the front and a pack of colored pencils with the school's name on them. She held the pencils as she watched her mother unfold a gold necklace with a tiny gold dove dangling from it.

"This made me think of you when I saw it," he said. "After all you been through, raising us by yourself and all . . . you still know how to fly like a beautiful dove."

Her mother's eyes filled with tears. She hugged JoJo for a long time while Mimi, wearing the frozen smile people put on for annual pictures at school, watched. When they broke the embrace, and while each of them wiped their eyes, Mimi slipped off the couch and quietly went to her bedroom. She could hear them laughing with Christmas music floating from the stereo.

The next day she sat in the kitchen staring at a bowl of cereal. The dreams were getting worse, and after each one, she found herself making a breakfast but not eating it.

JoJo sauntered into the kitchen scratching his chest and yawning. He jumped when he saw her at the table.

"Morning," he said.

"Good morning," she said. She didn't know how the next words made it out of her mouth. "That was a nice gift you gave Mom."

He was rummaging in the refrigerator. She sensed he knew what he wanted, but stayed there longer than necessary, moving and shifting items on the racks needlessly. "Thanks," he muttered.

"I thought it was very pretty."

"Thanks." His head was still in the refrigerator.

"I just wondered what I did that makes you think I'm still a kid who needs colored pencils."

The clanking of dishes as he moved them around in the refrigerator stopped. He slowly backed out and straightened himself. She looked over at him and thought he must be cold standing there in the open refrigerator door wearing only a tank top and shorts. The heat had not come on yet.

"What?" he asked. A quiver was in his voice.

"I just want to know what I—"

"You know what you did!"

"Wha—"

His hazel eyes darkened and the look cut off her response. He slammed the refrigerator door closed. Something inside clanked as it fell over. JoJo peered around the corner of the kitchen door, then moved next to her. It took him two steps.

"Don't you *dare* ask what you did." He grimaced and spat out his response through clenched teeth. "How the hell can you say you don't know what you did?"

"JoJo—"

"You're the reason our mother has to struggle so hard. You're the reason our father is in prison. Before you came up with that mess, I believed our family could have gotten back together."

"No, we couldn't, Jo—"

"How do you know? How do you know what could have happened. Dad was trying to get himself together. And he could have done it and came back home."

"He wasn't trying—"

"But then you came up with that lie and messed him up. You messed up our family. You messed up our chance to be together."

"JoJo, it was not a—"

"Shut up!" His voice was a little loud. He lowered it for his next statement. "You stupid girl! Was your daddy so precious to you, you couldn't stand to see anyone else get his love? So precious you had to tell a lie to keep him to yourself?"

Her insides became a pool of water in her feet. Had the ground moved beneath her, or was the room spinning and causing all of the lightheadedness? She placed her hands on her hot, fiery cheeks.

"It was . . . It was . . . It was true, JoJo." Her words sounded feeble in her own ears. A lump was rising in her throat.

"Something that nasty can't be true. Not at least for Dad. He was a lot of things, and he was struggling to get his life together because he missed her." JoJo pointed toward the kitchen door. "But most importantly, he wasn't that kind of man."

She couldn't breathe. "JoJo, listen. He—"

"What! You going to tell me the same lies you told in court?" He paused. She looked at him. His eyes bore into her own. "If it was so bad, and he was doing such terrible things to you, why the hell would you keep going to his house?"

And there it was. Something she was not sure she knew how to answer. She went because he was her father, her daddy. Mimi lost track of what to say and what came out was, "You didn't visit him at all, so who are you to talk?"

"He knew I had stuff to do with baseball. He understood. He told me. He told me to take care of what I needed to do and don't worry about missing some visits."

"You missed almost every visit. You let me go by myself."

"Don't even try to pull me into your lie!" By now their voices were loud and vicious.

"JoJo. Mimi," called their mother. "You guys are making too much noise. What's wrong?"

JoJo went to the doorway and yelled, "Nothing Mom. Go back to bed." He turned to Mimi. "Just stay away from me. I don't like you very much. No, now that I think about it, I hate you. Stay away from me and I'll stay away from you." He punched the door and left the room.

Mimi looked back at her bowl. Her cereal was drowning in the milk. It was soggy and limp. She knew how it felt.

Chapter 18
Twice the Loss

January 1, 1988

Dear Daddy,

I thought you might want to know how I'm doing now. I'm heading into eleventh grade. I want to go to college, some place far away – hopefully. I keep flip flopping on my major. I'm not sure where I want to concentrate, but I do know I want to help people. I want my life to mean something. I wasn't just put on this Earth for no reason at all, I hope.

JoJo is okay. He's still working for his girlfriend's father. They're talking about marriage now. I hope it works out for them. I think JoJo's got a lot going on inside and getting away from us and from this place may help him feel better. Of course, I'm guessing about what he feels and thinks. I really don't know. JoJo doesn't speak to me. He hasn't said much to me in the last two years. Oh well.

I guess you might care about Mom. She's okay. She started dating some man. Mr. Pepper. I can't stop thinking of Dr. Pepper, the drink, every time I see him. I want to say it so bad, and a couple of times I've slipped. He's nice enough. He makes Mom smile. She's smiling so much that I hardly ever see her. If she's not at work or running errands, she's on the phone with JoJo or Dr. Pepper.

I think you should know that Mom really hates you. I mean she hates your guts. If something comes up like a reference to something about you, she'll growl and call you a stinking dirty dog. Just yesterday I mentioned something about Grandma. I told her I thought my eyes were slanted down a little like yours and Grandma's and Mom went into a tirade. Oh my God, I didn't know she knew some of those words. I don't think I'll mention my eyes again to her.

Sometimes, when I do see her, we talk a little, but I don't see her often.

High school is a little hard. I don't mean the school work. I mean the people. People in high school are mean. I guess it's all those hormones. So I don't have too many friends in high school. If they're this mean and they don't even know a person, what do you think they would do if they knew about what happened? But sometimes I get a little lonely. That's okay.

To tell the truth, I'm not sure why I wrote you. I don't even know what to talk about next. I guess I'll just sign off here.

Love,

Mimi

P.S. How's prison?

Bad things always happen in twos. Or was that threes? She couldn't recall the exact saying as a swoosh of cold air followed her into the building. Mimi stamped her feet on the rubber mat to shake the snow off. Students filed back and forth through the hall. No one acknowledged her. She brushed snow from her jacket and hiked her book bag higher on her back. If she kept carrying her books instead of putting them in her locker, she was going to end up with a crooked back. She was sure of it.

But carrying the books was much more comfortable than the alternative. Other students stopped by their locker all day long to drop off and pick up belongings, but it was just unbearable for her to walk down the same lonely hall, stand in the same lonely spot to open the same lonely locker. Why bother? She just kept all her books with her and trekked from one class to the next.

Mimi began walking to her next class. Tenth grade contained important subjects that were part of preparing for college. She did not want to miss any of them, or mess up her grade point average. Doing well was important for getting away. Getting away from home. Going to another part of the world. She believed it was what would get her past a lot of things. The closer she got to senior year, the more she could see it happening. Leaving her mother. Leaving her home. Leaving behind her father. Her father. She still had not mailed the letter, and she was not sure she would. Mimi stopped to pull the book bag off her shoulder. It was getting too heavy, but not heavy enough to go to the locker.

She dropped the bag at her feet and stretched her back. As she was pulling on her shoulder blade, she caught a glimpse of him coming down the hall. His long legs moved swiftly, but his head was down. He was reading a piece of paper in his hand. She hadn't spoken to Xavier in over a month, and she still was not ready.

After her fumbling admission of feelings for him and his less than equal response, she knew they could not go back to the relationship they used to have. It was best to avoid him until they both left high school. She searched desperately for a way to get out of the hallway. If he saw her, he would open his mouth, and she didn't want to hear his voice. Mimi noticed that she was standing in front of the auditorium. She pulled the door open and lugged the heavy bag inside. She did this in one swift move and was amazed by her own strength.

On the other side of the door, she inhaled, praying he had not seen her. Her mind flashed back to when she confessed her feelings for him. They had been sitting at McDonald's. Their friendship had advanced to little excursions like this, under the pretense of studying for school. But she felt like these little rendezvous were not about studying. They hardly talked about school; in their sophomore year of high school, they did not have the same periods for the common classes they shared. There were other people he could have turned to for support if he really wanted, but she sensed he liked talking with her.

For several weeks, Mimi had been mulling it over. Should she say something to him? She played out all the possibilities, and the one that hurt the most was his rejection. But she had seen more and more of what she perceived to be signs over the weeks that followed. Xavier held a door open once and softly placed a hand on her back to guide her through the doorway. He purchased her meal during one of their times together. She caught him staring at her while she read an excerpt from the book Little Women. She had reread it and wanted to bring a point to his attention. He listened with his eyes glued to her face. Little signs kept happening and filling her with hope.

The one sign that gave her the most courage was a walk back to her house. At the front steps of her home, they shared idle chatter that she was not following, because she was watching his lips. They looked perfect. Thin. Flesh colored. A flattened heart. She wanted to touch them and had to pin her hands to her sides to stop from doing so. In the middle of whatever he was saying, he reached up and gently smoothed her hair on her head. His hand rested there for a brief moment, then fell back against his leg. He had stopped talking. The silence between them lasted for a moment but felt much longer. She thought he would kiss her next, but the moment was broken by her mother's announcement that she should come in the house because dinner was ready.

All this had given her enough courage a few days later as they sat discussing a movie they had seen separately. At a lull in the conversation, as he pushed fries around on his napkin, and she drew lines on her burger bun with a plastic fork, she started talking. Anyone watching would have thought she was talking to the bun. She did not look at him.

"Xay?" It was a nickname she had been using for a while before she even noticed she was doing it.

"Yeah."

"I . . . I . . . I want to tell you something . . ." Her heart flipped-flopped like fish just caught from the water. She willed it to be still. "I like you." She took a deep breath. "I think we have a lot of fun together. And I hope . . . I hope you like me."

He was quiet for a long time. She looked up to see if he had heard her. Xavier was drawing lines on his French fry with a fork.

"Xay?"

"Huh?"

"Did you hear what I said?"

"I did." His skin was suddenly blotchy. She had learned enough about him to know this was an indicator that he was uncomfortable. "You see . . . Mimi . . . I like you . . . I like you a lot . . ." The last sentence rushed from him and made it sound as if he was talking with his mouth full. He continued slowly, ". . . but as . . . as a friend."

The last word fell to the table and landed on a dried ketchup spot that had not been scrubbed away.

She began packing away her books, shoving them so hard into the bag, that she scratched her hand against the zipper. "O-kay. O-kay." Breathing was hard.

"Mee—" Another nickname that had appeared without each of them noticing it was being used.

"I need to go. I should go."

"Mee—"

"I'll see you at school. Okay?" She wasn't waiting for a response. She was at the door when she heard him call her again. "Mimi!"

And that was it. Even now she was having difficulty breathing. Recalling the memory had been like being there in the restaurant, feeling the air, smelling the aromas, and experiencing the pain all over again.

Leaning against the door, a voice from the front of the auditorium jolted her.

"We can decorate the whole front like that time period. I'm seeing red, green, and some blue, especially over here in this corner."

"My mom has a picture of a jukebox. Maybe we can make a cardboard version."

"Really! Cool."

The three girls moved about the stage, all talking at one time and not really paying attention to each other. Immediately, she saw Alaska's curvy frame among them with her mid-sized hoop earrings swinging back and forth as she swung her arms from one corner of the stage to the other and identified locations for the props they were discussing. She also knew the other two girls. One was in her English class and the other in her Chemistry class. Their names were

Dana and Kimberly. Two beauty queens, as she liked to call them.

Dana turned her head, and each move caused her long tresses to glide gracefully back and forth. She stepped to center stage and put her hands on her waist.

"This is *going* to be the best thing. You *know* people will be talking about it for years after." She had a tendency to place emphasis on the wrong words when she spoke, and the words "going" and "know" were a higher pitch that the other.

Kimberly walked over to her. Her blonde locks were pulled to the top of her head and dangled like bungee ropes when she moved. She was a strikingly pretty girl who was managing to get through high school without learning any tough subjects.

"That's what we want, right?"

Alaska remained in a corner of the stage, studying it. One hand was on her chin. "That's what you want. I just want world peace." The other girls giggled.

"Hey, how's the party planning going?" Kimberly said.

"I'm not having a party," said Alaska. "I'm having an experience. My parents are letting me do a girls sleepover in our newly finished basement. They built a fireplace down there and everything, so it'll be the coolest thing."

"Well, I'm coming, but I don't think you should invite your friend," said Dana.

"What friend?" Alaska asked, still studying the spot.

"That girl," Dana said. "What's her name?" Snapping her fingers, she added, "The one with the long neck, beagle eyes, and big head. She's always hanging around you."

Alaska turned to face the girls. "Mimi?"

"That's it. Her," said Dana. "I don't like her. She's weird."

"I don't like her either," added Kimberly.

Alaska seemed to mull this over a bit before answering. "To tell you the truth, she is a little clingy. The girl needs some friends. I think I'm the only person in this whole school who talks to her. It's sad."

"It's beyond sad. She needs a life, and you don't want that around you."

"I know. I know. She's a real bummer. Looking all pitiful. But what can I do? I said hi and next thing I knew I had a sidekick." Alaska moved to another corner of the stage.

"Well, if I were you I'd get roach spray. That keeps pests from bothering you," said Kimberly, and all three girls burst out in laughter.

When Alaska regained her composure, she wiped her forehead and said, "Seriously, I need to talk to her about how clingy she is. And I'd already decided she was too clingy to invite to the sleepover."

Mimi watched from the darkened shadow of the doorway. The girls switched to another topic and began walking to the back entrance of the stage. Their laughter clipped as the door slammed behind them. For a while Mimi stood still. A buzzer rang out signaling a class change, but she did not move. Her eyes stung, but no tears fell down her face. Not only was she lonely, but she was a pariah. A lonely pariah. A pariah no one cared about.

She remembered a Bible story her grandmother once taught her. The lesson she was supposed to get was that people were different, but Jesus loved us all. But all she kept thinking about was what it must have felt like to be a leper.

People shunning you. How did you eat? How did you make money to pay bills? Those were the only questions she had at the end of the story, and now she felt she knew what the leper must have known. He would always be lonely, even if he was healed.

Heartbroken, she grabbed her book bag and walked out of the auditorium. She walked back down the hall and out the door into the snow. It was coming down harder.

Chapter 19
And Now . . . Mom

A week after overhearing the conversation between Alaska, Kimberly, and Dana, Mimi sat in the kitchen with her mom. It was the end of a long day for both of them and her mother was recounting a useless suggestion a co-worker had implemented. Lost in thought, Mimi gazed ahead, still feeling the sting of the girls' comments.

Her mother reached for a roll in the bread basket. The table was covered with dishes of food. One bowl contained steaming green beans, another bowl offered fluffy mashed potatoes, and an accompanying gravy boat sat next to it. A plate, slathered with baked chicken, sat near the basket of rolls, and an apple pie rested neatly under the glass dome of the cake stand. Her mother had been unable to modify her cooking for just two, instead of three people, with one being a teenaged boy whose stomach was always empty. The dishes on the table would be wrapped and placed in the refrigerator to act as leftovers for the next few days. The only problem was, she did not like leftovers and neither did her mother. Eventually, most of the food would be thrown away.

Mimi pushed her green beans into the moat she had created in her potatoes. They drowned in the sauce she piled in the middle. Her mother's voice moved in and out of her head.

"I can't understand people," she was saying. "Why anyone would decide to make the report include numbers that we're never going to use is beyond me. Sometimes people can be so stupid."

Hours of listening to her mother gripe about work had solidified which career Mimi did not want to pursue. Over the years, her mother had been promoted to a supervisor in the Finance Department. Her days seemed to be filled with people who looked at numbers, argued over numbers, and sometimes celebrated numbers. How could her mother love this job so much? It was a mystery to Mimi, and she decided a job like that was not the job for her.

"I think I'll talk to him about it tomorrow. I'm trying to get them to recognize my talent. The best way to do that is to show initiative in finding the problems and bringing them to the surface."

Somewhere in Mimi's mind she remembered hearing those words before. Her mother was always talking about finding problems and bringing them to the surface. She had been at her current job for two years now and wanted to be in an upper-level position. She came home and strategized about how to make them see her. Yet, no matter how hard she worked, how many problems she found and brought to the surface, the promotion still had not shown up. Somewhere in the middle of talking, her mother switched topics, and Mimi missed it.

"Mimi?" her mother called. "Are you listening to me? What do you think?"

No, she had not been listening, and she had to confess it now. "Think about what?" She could feel herself getting irritated with her mother. She scrunched her nose involuntarily.

"Don't do that. You know I hate when you do that," her mother said, a hint of irritation lacing her own voice. "You heard what I said."

Weariness filled Mimi's soul. She let out a breath. "No, Mom. I didn't hear what you said. Do you mind repeating it?"

"Look, young lady, ever since you turned into a teenager you've had a little attitude about everything. You need to fix your attitude and watch your tone when you speak to me."

"What tone? I didn't even say anything. I just asked you to repeat it."

"You know what, Mimi, forget it. You don't have to come with us. I think you would mess up our good time anyhow with the way you're acting."

"Go where? What are you talking about?" She could feel heat rising in her stomach, another sign that her irritation was advancing to a next level.

Her mother stood and snatched her own plate from the table. She threw it in the sink with such a clamor that Mimi was sure it was cracked or broken. "You know, Mimi, I'm tired. I think I'll give your brother a call."

The statement punched Mimi in the stomach. Whenever her mother was annoyed or bored with Mimi, she used it as an opportunity to call JoJo. It happened all the time, but with Mimi's mind on Alaska's calling her clingy, her mother's words felt like another judgment call. Someone else was saying she was not good enough for them.

"You know what, Mom, why don't you call him. He's more your cup of tea, right? I can't do anything right, but there's nothing he can do that's wrong. So go ahead, call JoJo." She pushed her plate away and her moat-filled gravy sloshed onto the table.

"What are you talking about?"

"I'm talking about the fact that you love him more than me."

"What?"

"Mom, please stop. I've seen it for the last few years. He's like your golden child. I'm like the pain in your butt."

"Stop it. That's not true at all."

"But it doesn't matter, Mom. It really doesn't matter." She was warming up, and now she was cresting the hill of the rollercoaster ride. Gravity was about to take her on a high speed descent to the bottom, and there was no way to stop it. "It doesn't matter at all. One day you won't have to worry about me. I'll be out of you and JoJo's life for good."

"Listen, young lady, watch your tone. You know you're acting silly. You're getting upset for nothing. You're just like that, Mimi, melodramatic. Pull yourself together."

Mimi stood up so quickly she bumped the table and jostled her drink. A splash of water flew onto the table and mixed with the spilled gravy. She turned to go but stopped at the door. "You know, Mom, let's forget I even tried to say something."

As Mimi left the kitchen, she heard her mother say, "I think that's best. And you'd better stay in your room until you get your head together." She heard her mother move to the phone on the wall, lift the receiver, and begin punching in numbers.

"Hey, JoJo . . ."

Chapter 20
Mimi, the "L"

June 1, 1988

Dear Daddy,

I'm so scared. I keep getting these crazy thoughts. Like maybe life would be better if I wasn't around. I'm sure it would be better for Mom and JoJo. I doubt they'd even miss me. I'm feeling like the entire world would be better. No one wants me around. I'm ugly. I'm fat. I'm hideous. My nose is too pug. My hair is too short. My lips are too big. I hate being me, and I know people hate being around me.

I'm really, really thinking about doing something, anything so I don't have to be in a world where people don't want me in it.

Mimi

Alaska's party had come and gone with no invitation extended to Mimi. It was the first of three that Alaska had planned before the summer break. She hadn't mentioned them to Mimi, and Mimi hadn't asked, though high school being high school, almost everyone knew about these events.

In fact, after the auditorium eavesdropping session, Mimi had simply walked out of Alaska's life. It was her version of a pre-emptive strike. Leave them before they leave you. So she stopped accepting Alaska's lunch invitations. If she saw her in the hallway, she briefly nodded and quickly walked past her. Eventually, she took away the nod and looked the other way, or walked in another direction. At the beginning of the school year, she sat next to Alaska in the one class they shared. With the school year nearly complete, she feigned a sight ailment and asked to be moved closer to the board. Alaska acknowledged none of her actions and simply looked relieved that she did not have to interact any longer with Mimi.

On the night of Alaska's third party, Mimi closed her bedroom door and busied herself by cleaning out her closet. It had been a hot day, but she refused to open a window or turn on her fan.

With a light film of water building just above her upper lip, she dived into the explosive closet. Clothes lay in disarray to the point where none of the floor was visible. A sneaker and a jelly sandal stood lonely, their match nowhere in sight. At some point she had forgotten about a pack of cookies stuffed into the pocket of a pair of stonewashed jeans. She had managed to step on the pants, causing the pack to burst. Cookie crumbs sprinkled onto other shirts and pants. She knew she needed to clean everything before her mother saw the mess. Although they lived in a single dwelling, her mother still had fears of apartments and row homes and mice.

Mimi threw clothes on her bed and started sorting them by style. She began with her tops, neon colored sweaters in one pile, shoulder padded blouses in another. Next, she pulled her skirts together in another pile, but since she did not own many, the pile was miniscule. And finally, she attacked her jeans, organizing them by brand and color while absently picking off crumbs as she worked.

As she sorted, her mind drifted to her loneliness. Each time she thought about not being able to call and gab with someone on the phone, she would dig further in the closet and find something else to organize. When the closet was empty, she plopped on the one corner of her bed that was not covered by a neat mound of clothing and used her hands to wipe her face, which was glistening.

Her mind took her to the girls at Alaska's party. At that moment, they were probably in Alaska's basement, sitting on her couch or on her floor. Alaska probably had pillows thrown on the floor so some of the guests could lay across a pillow on their stomachs or backs. The girls were probably shrilling with laughter as they talked about people at school. Mimi saw Kimberly and Dana squeezed next to each other on a futon, and initiating a score card rating system for people in the school.

"I got it. I got it," shouted Dana. "Here's the system. Let's rate them from one to five. One means the person is awesome, and five means they are totally dweebs, real losers. Somebody throw a name out."

Mimi could see Alaska perched in the center of the floor. Lately, Alaska had straightened her mop of curls, and her hair now fell to the center of her back. It was a style that opened her face and revealed how slender it really was. She started wearing light pink lipstick that shined even when she was not in the sunlight. Her fashion style had also changed some. She now wore plaid thigh-high skirts to school, instead of her signature cargo pants. The latest change included a somewhat popular boyfriend.

Clearly, Mimi could see Alaska in a pink satin baby doll pajama set, raising her hand to give the first entry for the rating system.

"Ellis Moore," Alaska said.

All the girls moaned and cheered as somebody volunteered, "Definitely a one. If that boy didn't already have a girlfriend . . ." The volunteer pretended to faint.

"Nathan Cooper," someone else ventured.

"Poo-wee. I'll give him a 4.5. Seriously, if he'd just brush his teeth, he might have a chance." Everyone burst with laughter.

"I got another one," said a third person. "Monica Morehouse."

"Oh my God! Moany Monica. That girl needs a life."

"But she knows her stuff, and she's always willing to help you. So I'd give her a 3.5." The rest of the group shook their head in agreement.

So down the line they would go, picking people and rating people on the scale until someone, probably Kimberly, would say, "What about Mimi what's her name? I don't even know her last name."

"You know, she's JoJo Comb's sister. You know JoJo?"

"Now he's definitely a one."

"No way. He can't be related to her. That girl's got issues."

"I know. I say definitely a five. Loser all the way."

They would all burst into another round of laughs as the one who pronounced Mimi's rating sealed it by putting her fingers in the shape of an "L" and placing it on her own forehead.

Mimi pulled her legs up on the bed and hugged them tightly. Hot tears burned her eyes.

What would life be like if she was not around? Would anyone miss her?

Several ways to remove herself from the world consumed her thoughts. She had heard about a woman who cut her own wrists, but that seemed painful. Her threshold for pain was very low. She doubted she could thrust the knife deep enough to even make a sufficient slash through her veins. Mimi had heard about a boy who hanged himself. She tried to envision climbing up to her light fixture and wrapping a rope around it with a loop at the end. She tried to see herself putting the loop over her head and around her neck. Instantly, she dismissed this method. It was taking too long in her mind just to make the hanging rope and get up in the chair to rig the contraption. She knew she would chicken out before she even got it set. But she'd also heard about a girl who took sleeping pills, a whole bottle. It seemed easy enough. It would be like going to sleep, but not waking up. Mimi considered going to the bathroom and seeing if they had sleeping pills, but she knew without looking. Her mother had no problem sleeping these days.

She rolled off the bed and wiped her wet face with a shirt from one of the piles. *I don't even have a good way to kill myself.* Looking into the mirror, she made the "L" shape with her index finger and thumb and put it on her forehead. She spoke to her image, "You really and truly re a loser."

She got caught staring at the woman too long. Mimi knew she was, because the woman suddenly put her middle finger up. For some reason, the usual responses such as returning the finger, or rolling down the window and shouting something back at the woman did not come to Mimi. Instead, she was consumed by momentary grief for the woman.

The woman stood at the bus stop with several people, and Mimi's mother had just pulled up to the light signal. Mimi turned to look at the woman but could not look away. Even after the offensive gesture, she stared. Pity followed the grief.

Something in the woman's face sort of hung with Mimi, something the woman wore like a piece of clothing. And no matter what she did, she could not get rid of it. This something was in the slight downward curve at the corners of her mouth, and in the lackluster glow of her skin. In the wrinkle of lines in her forehead, and in the sag of the clothes she wore, lived the something Mimi could not yet place.

Sadness. The word permeated her thoughts. The something was sadness. Sadness covered this woman. Mimi saw it so clearly. The finger gesture had been quick and almost unnoticeable. Afterward, the woman put her head down and pretended to read the ground. Mimi knew this response. In fact, she gave the same reaction when she did not want to be seen yet wanted to be seen—a hunger for someone to notice you, but not hurt you. It was a desire to protect yourself, but also be open to anyone in anyway. Because it felt so familiar, Mimi could not look away from the woman.

The light changed, and as her mother proceeded forward, Mimi began to talk. She would never be able to explain "why" she started talking, but she would always be able to pinpoint "when." The instant the woman had used her middle finger to curse Mimi, but then wanted Mimi to forget about her.

"Mom," Mimi began. They had worked their way past their disagreement, and past their strained roommate situation, into a routine which included talks about college, JoJo (though her mother talked more than Mimi on this subject), and household chores. They talked about nothing more than these safe topics. But now, because of that woman, she was talking about something way beyond college scholarships.

"Mom," she said again, even though her mother had already answered, "Yes."

"What do you think about someone wanting to kill himself?"

Faye Combs jerked the wheel a bit. The car pulled slightly to the right, then headed forward again. She could see her mother squeezing the steering wheel, just like she had done the day she held the phone receiver to call her father after Mimi told her she might be pregnant.

"I think it's the most stupid thing. What kind of person thinks like that? It's dumb to have those thoughts. Only sad, sad people have those thoughts. It's just stupid."

The rush of words had been delivered with a nasty force that felt like a punch in Mimi's stomach. Her mother pushed violently on the turning signal. And as she moved the steering wheel, she added, "Stupid and sad. That's what I think of it." A bit of spittle was in the corner of her mouth, and after she completed her turn, she wiped it away with the back of her hand and drove on in silence. Her face, stony.

Mimi turned her head to look out the window again. Her body felt like it had been slashed, and she pressed her lips tightly together.

Chapter 21
Will

Mimi felt squeezed. Memories of the Squeeze-the-Lemon game appeared in her mind. JoJo, on one end pushing hard against her arm as her body wedged between him and the wall. The whole time she howled with laughter, begging him to stop. But the squeezing she now felt was not a game. Dreams pressed on her heart. Loneliness and shame pressed on her soul.

She functioned well amidst the pressure. If someone cared to try, they would not have found any outward sign of an inner problem. A loner or nerd to peers at school, a typical girl to her mother, Mimi came and went as a supposedly *normal* teen should. But she was not a normal teen. She was a teen who was being invisibly squeezed.

On a day when the squeezing had made its way to her brain, and a dull headache whispered in her ears, she found herself talking brashly to a boy in her neighborhood. She was someone else at the time. Some other girl.

The boy had walked past her house several times while she sat on the front steps reading a book. Finally, when she looked up, she saw him looking directly at her. After a week or so, he was brave enough to walk up to her steps and ask her name.

His name was William. "Will" for short. He was not a handsome boy. In fact, he was a little on the side of ugly, or actually, a lot on the side of ugly. A long head, large lips, and rat-like eyes made him unworthy of a second look, but she liked his voice. Deep bass with a bit of an accent. He told her he was from the Midwest, and an occasional clip on vowels reminded her of his origin.

She found herself sitting straighter in his presence, trying to appear svelte and big busted. She willed her hips to be rounder and her waist slimmer. She added seduction to her voice when she spoke.

Kind and attentive, Will sat on the front steps and talked about his hometown, the move to Pennsylvania, what he liked and disliked about both places. He asked questions about her family, her school, her hobbies, her favorites from color to food, and the book she was reading. He offered her pieces of his candy bar, and afterward, a stick of gum to remove the coconut from her teeth. As more conversations with Will emerged, Mimi told him one or two intimate secrets, but she never told him her big secret. She surmised that if she did, Will would think she was dirty, and he would not like her anymore. So she kept this part of her life closed.

Before Mimi knew what was happening, just a few weeks later, she was at his home. He lived three streets over. In their neighborhood, three or four streets could put you in an entirely different county or community. People were friendly and interacted more on his street, keeping an eye on each other's homes when they went out for store runs or long term vacations. But those people were not around the day she walked into his house and discovered his parents were out until evening.

Mimi should have suspected it was the case. Will had been talking about them going to a work-related event for a few days. She knew the date and the time when his house would be empty and should have been surprised when she found herself rolling around naked on his bed with him. Yet she was not. She didn't know when the decision to have sex with Will was made, but remembered feeling that the only way to make him like her better, was to do this thing. And she had made a decision to do it.

"Making love" or "having sex" with him—they seemed the same to her—was clumsy and quick. She sensed he knew no more than she did. When they were done, she lay on his chest and listened to his heartbeat as it slowed to a steady rhythm. He caressed her head and asked if she was hungry.

Sitting across from him and watching his lips engulf a sandwich, she asked questions about his home. A wooden grandfather clock peaked her interest. He said his mother purchased it from a Fingerhut catalog, and he and his father had built it together. After more talk and a glance at the clock, she realized the time was the same; the clock was not working. He apologized, informed her of the time, and told her he would walk her home.

On the way back to her house, Will talked, she listened. At one point, he asked if he could be her boyfriend. At the moment he asked, a streetlight came on as the sun, red and dull, began to set. They were standing in front of her home by then, and she watched the sun over his shoulder. She didn't answer, so he asked again. She laughed, realizing she had lain in bed with this boy, and she was not already his girlfriend. She agreed to the arrangement. He walked away bouncing on the balls of his feet. Occasionally, turning to wave to her.

Another month passed, three more sex escapades, one of which occurred in the basement of her own home, while her mother was on a date with Dr. Pepper. Then Will did something which changed her. He said, "I love you."

Mimi did not respond at the time. But later, she decided she didn't want to be a girlfriend anymore. She knew exactly when she made that decision. The minute Will asked if she loved him. How could she love him? She was still reeling from his own admission that he loved her. And if he knew everything about her, would he still love her? Probably not.

She told Will she didn't want to be his girlfriend as they left a movie theatre. At 8:00 at night, the sun was still bright in the sky and people ran about in a nearby park playing with a baseball. The sight of the ball reminded her of JoJo. She slapped away the thought, not needing JoJo present at that moment.

"Babe, you wanna stop over my house for a little before you go home?" He reached for her hand, but she conveniently shoved it into her pocketbook pretending to search for something.

"No. I don't think so. Not tonight." She took her hand out of the pocketbook and took a deep breath. *Here we go.* "And actually, I think we might need to take a break."

"Take a break?"

"From each other. For a while."

They had been walking, but he stopped and put his hand on her arm. "Babe, are you breaking up with me?" His face matched the stress in his voice. His rat-eyes watered under raised eyebrows.

"Yes." Why did she sound so callous? She didn't want to sound that way.

"Why?" Why did he sound so clueless? She hated that he sounded that way.

"Will, it's not you, its—"

"Do you think I'm stupid?" He stepped away from her, then stepped toward her again. "Don't give me that it's-not-you-it's-me speech. Whenever people say that, it always means it is you."

The truth of his statement was hilarious and she stifled a giggle. Normally, in a normal situation, with a normal girl, it may have been true. But not this time.

She reassured him, "No, it really isn't you. It's me."

As they rode the bus home, she tried to convince him with words like "not ready," "too fast," and "good guy." She didn't mention his admission of love as a source for the break up. She didn't tell him if he knew her truth he might be repulsed.

On the street corner that took her one direction and him another, she looked over his shoulder at the setting sun, and listened to him whine, "I don't understand. If I'm such a good guy, why break up with me?"

She had no response. She kissed him one last time, said "Goodbye, Will." and walked home alone.

The next day he came over, having sensed something in their last kiss. According to Will, something told him she wanted to be his girlfriend, still. Mimi explained one more time it was not him but her, and watched as he walked away. He came over again the following day, and she hid behind the door and pleaded with her mother to tell Will she was not at home. It took a full week of hiding before he stopped coming over.

September and the beginning of school quickly came. Mimi never saw Will again. Sometimes she thought about him and craved to go over to his house and reconnect. Will seemed to be standing next to her and whispering "I love you" in her ear. Each time she heard those words, she quickly sobered.

She began the school year in solitude, which occasionally required its owner to do things or go places alone. Her mother would drive her to these places. Mimi believed her mother thought she was meeting friends at some of the destinations. A thought her mother never voiced, a thought Mimi did not correct.

Chapter 22
For Safekeeping

February 14, 1989

Dear Daddy,

I have a boyfriend. His name is Duke. He attends a program that I participate in after school. It's for kids who want to go into business. Duke and I are on the same project team. He's a nice guy. I like him a lot. He takes care of me. He's kind to me. He doesn't hurt me at all.

Mommy's fine. JoJo? Okay, I guess. He doesn't really come home. He's in his last year of school, and he's preparing for a job with his girlfriend's father's family. Something about investments. Whatever that means. Sorry he wasn't able to play pro ball. Seems a pity to spend all your life concentrating on one thing and then not to get it. He should have been more well-rounded.

That's what one of my teachers tells us all the time. Have more than one option. I'm still sitting on that fence regarding a college major choice, but this year I took a Creative Writing class for 11th grade elective. I thought it would be an easy A, and it is for me. I like writing. Not sure I can change the world with writing as a major, but who knows.

I took the PSAT's last year. I'm glad we did that. It showed me what I needed to work on. So far so good. I've got all A's, and now I'm getting ready for the SAT's and I'm narrowing down my college choices.

Duke is still thinking about colleges and about his major. I hope he chooses my college. I'd love to have someone I know in my corner with me.

Well, I didn't want anything. I just keep seeing your face in a dream, and I thought I'd write you.

Love,

Mimi

She reached out and fumbled her hand along the neck of the lamp. Where was the switch to turn the darn light on? She had turned this thing on and off for years, but tonight she could not get her hand to the familiar location. Her hand was too wet with perspiration and kept slipping off the neck of the lamp and the knob of the switch. She wiped her hand on the bedspread and reached for the knob again. Mimi turned it, and her room filled with the first level of light. She turned it again, and the light in her room became a bit brighter. A third turn and her room filled as if it was daylight, but her clock told her it was 3:21 a.m.

She needed light at this moment. Light and a lot of it. The dream had been too dark. The weight of her father's body on top of hers blocked the light from her eyes and the breath from her nostrils and mouth. Her fists beat against his chest. Mimi needed to see and breathe. She wanted to see the dingy wall behind him and inhale the staleness of the room. But the more she beat his chest, the darker it became and the less she could breathe. Just when she knew she would die, her eyes flew open and she saw her own bedroom, which was barely lit by the moon. She needed more light and reached for the lamp.

The letter she'd written to her father before going to bed lay on the nightstand. She picked it up. As she reread the letter, she thought about the part she was leaving out. What she was omitting from this letter was that there had been a couple of boys between Will and Duke.

Intentionally, the letter painted the idea that Duke was her first boyfriend. Her father did not know about Will, but if he did and built a timeline to Duke, she wondered what he would have thought of her. Shame flushed in her cheeks. She had not been ashamed of her relationship with these boys until she thought about her father's reaction.

Her history had been that each relationship began and ended in similar ways. She and the boy got to know each other and became friends. They moved to boyfriend and girlfriend; she had gotten smarter after her relationship with Will. Then, she and the boy slept together. They stayed together for just a little while longer, and suddenly, as if it was a brand new idea, Mimi found something wrong— something that she had to do to end the relationship. Sometimes the something was about the boy—ears too big, nose too small, breath too bad. Sometimes it was about her. A sense of being unworthy of someone's trust and care would erupt in her like a volcano, and she would end the relationship.

She was not sure how long it would last with Duke. But she put a smile on her face and pretended she had a real future with him. Mimi left all of this out of the letter because she had not decided if she was going to mail it. She had several letters already, and none of them had been mailed.

Perhaps she believed the letter would squash the dreams. And yet, the dreams continued. When they did, she would wake up with sweat rolling down the back of her neck and into her sleep shirt. The early morning stillness would begin to dry her drenched face. She would lie in bed staring at the ceiling until the sun peeked into her room. The worst dreams made her write her father. The sanity of morning made her tuck the letter away.

She put this letter in an envelope that was already addressed because she had already done the research. Mimi knew where her father was. Knew the prison address and his prison number. All she had to do was seal the envelope, stamp it, and drop it in the mailbox. But it just didn't feel that easy to do.

Rolling out of bed, she dragged herself toward her home safe. She carefully turned the dial to the combination code and then pulled on the handle. The door easily opened. She was thankful it did not behave like her locker at school. After she put the envelope in the safe, she patted the metal box and recalled the day she begged her mother for the safe.

They had gone shopping for a new computer. Her mother preferred to search for one early for college instead of waiting until the last moment. This was an example of how Faye Combs liked to prepare for life. Inside the electronics store, a stand up neon colored sign alerted them to a sale. The sign boasted that for safekeeping, no brand was better than the brand they were selling. A photo of a policeman standing near the home with a thumbs-up signal was supposed to lure the customer into the purchase.

Mimi took the bait and announced that she wanted the safe.

"Why? You don't have anything that valuable," was her mother's response. "Do you?"

"Maybe not, but if there's a fire, I don't want to lose the things that are important to me."

Her mother considered this while they walked around the store lifting items, checking their prices, and putting them back on the shelf. They had come for a new computer but left with two home safes.

"You make a good point," was the response as they lifted the oversized boxes into their cart.

Mimi locked the safe now and put the key in the envelope that she taped behind it. She knew that as long as her room looked presentable, her mother would not come in to check on anything.

One day she would mail the letter. Today wasn't the day.

Chapter 23
Anyone Can Do That

Twelfth grade. Thank God it was finally here. She would have run directly to college if only the road had not been paved with senior year time wasters like class rings, proms, and pictures.

She walked into the Yearbook Committee office and sat where the photographer directed. He was a pudgy man with rosy cheeks and a half-bald head. "Call me Mr. Richardo," he introduced himself then told her about the photos they would be taking while he cleaned the camera lens.

"Did you bring your cap and gown?"

Mimi held them in her hands but nodded assent as Mr. Richardo pointed to a small closet that acted as a dressing room. "We'll start with what I like to call the glamour shot. The cap messes up your hair, so we'll do that one last. You can change there."

The photos took about fifteen minutes with Mr. Richardo stopping every two minutes to adjust something on his camera or on Mimi. When he was all done and had dismissed her, she walked out the door just as Alaska entered. While shouting over her shoulder to someone in the hall, Alaska held the door open for Mimi.

"Thanks," Mimi said.

Alaska responded, "You're welcome."

She rushed into the room and Mimi felt like Alaska had just extended an automatic absentminded courtesy to a stranger on the street. The kind you give where you know someone is in your path, but you do not truly see them. Giving a description to a police officer would be impossible. Alaska had not seen Mimi, even though she knew someone was there.

Mimi received this reaction everywhere she went. People saw her but did not acknowledge her. So by twelfth grade, she had no friends inside school. Occasionally, she would see Xavier. An exchange of looks between them would last a few seconds, and then he would turn his head, erasing that he had noticed her. Mimi grew accustomed to this behavior in people. She learned to expect it.

In her final year of high school, she busied herself with all the preparations for leaving, or as she liked to refer to it, "getting out." She devised a plan that she titled the "Freedom Plan," which, if well-executed, would be the move that would change her life. She would leave everything behind. Her mother. JoJo. Her school. Her empty bedroom. Her latest ex-boyfriend. And her father. They would all become monuments of a past she no longer needed to regard or remember; this is what she told herself.

The Freedom Plan was all about choosing the college that was furthest away. She had been the best student she could be, and she felt somewhere along the line, all the funds, grants, and scholarships she applied for would pan out. Someone would choose her for their school. Someone would give her a full scholarship. This is what she hoped for.

Every day Mimi stood at the mailbox, closed her eyes, and said a silent prayer. She did not know who she was praying to. A long time ago she stopped talking to God, but someone, somewhere, had to be listening to prayers and answering them. She hoped they would show her mercy, throw her a bone, and give her the college and money that would make the Freedom Plan work.

She purposely excluded her last real boyfriend from the Freedom Plan. She knew the first time she met him that their relationship would not last. She already saw what would be her reason for ending it. They met in the library where he worked. Amidst flirting, she discovered he was three years older and already attending college. She was impressed and felt grown up. When she told her mother about him, a frown had grown on her mother's face.

"Isn't he a little old for you?"

"Mom, it's just three years. No big deal."

Her mother shifted in her seat and uncrossed and re-crossed her legs. "I want to meet him."

That meeting turned out to be uneventful. The boyfriend came, ate dinner with them, used his "educated" voice to talk with her mother, and went home. Afterward, her mother, still wearing a frown said, "I think he's going to get tired of you. Some high school chickie . . . What conversation do you have for him? Listen, watch yourself and don't come back here pregnant."

Mimi then realized she and her mother never had a real sex conversation. It was as if her mother had assumed that incest with her father served as the conversation Mimi needed. "Do not come back here pregnant," was all Faye said to her. In this command, she seemed to be acknowledging that Mimi was having sex and was old enough and smart enough to know what to do to prevent a true pregnancy.

The boyfriend's name was Spencer, a junior at a local technical school. He looked every bit like a tech geek—wiry, thin and short with a round head and thick glasses.

Whenever he was on a roll in a conversation, he would push his glasses up to better focus on the person he was talking to, but his face was oily, so the glasses slipped back down his nose. Spencer would push them up again and continue talking, slashing the air with his hands to make his point.

She liked to listen to him and let him think he was teaching her something. It was somewhat of a game to her. The trouble with the game was she already knew what he was talking about and often thought he was an idiot. But just having a boyfriend, just having a prom prospect, made her put up with a great deal of his blabbering.

The first time she let him touch her was when she made her first visit to his home. He lived with his parents and stayed in the basement. Spencer had guided her to his basement apartment late one evening, while the upstairs TV blared a crime drama complete with bullets flying and sirens screaming.

They sat on his bed while she used her own principles of letting a boy know she liked him. She held an aimless conversation about nothing while she crooked her head to the side and massaged his leg. Then she moved the aimless conversation into targeted banter.

"So what type of things do you like to do with your free time?"

Spencer watched her hand moving smoothly up and down his leg. "I like watching TV and playing my video game."

"What does that game do for you?"

"It relaxes me." His eyes were still on her hand.

"I can think of another way to relax you."

His eyes moved from her hand to her eyes, and she leaned forward for him to kiss her. She had mastered how to seduce a boy without thinking about it. During these moments, she forgot how the "L" looked on her forehead.

That night they had sex. Spencer walked her to the bus stop afterward, and waited until the nearly empty bus pulled up to the corner. He pecked her on the lips and watched her climb on and take a seat. Mimi waved at him as the bus pulled off. On the ride home, she kept the image of him standing on the corner, his jacket buttoned up to his chin, and his hands shoved into his jeans pocket. His breath came out of his mouth as white smoke. He kept stamping his feet while he waited with her.

The image made her say aloud, "What do I see in him?" A man and woman glanced at her, then continued their conversation. She wondered again what she saw in this "boy-man." Spencer was a clumsy geek. A grown man living in his parents' musty-smelling basement and reeking of its ever present dankness.

What did she expect to happen? She didn't see in him what she saw in other boys she had been with. She had built fantasies with some of them. Mimi had seen herself being the center of their worlds while they defended her in front of a group of people who taunted her. She had seen herself getting older and going to college with them. She had seen herself marrying one or two of them. Sometimes she had seen drama. Once she saw one of them grabbing her shoulders, shaking her, then pulling her in for a long, hard kiss. She knew that was a cliché from a movie, and she didn't care.

Mimi had seen so many fantasies, but with Spencer she saw nothing. She realized she just wanted someone to hold her. Spencer offered no special qualifications for this. Anyone could do that.

The day after she had been intimate with Spencer, JoJo
called the house and announced his plans to marry his
girlfriend. Her mother was hysterical, crying and gasping for
breath. Crying again. She sat down then stood back up. The
whole time she screamed into the phone, "I can't believe
this! It's finally happening! Oh my God! What will I wear?
Oh my God! Tell her I said congratulations. My boy is
getting married! Oh my goodness!"

Mimi was less enthusiastic. This was one more way for
JoJo to get attention. And he was planning a short
engagement, so there would be a great deal of focus on his
wedding date and less focus on her graduation date. Then
another thought occurred to her. There would be less money
for college as her mother bought outfits and plane tickets
and tried to contribute in some way to the wedding, though
she had nowhere near the money JoJo's soon-to-be father-
in-law possessed.

She was a wreck with worry about responses from colleges
and scholarship applications, and JoJo's impending wedding.
She tried to express herself to Spencer.

"I can't believe he's getting married *now*. You'd think he'd
wait." They were lying in the basement again on another
night when he had secretly brought Mimi in while his parents
were locked away in their bedroom. She still had not met
them, but at this point she did not want to. She decided this
closeness and the idea of someone listening to her was all
she wanted from Spencer.

He still wore his undershirt while Mimi lay completely
naked with the sheets pulled up around her neck. Her body
faced his, and her leg draped over his stomach as he watched
television.

"What does it matter? You said you and he weren't close.
So what do you care if he gets married?"

"It's not that I care that he's getting married. I care that he's getting married now. What about me and graduation and college? I know my mom is going to try to do everything for her baby." She rolled her eyes as she said the word *baby*.

"You know you're being melodramatic." He reached for the remote and switched the channel. Something inside Mimi switched. She actually saw it like a scene in a movie flipping from one frame to the next.

"What?"

"Come on. Stop acting like a baby. Just do what you got to do and ignore this mess." He rolled over. Her leg fell off him.

She hopped out of bed and started pulling on her clothes.

"Hey, where ya going?" he asked, pushing his glasses up his nose. They slipped down again.

"I'm going home."

"Now, Mimi? Wait until my show goes off."

"I don't need you to walk me to the bus stop. Stay here."

He glanced at the television, unsure if he should agree or try to convince her to stay. "Just wait a minute. It's about to go off."

She was fully dressed. "No, I don't need you. You stay here with your show."

As she struggled into her coat and grabbed her bag, he stumbled out of bed. "Mimi."

She was up the basement steps and headed to the front door. A woman stood on the stairway leading to the upper level of the house. She asked, "Who are you?" Then she shouted toward the basement door, "Spencer, get up here!"

Laughter poured from Mimi once she noticed his mother's thick glasses also slid down her long, oily nose. Mimi opened the door and ran into the night.

Chapter 24
Bizzy's Back

March 23, 1990

Dear Daddy,

Someone ought to tell you that JoJo is getting married. It's scheduled for the month before my graduation. Mom is ecstatic. She's got a dress for the mother of the groom, and the girl asked me to be one of her one hundred bridesmaids. I'm not joking. No, really! She has about ten and I'm all the way at the end. The last person to come in and the last person to stand in the line behind the bride. The dress is hideous. A pale silver A-Line with puffy shoulders and a wine colored bodice. Where did she get this idea? Even the fat bridesmaids are arguing about how it makes them look. I'm big, but I don't look like a whale with some book on my chest.

Anyway I'm all set for college. I got accepted at a college in Ohio. It's nearly an eight hour drive away. Not as far as I wanted to go, but far enough. I'm sure there is no way Mom will drive to see me more than once a year. Besides, JoJo and his new bride will be capturing all her attention since they're building this huge house with an in-law suite. I think an in-law suite is a room hidden in the back of your house so your visiting in-law doesn't get in your way. Honestly, I think JoJo's girl hates Mom. When Mom speaks, she gets this frozen smile on her face.

I don't have a boyfriend. My last one was a boy in college. I decided he didn't care enough about me. So I dumped him. I'm not going to mail this letter, but I just wanted to tell you what I think you ought to know.

Love,

Mimi

Before I die, I should burn these letters.

Why in the world was she feeling so calm about this thought? And which was more soothing, the dying or the burning? She wasn't sure. But before anyone had an opportunity to read her letters in some public place again, like a courtroom, she would need to destroy them.

She sealed the letter, addressed it, and then tucked it away in her safe. Her letter writing to her father had increased but none had been mailed. Strangely, she found pleasure in pretending she could write to someone who actually cared about her. She assumed her father still loved her, although she hadn't seen or spoken to him in five years.

The phone rang while she was turning the handle on the safe. Without saying so, the cordless phone had been a peace offering from her mother after their huge fight about how Faye loved JoJo more. By giving her this piece of technology, her mother was saying "see how much I love you" and "JoJo did not have his own phone."

Mimi liked having her own line, but wondered if her mother noticed she rarely received phone calls. No one except boyfriends telephoned, and she currently did not have one of those.

She fell across the bed and grabbed the phone.

"Hello?" she puffed into the phone.

"Mimi?" The voice was high-pitched and shrilly.

"Bizzy!"

"Yes, girl, how are you?"

How was she? She had not spoken to Bizzy in years, and now she was packing to go to an orientation weekend at Foster College in Columbus, Ohio. She and her mother were driving up next week.

"I'm fine, Bizzy. How are you?"

"I'm fine. Hey, I'm back on Terrace Street. Do you want to get together or something."

Mimi's head spun. Bizzy? A friend? An old friend? Someone she used to care about. Someone who once cared about her.

Why was Bizzy calling her? She didn't care why.

"When?" she asked.

Bizzy was already sitting at the table when Mimi arrived at the restaurant. Mimi was telling the host she was meeting someone when she heard her name. The girl at the table facing the door waved frantically. Mimi smiled at the host and made her way to Bizzy.

Her friend hadn't changed, except she appeared to be plumper. Her light skin spread across a wider face, and her amber colored eyes peered from chubby eye sockets. She wore a sleeveless shirt, so instantly Mimi recognized the absence of the firm, muscular arms that athletic Bizzy once possessed. These new arms jiggled when she waved. This version of her childhood friend would most likely have trouble running around a softball field or dribbling down a basketball court. But this did not change the fact that the girl in front of Mimi was still the Bizzy Albright she knew from elementary school.

Bizzy grew more animated when she got excited, using every part of her upper body as she spoke. A pair of large gold studs with large green beads extended by gold chains dangled from her ears. When she talked, the earrings bounced violently. Mimi smiled as the sight brought familiar memories to her.

"Oh my gosh, Mimi! I'm so happy to see you!" Her arms, hands, and head flailed and twisted with excitement. Her wide smile took over the bottom half of her face. "Let me give you a hug."

As Bizzy stood to greet her, Mimi stopped. She was prepared to embrace Bizzy, but now her own arms hung in the air.

"Bizzy, you're pregnant!" It dawned on her that she was telling this to Bizzy as if Bizzy didn't know.

Bizzy put both hands on her stomach. "I am?" She broke into huge laughter that made others in the restaurant turn to look at them. She pulled Mimi close to her enlarged stomach and wrapped her arms around her. "I missed you."

Mimi returned the hug as a swarm of questions filled her mind, many of which she felt too embarrassed to ask. "I missed you too," she said.

As they sat in their seats, Bizzy said, "I'm in my fifth month. Looking forward to it being over. The doctor tells me I'm going to get bigger. Can you imagine more weight on me?"

Mimi shook her head no.

Bizzy squinted. "Am I that fat?"

"No, no." Mimi scrambled and tripped over the two simple words. "I meant—"

Bizzy reached over and touched Mimi's arm. "Stop, Mimi. I'm just kidding you. I'm pregnant. It's okay . . . Now, let's catch up."

They spent two hours painting the story of their last few years apart. Bizzy left for Atlanta shortly after Mimi moved. Her mother died, and her father moved them both to the area to soothe some of the memories with a change of scenery.

"So sorry about your mom," Mimi said, reaching over to pat her hand.

"Thank you." Bizzy took a deep breath and continued her story without taking another.

She had been on track to go abroad for college, which was something her parents had been talking about since Bizzy was small. Each of them had come from different countries—her mother was from Paris and her father from Kenya. They had met and married in the United States and wanted Bizzy to see the rest of the world. But last year, Bizzy met a boy at her high school, gave up the "goodies" (Bizzy's choice of words, not Mimi's) for the first time, and got pregnant. Her father decided to bring everyone home where their family could support them in caring for Bizzy's new baby.

"It's okay," Bizzy said again. Then she added, "The baby's father will be going to school here at Temple University. So he should be able to provide some support as well." Bizzy's eyebrows went up, and her forehead crinkled as if she did not believe in what she was saying. She picked up the last slice of bread and started nibbling. "How's your family? How's school? How's letter writing?"

Mimi updated Bizzy formally, laying pieces of her life out like a newspaper editor organizes stories—being selective with information. Bizzy learned Mimi's parents were divorced, but Mimi did not disclose her father's imprisonment. She told her JoJo was getting married, but left out how much he hated his own sister. She found out Mimi was not dating anyone, but not how many liaisons she had been exposed to since she was fourteen. From Bizzy's update, Mimi had deduced that Bizzy was a virgin when she got pregnant. Mimi had been anything but a virgin by the time Bizzy got pregnant.

She was talking on auto pilot and didn't notice the change on Bizzy's face, her skin reddening while her wide smile regressed into a shorter, straight line.

"You know you're telling me a story, but you're not telling me *the* story," Bizzy said.

"What do you mean?" Mimi glanced down at her plate.

Bizzy was some sort of psychological genius when they were younger. Apparently, this hadn't changed either. She could sense when people were distressed. But Mimi was not telling Bizzy any more than she had already given up. Bizzy seemed to know and understand this.

"Well, you haven't mentioned your letters. I could have used them in Atlanta."

It hit Mimi then. She could have mailed letters to Kayla and Bizzy after she moved, but since the telephone worked just fine, she hadn't bothered.

"So sorry, Bizzy. I guess I could have done that. Maybe I should have done that."

"Why are you apologizing? Sounds like you're still writing them."

"I am," said Mimi, letting a smirk cross her face then quickly disappear.

They continued the rest of their lunch with an update on Kayla. Bizzy's first actions upon returning home were to look up both her childhood friends. Her research on Kayla brought her to a distant cousin who informed Bizzy that the family had moved to California just before Kayla's freshman year of high school. Her father's afro-centric focused lifestyle had earned him a position teaching African studies at a California university. The last time the cousin heard anything from the family, Kayla was interested in becoming an entertainer, which was giving her father a great deal of stress.

As Bizzy shared all this, Mimi mourned the loss of her friend. They had been a tight trio. Would that trio have helped her through this tough time in her life? Bizzy interrupted her thoughts with a question about dessert.

"Sure." Mimi smiled.

"Then it's my treat. Actually, I got our meal today." Bizzy's red, wavy hair was pulled back into a ponytail. Using both hands she brushed her hair back, then rested her head in her hands and closed her eyes. A few seconds passed before she opened her eyes and flashed a broad grin at Mimi. "Hmm . . . you don't know how great it is to see you." I really needed to see you. I really needed to see my friend."

Bizzy's eyes bore into her with a sincerity Mimi had not experienced in a long time. For a moment, she felt useful, as if she mattered to someone and that someone needed her.

In the next moment, she made a decision not to tell Bizzy her secret. Mimi believed what Bizzy saw across the table was this person who could be counted on. Someone supportive, who didn't have any worries. Someone whole. If Bizzy knew the truth and knew the secret, she just might shut the door on their relationship. Mimi needed the door to stay open as long as possible.

Part 4

Do Kings Go to College?

Chapter 25
Repaint

The boy had wandered into the girls' bathroom of the dorm floor. Sitting on the dingy tile next to one of the stalls, he blubbered about a hole being ripped through his stomach. As tears began to mix with snot, he wiped his face on his sleeve. A disgusted chorus rose from the crowd of observers. Several girls, some from Mimi's floor and some from other floors in the dorm, stood outside the bathroom and giggled or held their noses. The gigglers took joy in the boy's demise, while the nose holders balked at the putrid smell of vomit he'd failed to place in the toilet.

Mimi peeked around the small crowd and saw the boy holding an empty bottle of beer between his legs. The only hole being ripped in his stomach was actually coming from his inability to hold his liquor.

That concluded day one of her stay in the Piper's Hall dormitory.

On day two, she retrieved the half-sheet size of paper from her desk and sighed. Such a small object regulated her every move from 8:00 a.m. to 3:00 p.m. each day. The paper was her first semester schedule for Journalism. A smile spread across her face. She had finally decided what to do with her life. She only hoped she could impact the world with her choice.

Her mother smiled when she happily announced her chosen major and said, "As long as you can eat and pay your bills."

As she studied her schedule and the requirements to take classes like Elements of Writing, Analytical Reading, and College Math, she was suddenly a bit doubtful. The class titles on her schedule sounded far more challenging than the English, Biology, and Algebra titles she had endured in high school. A wave of fear covered her body, followed by pure calm.

She assessed there was no doubt about it. College was crazy—in good and bad ways, but she was determined to become a master of her environment.

Mimi jumped right into the routine and had called home only once, which was during her first night. Ashamedly, she had not reached out to Bizzy all summer, and was unaware of the sex of her baby. But she felt too wrapped up in her new life to be seriously concerned about this. Everybody was far away from their parents, and without that supervision, they did whatever they wanted.

As master of her new world, she wanted to do was take advantage of the opportunity. It was a fresh way to start over with people who did not know her, her past, her loneliness, or her self-loathing—people with whom she could pretend to be another person. This new person did not wear a painted smile, or dream about killing herself. This new person's father had not touched her in a way that a court labeled deviant. She could be the girl who people admired as she walked across the quad with her hair waving in the wind, her fashionable clothes striking the sun, and an expensive perfume trail flowing behind her.

The first problem was that her hair was not designed to wave in the wind. Its length was too short, and she wore a loosely curled style, achieved by forty-five minutes of maneuvering a curling iron. Windy days turned her hard labor into an untamed forest.

The second problem was she still owned the clothes she'd worn in high school. They were a little behind fashion then, and they were probably unfashionable three months later in college. Her clothes struck a note of being more functional than fashionable.

The third problem was the only perfume she owned was an abandoned bottle she snagged from her mother's bureau. Some unknown name that promised to smell like gardenias; however, when she put it to her nose she only smelled sugary sweetness, a close kin to molasses.

Yet, she did not let those problems deter her as she ventured into her new world. She was on a mission to recreate herself. She would repaint her life. She had started out well enough. The first class she attended was Math 101, a requirement for all freshman students, even if your major had nothing to do with the course. She groaned as the word brought images of her mother talking about the Finance Department she worked in. Pictures of numbers danced around in a circle in Mimi's head and gave her an instant headache.

She arrived at the class and slumped in her seat with an air of abandon that she really did not possess. Her theory being: it was good to look as if you had done this before, and it bored you to be doing it again.

Before the instructor appeared, a tall, Caucasian girl with curly blonde hair, an oval shaped face, and black-rimmed glasses plunged into the seat next to her and began unpacking her bag. Mimi had resolved that the new Mimi was free spirited and friendly, which was the reason she would speak to anyone before they spoke to her. She was the new Mimi for about a week before she realized she was copying Alaska's style. But it worked, so she kept it.

"Hi," she said to the girl. "How are you?"

The new Mimi was following a textbook strategy she had created herself. *Rule number one: always act like you care about their well-being.*

"Hi. I'm fine. I'm Peyton." The girl extended her hand to Mimi.

She shook it and said, "I'm Mimi." They had only been able to tell each other their hometowns before a light-complexioned guy with curly red hair plopped in the chair on the other side of Mimi.

"Hi, ladies." His voice was deep and thick with an accent Mimi could not place. "I'm Billy Tomlinson. Who are you ladies?" He almost sang the word 'ladies.'

The new Mimi spoke up. "I'm Mimi Combs and this is Peyton." *Rule number two: be helpful.* Show them you can provide help in the smallest ways and are more than happy to do it.

"Oh, so nice to meet you both, Peyton and Mimi." Mimi cringed. He'd said Peyton's name first. Had a rule been violated? She was not sure.

"I hope you both know something about math because I'm not so good at it," Billy said.

He smiled, and it changed the makeup of his entire face. It became brighter. In that moment, Billy Tomlinson had sealed a connection between him, Peyton, and Mimi that would last for some time. Later, Mimi would find out that Billy was exceptional in math.

Yet, she did not rely on this relationship singularly. The new Mimi would know people who knew people, because of *rule number three: network out the wazoo.* So on the first day of each of her courses, she struck up conversations with strangers with an intention on making them friends. By the time she was done, everyone in each of her classes knew Mimi and described her as friendly and nice. Great. Her plan was to keep knowledge of her past and her true self under the radar. A significant label, such as being called "clingy," could put anyone in a limelight. The limelight could be good, or it could be bad, depending upon the label. What mattered most to her was to avoid any limelight of any kind. She desired an undercover popularity. Thus far, she had achieved it.

Though acquiring friends in the classroom, the cafeteria, the library, the quad, and even the school store, had been easy enough; it was harder to maintain those friendships when you lived with the person. Her roommate for freshman year was a girl who came from a life much different than Mimi. Mimi's mother was not poor, but she wasn't rich either. She held a much desired management position at an insurance company after finally leaving her old job. But Faye was not able to vacation to islands and other countries like Natalie Piermont's parents. She was a single mother financially assisting two kids through college.

Like Mimi, Natalie came from a small family, which comprised her brother, and her mother and father. Like Mimi, Natalie's brother was older. But unlike Mimi, Natalie's entire family smothered her with attention. Her brother called once a week to check on her status and her needs. He was a senior in a college that was a day's ride away, but if his little sister needed something he found a way to get it to her.

Her parents, who were successful business people, owned a chain of restaurants. They also called weekly and frequently sent care packages. They deposited money into a bank account for Natalie on a regular basis. And when they saw the room their daughter had to share, they both sucked in a deep breath. Her mother said, "Well, you wanted the dorm experience for the first year, but really, next year, let's look for a bigger room or get an off campus apartment."

Anyone visiting the room could clearly see which side belonged to which girl. Natalie had a green and yellow pastel comforter with red and orange throw pillows all over it. A yellow, plush throw rug sat on the floor beside her bed. Pictures of her boyfriend and her family covered a black end table next to her bed. A brass lamp with an orange shade stood on top of it. Because she was "watching my weight" she had a small refrigerator stacked with fresh vegetables at the foot of her bed. On the wall, she placed a framed print of an island. At night, Mimi would watch the print in the dimness of moonlight and pretend she had been there as well. Because of the size of the room, Natalie was limited in her decorating, but Mimi had a feeling her parents had filled a car with implements that would mirror the room she had back in their Boston home.

Mimi's side of the room told a different story. Her pale blue comforter was the one from her bed at home. It was neat but stained on the end with cranberry juice she spilled while trying to turn the page of a novel and drink at the same time. The only pillow she owned was the pancake-like one she had also robbed from her bed at home. As she watched Natalie's side of the room, she realized she would not have a pillow or a comforter on her bed when she returned home for winter break. She had nothing on the wall and had not considered that she needed a rug for cold mornings. Thank goodness she did remember her worn slippers, which sagged as they faced Natalie's side of the room. She didn't have any pictures of her family or a boyfriend, and her trunk, which seemed the only way to pack her books and her clothes in one piece of luggage, was her nightstand. However, she didn't have a lamp to put on top of it.

The difference in the girls' two worlds did not collide until their third week of school. Mimi had been sitting at her desk studying when Natalie came into the room. She had looked at her own bed and not seeing any room for her Coach book bag, dropped it on Mimi's bed while she gathered her bathroom supplies.

"I don't think I'll ever be able to get used to a shared shower situation. I can't wait until next year when I can get a bigger room or go into an apartment."

Mimi's head was stuck in her book. She had already developed a technique for ignoring whatever Natalie said. "Uh huh," she answered.

Natalie had stripped and was wearing a white robe with the monogram NEP on the pocket. She was singing to herself as she walked out the room to the showers. She stopped at the door, and as if she had stubbed her big toe, she flung out the statement, "Oh, Mimi, please don't leave your towel to dry on the back of the chair like that. It'll fill the room with an odor that I won't be able to take."

Mimi half turned her head after she finished reading a sentence. It took a moment for Natalie's words to register. She looked at the closed door as she processed Natalie's comment. Then she glanced at the towel on her chair and then at her bed. A black mark covered the bottom of Natalie's book bag and traveled up the side of the bag, which lay on Mimi's comforter. She hopped up and grabbed the bag. Sure enough, the black mark looked like some kind of gravel from the street and it now lay on Mimi's comforter. She swiped it away with her hand and the mark smudged the comforter.

Natalie entered the room with a nonchalant attitude. "I forgot my body wash. Smooth skin is a woman's nectar. That's what my mother says."

Mimi turned toward her. A fury she had not experienced before reared inside her. She held the bag in one hand and flung it on Natalie's side of the room. It hit the wall and then fell onto Natalie's bed.

"Natalie, before you make comments about what other people should do, check yourself. Are you taking care of your own business?" Something inside her told her they were headed down a path that she did not want to walk.

"Why did you throw my bag?"

"I threw it because it was on my side of the room on my bed."

"Well, just ask me to take it off. Don't throw my bag. It's very expensive, and I have very expensive things in there."

Mimi felt the last sentence was a comment on her entire life's financial structure. She responded, "Well, I'm sure it's not books because you don't seem to study."

"It's none of your business what's in there. Don't touch my stuff."

"Don't leave your stuff on my bed, or on my side of the room."

"Don't worry. I wouldn't want anything to get messed up." The words "messed up" came out with a slice of sarcasm. Mimi's neck had been getting hotter with every word she and Natalie exchanged, and now it was scorching. Natalie left, slamming the door behind her.

Mimi screamed after her, "You forgot your nectar!"

That was their first fight, and it wasn't going to be their last. They argued over everything from leaving the door open to how late someone left the desk light on. Mimi could not believe the words that flew from her mouth at times. "Stuck-up tramp" came after she had entered the dorm and caught Natalie and a boy, who was not Natalie's boyfriend, wrapped in Natalie's comforter. Neither of them had on any clothes. "Rich dummy" came after Natalie left a test on her desk, which revealed she clearly did not understand English 101 and was struggling horribly. Mimi held the paper in her hand. She knew she could help her roommate but decided she would rather watch her suffer.

By winter break, she and Natalie were not speaking to each other at all. Neither of them sought other living arrangements. They just maintained silence sprinkled only with necessary communication.

She was lonely in her dorm room as she watched Natalie race around the building making friends who stuck. By the end of the semester, Mimi's initial foray into friends culminated with only Peyton and Billy enjoying her company. She discovered some people had not matured as much as they needed to, even after being out of high school for six months. Mimi felt like a driver going on a long distance trip with no map. Her plan for mastering her environment had not worked as well as she planned. All her rules had been broken or shattered. She had no idea what she was doing in college.

Just before going on winter break, she had a big blowout with Natalie that almost made her rethink her whole college experience. A common, tense conversation between them was about the food in Natalie's small refrigerator. She swore that Mimi stole from the refrigerator whenever she got a chance. They were arguing about a missing pear, which Mimi knew Natalie had already eaten, or had been eaten by one of the visiting "boyfriends." Mimi tried to explain that she did not care for the taste of pears.

"I hate them, so I wouldn't take it."

"You would take it just to goad me."

"You need to get over yourself, Natalie. And do you even know what 'goad' means?"

Natalie's face went red at the insult. "I know what goad means," she replied. "And you need to get over yourself. Now I understand what people are saying . . ."

Mimi halted. Her pencil suspended half-way to her notebook. She felt something crawl up her spine. Later, she would identify this as a warning of something she should run from.

"What are you talking about?" The words came out slowly.

The color left Natalie's face. "Nothing."

"No. What do you mean?"

"It's nothing."

"What do you mean?" She stood up and walked over to where Natalie sat on the bed. At college, she saw sides of herself that she could not believe were part of her. The latest side was particularly aggressive. She towered over Natalie and asked again, "What do you mean?" Natalie shook her head and looked down at her hands. "Natalie," Mimi demanded.

"You certainly can't be oblivious to it."

"To what?"

"To what people say."

"And what do they say?"

Natalie eyes focused beyond Mimi to the picture-less wall
that acted as a background. "People say you're too . . . too . .
. clingy."

Mimi stepped back. Breath left her in one huge expulsion.
A full five seconds passed before she inhaled. "Who says
that?" she asked.

"People."

"What people?"

"I shouldn't have said anything. Forget it."

"What people?"

"Mimi—"

"What people?"

Natalie threw up her hands, and well-manicured nails
flashed across Mimi's vision. "If you really must know.
People in your classes and in this dorm say you're a phony.
You try to get close and pretend as if you know people. You
try to act as if you're popular. Really, Mimi, high school is
over. If you weren't popular then, you won't be popular
now." Natalie stood up. "There. Is that what you wanted to
know?" She stomped out of the room slamming the door
behind her.

Mimi sat on the edge of the bed, hot-tempered and
nauseated. Her stomach roiled. People could see through her
plan, and according to Natalie, Mimi's plans made people
think she was needy. The words Alaska had used in high
school came back to her now. People thought of her as
clingy. She put a hand on her mouth and wiped. The taste of
bile was there.

She needed to talk to someone, anyone who was not at her
college and who was not her mother. Mimi wracked her
brain, but besides Peyton and Billy, she did not know who

she could talk to at the moment. She feared a conversation with them might only drive them away.

A knock on the door made her jump.

"Mimi, phone call." A phone call in a dorm was a big deal since the phone was never free.

As she put the receiver to her ear, she heard Bizzy's high-pitched, high-speed wail.

"You could call, you know. You've been at college how long and still no call from you. I thought perhaps I could bring the baby up to visit you. I had a girl. Can you believe it? I felt so sure he'd be a boy, but he is a she. I named her Barbie."

She had forgotten about Bizzy. College was frying her brain. The call was like an answer to a prayer she had not spoken. She let herself go to a temporary place of relief and began to bombard Bizzy with questions about Barbie. Natalie Piermont and the fakeness of Mimi's own life melted into the background.

Chapter 26
Pitiful Me

Loneliness permeated Mimi's soul. At times, it talked to her. It told her without someone to love you, you were nothing.

One day loneliness spoke to her while she was on her way to her Analytical Reading class. She passed various groups of people. Some included couples clinging to each other and laughing. Others included friends standing close to protect against increasingly bitter fall winds. Occasionally, she saw someone she knew in one of these groups. They nodded at her or waved loosely. None of them invited her into their group.

Loneliness said, "You have no one."

Mimi tried to reason with loneliness and said, "Peyton and Billy are my friends."

"You hardly see them outside of class. You have no one," Loneliness responded.

She tried again, "What about Bizzy?"

Loneliness laughed. "Leave Bizzy alone."

She pulled the collar of her jacket closer to her neck and walked faster. She arrived at the lecture hall fifteen minutes early. Other students were milling in and finding seats near friends.

Loneliness spoke again. "Sit there."

There was an empty seat next to an average looking black guy. She had noticed him in class before but had not paid much attention to him. Besides neatly trimmed hair and full, dark lips, nothing grabbed her attention. She thought she remembered the instructor calling him Devereaux—Caleb Devereaux.

Loneliness said it again. "Sit there."

So she went to the seat next to Caleb Devereaux and sat down.

"Hey," she said.

"Hey," said Caleb.

She started digging in her backpack for her supplies for class. Caleb already had his notepad, text book, and pen resting on the small desk. She glanced at his legs protruding from under the desk.

"They don't make these seats comfortable, do they?" she said.

He looked at her, then at his legs, and back at her. He smiled and took a deep breath. "No, they don't." He extended his hand to her. "Caleb Devereaux."

"Mimi Combs." She shook his hand.

She flew through her brain for what to say next. Normally, she would find a way to seduce him, but loneliness was leading this one.

Caleb spoke up. "What did you think of that assignment?"

"Not too bad. I like this class. I like anything related to reading and writing, so this class is a nice fit. I was good at subjects like this in high school, so it's not so bad here at Foster." Too much. She was talking too much. Where was loneliness?

"Well, I'm awful at it." He rubbed his eyes with his hand.

"I can help you."

"You don't have to." He chuckled.

"I can. Let's meet tonight and go over some things."

"Really, you don't have to."

"I don't mind."

The instructor walked to the front of the room, and Mimi scribbled her dorm room and phone number on a piece of paper. "Call me," she whispered. "I'll be back in the dorm by four p.m. We can set up a time then. I really don't mind helping."

Caleb took the paper and placed it in his notebook. "Thanks," he said.

They agreed to study in one of the quiet rooms at the library. Mimi found one of the most secluded ones and brought Caleb to it. He glanced around the room and said, "Small and tight. They don't make these rooms comfortable, do they?" She was not sure what he meant. He laughed. "You know. Chairs uncomfortable. Rooms uncomfortable."

It took her another second, but finally she got the connection and laughed. Caleb was corny, and now, suddenly cute.

As they began to study, Mimi found Caleb was awful in the subject, but he was an eager and easy student to work with. After an hour and a half, she rubbed her neck and asked if he wanted to take a break.

"Sure."

Grabbing sodas, they returned to the study room.

Looking through his notes, Caleb said, "I usually don't ask for help, but this has been very helpful. I can go out to that party this weekend because you helped free up my time." He was thumbing through his notes.

"Party?" Mimi asked.

"Some boys from one of those frats." Again, his eyes were glued to something he had written on a page.

"I'd like to go." There it was. Loneliness had returned.

Caleb looked up. She could see confusion on his face. He searched for words and finally said, "I was invited by a friend."

"And you can bring a friend, right?" She slid her chair closer to his. She let her hand go to his face and caressed it. Caleb's eyes grew wide. She pulled his face to hers and was about to kiss him, when Caleb pulled away and stood up.

"Mimi." He was agitated and started pacing the floor. "You know I have a girlfriend."

She sat back in the chair, "Nope, I did not know."

"Sorry, if you thought something."

She said nothing. Mimi stared at him, and loneliness told her to make him change his mind.

"I thought we were just getting together to study," Caleb said. "That's what I told my lady."

Mimi folded her hands on the table and leaned forward. She had changed to her favorite white blouse. When she leaned forward like this, it gave a clear view of her cleavage. "Maybe your lady doesn't have to kn—"

Caleb began packing his things. Mimi was confused. They did not normally respond like this. "Caleb, wait. Wait. What's wrong?"

"Mimi, I think you're a nice girl. A smart one too." He stopped packing and looked at her. "But you don't have to try so hard to get friends, especially boyfriends." He continued packing. When he was done, he stopped at the door. "You don't have to do this to yourself." He walked out.

Mimi had not moved her position. She had not looked at him. Her hands were still folded on the table. Her blouse was still open and revealing too much cleavage. She mused about how she had never gained and lost a friend in such a short time. It must be a record. He said she had tried too hard. He said she did not have to try this hard.

"Yes. I do," she said to the empty room.

Chapter 27
The Way Bizzy Says God

From one state to the next, the picture was the same. The unblemished snow sparkled in the light. Packed hard and tight, the powdery mixture rolled over the hills and valleys of the landscape. The trail of footprints of some lone animal was evidence of a quest for food. Bare trees stood, sometimes alone, sometimes in groups, and sometimes next to prickly spruce or pine.

For miles and miles this was the scene, then slowly, the bare trees became dense clusters of twigs and bark planted next to a sea of cold stone buildings, which comprised a city's skyline. Billboard advertising quietly promoted the benefits of Coke or Pepsi, and the joy a set of diamonds might pull from a love interest. People replaced animals. The snow became black with the dirt from the wheels of vehicles and soles of shoes.

At these times, the din of the train's engine grew louder and the smell of diesel more profound. The conductor would announce the destination. A host of United Nations characters would board and disembark. And the train would roll on while the record began again with a white canopy, a single trail of footprints and barren trees.

From Charleston, West Virginia to Charlottesville, Virginia to Washington, DC, to Baltimore, Maryland to Wilmington, Delaware and finally to Philadelphia. By this time, Mimi was familiar with the scenes displayed before her window seat. At the sound of the Philadelphia destination, her stomach burned with a mix of anticipation and fear. She was glad to be home, but her last conversation with her mother had not gone well.

Pleading had been the aura of the first half of the conversation. Her mother had broached the subject of JoJo. She sensed tension between her children and coaxed Mimi to call her brother. But since her relationship with her brother had melted into small pleasantries, Mimi saw no need to do this. Her non-hesitating response had been a flat and final "No." The latter half of the conversation had ventured into a threat. At the sound of her matriarch's do-this-or-else voice, Mimi folded for a second, then pulled in her strength. She reminded herself she was eighteen now, and conversations with her mother should not be this way. But she also knew she could not be disrespectful. She simply said, "I'll think about it." Then added, "I gotta go, Mom. I'll talk to you later." Mimi barely heard the good-bye as she pressed the button to end the call.

But her mother seemed to have forgotten the end of the conversation as she flooded Mimi with question after question about school. Mimi answered each while confirming what she already knew. She didn't have the relationship with her mother that her mother had with JoJo. She did not call every week, and she did not seek advice, or keep her mother informed. Her mother needed this moment of reconnection. Mimi allowed it.

Her only sore point was when her mother squeezed Mimi's face between her hands, wrapping the leather gloves that encased them around each cheek. Mimi thought she was about to say, "I missed you," to which she was prepared to faint. But her mother said, "You've put on a few pounds, Mimi-cake." And Mimi rolled her eyes, snatched her face away, and groaned, "Mom!"

Besides this hurtful moment, her time with her mother had been uneventful and limited. The rest of her winter break, and thus, most of her winter break had been spent with Bizzy and Barbie. Five-month-old Barbie was a mini version of Bizzy. She had her mother's bright eyes, and shapely nose and mouth. She had her mother's red frizzy hair. Bizzy claimed she did not see herself in Barbie, but all Mimi saw was Bizzy in every inch of the little girl's face.

Spending time with Bizzy and the baby allowed Mimi to escape. Playing with baby Barbie took her to other places where she did not have to think as hard about her life. Conferring with Bizzy about Natalie gave her release. Although she did not think she could follow the advice Bizzy gave, it felt good to talk to someone and to have someone listen.

"You probably should step back for a moment. You have to spend the next few months with this girl, Mimi." Bizzy was feeding Barbie, who was growing into a hefty baby with a big appetite. It showed in her round cheeks, her thick hands, and her plump legs. Occasionally, Bizzy bent down and kissed the top of Barbie's head. "You should probably start with an apology."

Mimi was sipping a drink as Bizzy talked. She sputtered soda on the front of her shirt when she heard the word 'apology.' "Why should I apologize?" she asked. "She's the stuck-up one. I'm not kissing her butt."

Barbie finished her bottle. Bizzy shifted the baby to her shoulder and began patting her back. "I think I'm going to start her on some baby food next month. She should be ready," Bizzy said. "I'm saying, sometimes apologizing and really meaning it sets people on new ground. Like with Barbie's dad and me. I was angry at the end of my pregnancy." She peeked over at Mimi. "I don't think I ever told you that. But I was. He was off with his new girl, and I . . . Well, I was trying to be like a martyr. But that lasted a couple of weeks. Then everything blew up on my body, and I felt like Barbie—though I didn't know she was Barbie— was sitting on my bladder all . . . the . . . time. All I could think about was what I was going through, and I was doing it alone."

Barbie let out a loud burp.

"Good girl," Bizzy said.

She placed the little girl in her crib and sat in a chair next to it. "I was so angry I called him up and told him. I wasn't nice and said a few things that weren't at all true. I'd been saved for only a short time, but I'm pretty sure Christians aren't supposed to say what I said." Again, Bizzy peeked at Mimi and a smile spread across her face. "Then I had Barbie in my arms, and I felt something, the Holy Spirit really, telling me this little girl needed her mother and her father to be on good terms even if they weren't dating anymore."

Bizzy's voice had been moving quickly, and she paused to look at Barbie as the fond memory of her child's birth etched itself into her thoughts. She continued, "I called him from the hospital, apologized first, and then told him his little girl was born. He was actually happy. Happier than I thought he would be. And you know what? He takes better care of her than I thought he would. He even makes sure his girlfriend doesn't get all crazy about him picking up and dropping Barbie off. I don't think we would have gotten as far as we have, if I hadn't called him and apologized."

Mimi sat in a chair on the opposite end of Barbie's crib. Sometimes Bizzy used words, like "saved" and "Holy Spirit," that Mimi did not fully understand. She let them enter and leave her head.

Barbie had been squirming and flailing her arms, but now they slowly fell back on her mattress. Her eyelids closed slowly. Her little chest moved as she breathed in and exhaled the aroma of a deep sleep. Mimi had grown to love this little girl in the few days she was home. She almost regretted having to go back. She was going to miss Barbie. Truthfully, she had been thinking about staying home. Mimi was sure the world at school knew she was unstable. She knew people would look at her, and some of them would smile in her face and all of them would think of her as being *clingy*.

She informed Bizzy of her decision. "It doesn't matter anyway. I'm thinking about transferring to a school back here." She covered Barbie with her blanket. "Besides, it'd be good to spend some time with you and B-baby here." Mimi fussed with the blanket unnecessarily, trying to get it perfect to Barbie's form. Bizzy was unusually quiet. Mimi looked over at her.

"Are you crazy? Why do you want to transfer back home? Just because you're fighting with your roommate? Don't let someone else stop you from doing what you need to do. You chose a major, right? And this school has a good program for that major, right? Then stay there and do what you need to do."

"You don't understand, Bizzy. It's hard." Mimi leaned her head against the bars of the crib.

"No, it's not as hard as you think, and if you let God help you, you'll find out it's not hard at all."

It had been a long time since she had heard anyone say God the way Bizzy did. Bizzy said it as if she knew him personally. Like she had met him at some event, and they had struck up a conversation that led to them being the best of friends. The only person she knew who spoke of God as if he was a personal friend was her grandmother.

Bizzy said, "Go back to this school, set things straight with your roommate, and whatever problem is going on, ask God to help you with it." She laid a hand on Mimi's leg. Bizzy's voice became softer and slower. "Mimi, I know it's hard, but I also know the only way to survive is through the Father and his Son. That's how I'm able to survive on a daily basis. That's how I'm able to take care of this little girl." She put the other hand on Barbie's leg as she spoke. Barbie stirred but fell quickly back into her deep rest. "Please, Mimi, stay in Ohio. Get your education." She straightened in her chair. "Then Barbie and I can be real proud of you." She smiled.

Sometimes Mimi saw Bizzy when they were young. Huge afro puffs bouncing all over her head. A laugh that no bottle could keep. It was those times when her heart hurt so much for her friend. Bizzy was not so young anymore. Instead of looking eighteen, Bizzy looked thirty. Life was tough, but Bizzy kept smiling.

"Okay," Mimi said, leaning back in her own chair and watching Barbie. Without taking her eyes off the round, sweet cheeks, she added, "Thanks, Bizzy."

Tempted to take Bizzy to the secret place where darkness would not let her go, Mimi almost opened her mouth and told her friend about Joe Combs. But trouble with a stuck up roommate was mild compared to what her father had done to her. Sitting next to Barbie's crib with Bizzy and letting out that story would fill the room with ugliness. No. She had made a decision to keep the door of their relationship open, even if it was really closed from her viewpoint.

Chapter 28
The Safe and the Lie

The ball of electric pink socks fell from the bed and rolled under the nightstand. She knew she was trying to pack too much, but her mother had experienced temporary insanity by purchasing new clothes and new furniture for Mimi's dorm room. Since the return trip to college would be made via car, Mimi had no intention of leaving any of her new belongings behind.

The socks were cotton and thick. Good for sleeping at night when every draft in the dorm room's window seemed to be extra busy. She knelt to see how far away the socks had rolled. Under the nightstand, she saw a piece of paper taped to the underside. She reached in and pulled the paper away. Unfolding it, she quickly recognized the scrawl of her own middle school handwriting. This was the letter Mimi wrote to her grandmother telling her that she might be pregnant.

After everything exploded because she had told her mother about her father, she completely forgot about the letter. The paper was thin, and the tape had ripped some of it off like a layer of skin, but the handwriting was still legible. She saw the words "Dear Grandma" and a lump formed in her throat. Mimi sat on the floor with her back against the nightstand. This letter made her miss her grandmother with fresh pain. She wondered if she would have told her grandmother about everything she felt now. She was still lonely, still feeling unworthy, and still unsure about herself. What would her grandmother advise?

Grandma was both kind and sweet; at times she could be tough. When that side came through, the way she talked to Mimi and JoJo was cold and somewhat harsh. When she used this side, Mimi and JoJo knew they had better listen and do what their grandmother said.

Mimi recalled a time when her grandmother caught her in a lie. She'd spilled orange juice on the floor but wanted to get back to her room to work on something, probably a letter. She assessed the mess. Cleaning it would delay what she had been doing. She was in a good rhythm. The juice spill was under the table, and unless someone bent down to look, they would not notice it. Dismissing it, she told herself that no one would look under the table for a while, and she left the juice on the floor. She underestimated the power of grandmothers that day. Within a half hour, her grandmother was at her door.

"Mimi."

"Yes, Grandma." She did not look up from her work but kept writing furiously.

"Did you leave the mess on the kitchen floor?"

"What mess, Grandma?"

"The mess under the table. The spilled juice."

She was still writing, and the first answer that popped in her head was the one she let come out of her mouth. "No, Grandma."

Her grandmother crossed the room and sat on the edge of the bed. Her weight shifted Mimi's hand, and it slid across the paper.

"Grandma!" Mimi shouted.

"Let me tell you something, young lady." She cupped Mimi's chin gently and turned her head so Mimi had to look into her grandmother's face. Mimi remembered thinking the touch was gentle, but it was minimized, nearly erased by the firmness of her words. "It's best to be honest than to tell a lie, which only lets people know you have very little character. If you will lie about little things, you will lie about big things. When you lie, Mimi, you showing the world your tail, and your tail stinks." She released Mimi's chin and stood up. "Go clean the mess you left. I cleaned that kitchen before you went in there. I know it was you."

She felt horrible. Her grandmother's words stung. She got on her hands and knees and scrubbed the juice from the floor until it sparkled. Her grandmother returned to the kitchen while she worked.

"Something you'd like to say to me?"

"I'm sorry, Grandma."

"Thank you. This is the side that I know is really you."

What would her grandmother think of the side she was showing now? Practically begging for friends. Sleeping around with boys. She knew it wasn't right, but it was addictive. It made her feel better when she impressed others to gain a friend, or an intimate boyfriend.

A knock on her door made her jump to her feet. Her mother opened the door and stuck her head in the room.

"Mimi, you should know that your brother purchased all this stuff for you today. I didn't do a thing. He and Tomas wanted to do something special for you, so they sent me a blank check and told me to fill in a number. They did it for you, so . . ." She paused as if choosing the best way to proceed. Finally, she said, "Just don't forget to thank them."

"I won't, Mom." She folded the letter and moved to the safe. Mimi was planning on taking the safe back to school with her.

"You know I chucked mine. Nothing I need to keep protected anymore," her mother said.

Mimi stood in front of the safe, unwilling to bend and put in her combination code, not with her mother looking over her shoulder. "Mom, I'm going to finish packing so we can get on the road."

Her mother turned to go. "Don't forget to thank your brother. Okay?"

"Okay. I got it, Mom," she purposefully responded in a flat tone, not wanting to incite any additional emotion from her mother.

Her mother looked as if she wanted to remind Mimi one last time, but chose to walk out of the bedroom instead.

Mimi looked down at the letter in her hands and knew her grandmother would have been ashamed of her. She was ashamed of her own self. Realizing this felt like a dump truck sitting on her heart. She couldn't bear it.

Rip.

She continued shredding the paper with her hands until a mound of tiny pieces was left and her heart felt lighter.

Chapter 29
Tate King, RA

Returning to school was nerve-wracking. Mimi picked orange nail polish from her finger nails, and then bit her nails to the skin. She twirled her hair until strands of it fell to her shirt. Paranoid, she entered her dormitory feeling as if everyone was staring at her.

"Walk faster, Mimi," her mother said. "I need to get back on the road before the traffic builds up."

She was returning to her dorm room with not only her cherished safe, but also new supplies. A new comforter and pillow. A new throw rug. A new nightstand. A new picture for her own wall. These were all items purchased by JoJo. On the drive up to the school, her mother reminded her to call JoJo to thank him for buying everything.

"Don't forget, Mimi."

"I won't, Mom."

Her mother drove in silence for about another twenty minutes before she reignited.

"Well, don't forget, Mimi."

"Ugh!" she puffed. "I won't, Mom."

By the time she arrived at her room, Natalie had not checked in. Natalie's side of the room was sparse, with only a rolled up mattress atop an iron bed frame and the floor beneath swept and mopped clean. She said good-bye to her mother, made one more promise to call her brother, set up her side of the room, and unpacked her clothes, but still Natalie had not arrived. She was preparing for bed when she heard a knock on the door. Her heart leaped as the picture of Natalie on the other side of the door, arms loaded, and using her foot to knock, crept into her mind.

She took a deep breath and opened the door to see Tate King, the dormitory resident advisor, leaning against the frame. He was dressed in jeans and a sweatshirt with the letters RA on the front.

Tate was a twenty-eight-year-old graduate student who made extra money by being somewhat of a babysitter to the students who lived in the dorm. His job was to make sure everyone followed the dorm rules. He was, however, not as compliant as other RAs. As long as the students did not kill each other, Tate left them alone. The first day Mimi saw him, she thought he was kind and handsome. His baldhead, long lashes, and provocative smile made him sexually appealing, but he was always formal toward her.

"Hi Tate. How was your break?" she asked.

"Not nearly long enough, Combs. Not long enough." Tate preferred to use their last names. Mimi had no idea why. Maybe it made his job seem more important. Or, maybe it helped him maintain a distance from them. "But thanks for asking. Just wanted you to know that Piermont won't be returning to us."

Mimi felt the floor drop from beneath her. She knew it was something she had done. "Wha-wha-what happened?"

Tate did not say anything for a moment. She could see the faint line of a shaven beard etched in his cheeks. "Don't worry, Combs. The Princess decided she didn't want to do college anymore. It was—now let me see if I can tell you the way her mother put it—oh yeah—a boring waste of her time. She's off to some other country to study fashion."

Mimi wasn't sure she didn't have something to do with Natalie's new direction in life. She leaned against the door, knowing she wouldn't be able to apologize as she had made the decision to do. Her body jerked slightly with a new revelation. But now she would not have to apologize, would she? She felt a small amount of exhilaration. And perhaps, with Natalie away, people would not remember anything about Mimi being clingy.

"Thanks, Tate," she murmured, her thoughts truly elsewhere.

"I know you two argued a lot that first semester, but don't go blaming yourself, Mimi. These things happen." He checked the clipboard he held in his hand. His fingers were long and virile. "You may get another roommate. You may not. We might do some reshuffling. If we do, I'll let you know. Good night."

He walked away, and Mimi closed the door. She was climbing into bed and turning off her new lamp when she realized two things. First, she forgot to call her brother. Admittedly, she had no intention on calling either. And second, Tate had called her Mimi instead of Combs.

Tate seemed to understand her, and because of that Mimi developed a near instantaneous relationship with him. They talked about everything. He brought small gifts for her. He took her to eat at places far away from their college campus. In all this, he never touched her. He never kissed her. They only talked. In his presence, she felt like an older woman.

Mimi hid the relationship and publicly maintained dorm required communications only. To outsiders, she and Tate were acquaintances because of circumstance. Even Peyton and Billy were unaware of their relationship.

In her second term, she shared a couple of classes with Billy and Peyton and was their study partner, but each of them had love interests on campus. Peyton had met a basketball player. Billy had met a quiet but strong-willed girl in one of his classes. As the relationships grew, neither Peyton nor Billy had much time to study in a group.

Tate became Mimi's primary, yet secret companion. He slipped notes under her door. She blushed as she read what he wrote about her inviting smile or her intelligent conversation or some other aspect he adored. He saw pieces of her soul that she hadn't noticed herself. By the time he invited her to his friend's apartment, forty-two days later, she was in love with him. From her perspective, no one loved or cared about her the way Tate did. She was the most important person in his life, and he was the most important person in hers.

One of his greatest areas of concern for her seemed to be her education. He encouraged her to maintain her studies and loaned her notes he got from other people who had taken her classes.

"School's first, Mimi," he said, handing her a neat stack of papers one day. "Always remember what you came here for and what you're trying to achieve."

Words like these buried themselves deep inside and convinced her that he cared not only about her but her future. She was beginning to believe he wanted to take care of her. As she mused with thoughts of being with him for the rest her life, she toyed with the idea of telling him about her father. But no. Such information would be a relationship destroyer.

The night she went to his friend's apartment, they decided it would be best if he gave her directions. He didn't want anyone to see them leave the dorm together, or walk together to the place. Mimi was not naive. She knew she was going to this apartment to make love. She intended to demonstrate just how great her love was for Tate.

To prepare for the night, she bathed before she left and selected a pair of pink panties embroidered with white lace. Her bra carried the same design. In one of Natalie's drawers, she found a small bottle of expensive perfume. The cube-shaped bottle of Liz Claiborne Realities reminded her of a baby's building blocks, though the scent was far from those associated with children.

She moved freely about the dorm room because she still didn't have a roommate. Tate was probably behind this. Other people, who had been without roommates, had already been paired. Had Tate prevented someone from moving in with her because he wanted her all to himself? Smiling, she brushed her hair back into a bun. She was willing to oblige his desire.

Smelling like an exotic flower, she arrived at the apartment wearing the one short skirt she owned and a button up blouse. He opened the door, and she entered the small apartment. A quick survey of the place told her a poor man had furnished it. Consisting of just three sparse rooms—a front room, a kitchen area, and a bathroom—it lacked the comforting feeling of a true home.

"Welcome," he said.

"Thanks." Mimi smiled sweetly.

Tate explained, "I'm thinking of renting a home next year when I'm done with RAing. Something like this is really too small, but my buddy, he likes it. Ya know. What he can afford."

She interrupted his rambling by placing her hand on his. "It's okay," she whispered, wanting tonight to be perfect.

In the middle of the room lay a flat mattress covered with a heap of white sheets. In the dimmed lighting, several lit votive candles floated in tiny glasses in various areas around the room.

"Here, sit here." He pointed to the mattress. "I'll get you something to drink." Tate disappeared into the kitchen and returned with a red plastic cup. She sipped and tasted Pepsi.

"Thanks, Tate. So tell me . . ." She placed her cup on the floor. ". . . How was your day?"

"Good." He settled next to her on the mattress. "I spent most of the day thinking about you. I couldn't wait for the day to end, so I could come here and wait for you. You know, I really missed you today."

Mimi shifted her position to face him while he talked. "What did you miss?" she asked.

"Everything. Mimi, I think about you all the time. You make me feel good . . . right here." He took her hand and placed it on his chest. She could feel the quick pounding of his heart.

"Mimi, I care a lot about you." He paused. "Do you care about me?"

"Yes, I do, Tate."

"You do? Girl, you don't know how happy that makes me." He leaned over and kissed her hard.

"Tate, I love you," she breathed.

"You know I care about you, baby." He moved his hands quickly across her upper body, rubbing her arms, her stomach, and her breasts while placing little pecks all over her face.

"Tate, I love you so much. Do you love me?"

"Baby, don't worry. I care about you a lot. Let me show you." In one swift move, he had Mimi on her back, her skirt pushed up, and he was on top of her fondling and pulling at her underwear. She twisted her face in confusion.

This was going much faster than it did in the movies. Where were the slow and passionate kisses? The gentle massaging? Those things were part of lovemaking.

"Tate, let's go slowly. I want to make love to you."

"I know. I care about you, baby. A lot. Just let me show you."

Before she could protest, he was inside her. She tried to push him out of her, her hands mashing against his chest. "Stop, Tate. It's not supposed to be like this. I don't want it this way."

"Yes, you do."

"Stop, Tate!" she screamed

"C'mon, baby. Show me how you love me."

A tear rolled from one eye, followed by another. Soon her vision was blurred by the tears and she screamed, "You're hurting me!"

"It'll feel good in a minute. Just wait. I'll make you feel good."

"Please! Stop it, Tate!"

He moved like a wild animal. She murmured, "Stop," but he ignored her pleas. When he was finally done, he rolled off her. She curled into a ball, and her back rested against his clammy arm. It occurred to her that she was still wearing her underwear. She could feel the lace edge of the panties against her belly skin as if it were a chain of iron links surrounding her.

Tate, panting next to her said, "Baby, that was so good. You want something to eat?"

Something to eat! She began a quiet whimper. When he tried to console her, she stiffened.

"Mimi, come on, girl. I know you ain't a virgin. I can tell you been with other guys. At least I care enough about you to do it right. It's not just a hit it and quit it, right?"

Wasn't it? The response formed in her head but didn't leave her mouth. She tried to stand, but her legs felt loose and she stumbled. He reached out to catch her, but she jerked away. She fumbled at the underwear and noticed the lace had been ripped in one section and was no longer attached to the rest of her panty. She tugged the skirt down, willing it to cover her entire legs, but it stopped mid-thigh.

Standing and clutching her sides, she announced, "I need to leave."

"Why?"

"I need to leave," she said again, her eyes averting his as she watched a votive candle bounce against the walls of the glass it floated in.

Tate sighed. "Well, at least, let me walk you. I really don't get what you're so uptight about, but I won't stop you from leaving."

Mimi cringed at the word "stop."

"I can go as far as two blocks away from the dorm, okay?"

She watched him pull his pants up, zip them, and hunt around for the apartment keys. The whole time Tate chatted about her coming over again and having a meal prepared for her the next time. She was bombarded with emotions as his voice floated in and out of her head. Hatred and disgust came first. The image of her finger in his eyeball was oddly prevalent. But hatred and disgust moved over for shame and fear. How could she allow it to happen? What had she done to make it happen? And, would he touch her again? By the time they walked out of the door, the final emotion had rested on her—lost. She actually felt like she was losing something.

As they walked toward her dorm, he finally stopped speaking. The clicks of her heels on the pavement were the only sound in the nighttime air.

When Tate had gone as far as he allowed himself to go, he glanced around and bent to kiss her on the lips. She let him, though her lips were unresponsive.

"Okay, Mimi, baby. Um . . . I'll see you in the dorm tomorrow. Okay?"

She shook her head in agreement and walked toward the dorm, hugging herself.

Chapter 30
I've Made Up My Mind

April 1, 1991

Dear Daddy,

I hope you're happy. Someone finally showed me what I'm worth. And I'm worth nothing. I'm like some blowup doll that men use for their own pleasure. That's right, Daddy, and it started with you. You used me for your own pleasure. And now that's what men do. They use me for their own pleasure.

I hope you're really happy, because I'm dead and gone. I want to run away, but I won't. I'll stay here in college and finish up because I don't have anything else to do in life. You know what my life purpose is? I'll tell you. My life has two purposes—get a job and be a blowup doll for some man.

A man told me he loved me, Daddy, just like you did. Then he just took from me. Just like you did.

As you can see from my other letters, I've been writing you since you went off to jail, but I didn't mail any. Now I'm mailing everything because I want you to see what you messed up, what you gave up, what you missed.

Daddy, I hate you. I hate the air you breathe. I hate the ground you walk on. If they gave the death penalty for what you did to me, I'd have a front row seat, and I would sign the option on the form that allows me to watch you die a slow death. Do they do that, Daddy? Do they let you decide how your tormentor must die? I wish they did because I have big plans for you.

No love whatsoever,

Mimi

Bobby Benson.

She had forgotten him. Many memories from her childhood had slipped away throughout the years. Gone to the strange and unobtainable parts of her mind. Her required psychology course told her they were not lost, but simply hiding until something or someone invited them to the forefront. A specific memory about flat-faced, big-nosed, pop-eyed Bobby Benson had been summoned for her to evaluate.

His unattractive features were not the reason Mimi disliked Bobby Benson. She was not cruel; not the kind of child who made fun of how others looked. Not at all. Bobby Benson had been disliked and practically hated by almost everyone because he was annoying.

Bobby created and executed ways to bother kids on a daily basis. The lifeless cockroach on its back, legs protruding in the air, lying on your desk as if it were a gift. The tip of a paintbrush dipped in blue paint, so small that the owner did not notice as he plunged the brush into a jar of yellow paint to color in a picture of the sun. A cluster of Gail Jones' own stiff, auburn brown hair strands resting in a plastic bag inside her lunch box. Gail had touched her ponytail, and realizing it was about an inch shorter, she shrieked. These were all signatures of how annoying Bobby Benson could be.

Mimi ignored him as much as possible, but she remembered a day when no one could ignore Bobby Benson any longer.

The day had been dark and rainy as clouds moved in during morning reading. They settled in one spot and glided back and forth but did not lift. Planned outdoor recess had been abandoned for fun and games in the classroom. And Bobby, in typical Bobby style, had devised a plan, which angered its victim, their teacher.

Untangling the tape from every pen on her desk had been disastrous, and before she could complete the task, the teacher threw the mess in the trash can and singled out Bobby Benson. Everyone knew Bobby had done it, because first, he did not deny it, and second, he was the only child in the room laughing.

The punishment had been to stand in the storage closet until he was called out. To solidify his punishment, the teacher locked the door. And Bobby Benson demanded to be released while the other students sang songs. The louder he called, the louder they sang. But a deafening crash singularly snipped every voice, and as the teacher approached the closet, she heard Bobby yelling, "Open the door"—and then a whacking sound. "Open the door!" Whack. "Open the door!" Whack. Over and over and faster and faster until she opened the door to find six-year-old Bobby Benson sitting on the floor hitting his own legs with a broken broom handle.

The teacher cried out for Bobby to stop, but he didn't seem to hear her. Over and over. Faster and faster until she shouted into the closet for him to stop hurting himself. Bobby froze, dropped the bloody handle, and limped back to his desk.

In an unemotional voice, Bizzy, sitting next to Mimi, had proclaimed Bobby Benson unstable, but she used the word "crazy."

As Mimi sat on the edge of her bed cradling the letter she had just written, she realized she had been relentless in trying to hurt herself. Like Bobby Benson in that storage closet, something told her to stop writing because it was painful.

But she would not heed the warning. This was the ninth or tenth letter she had written to her father since she began mailing them. She was losing track because they all sounded the same. He needed to know how much she hated him. He needed to know about her awful life, and how he contributed to it being that way.

By now, her father had served over seven years of his prison time. But before he left that jail cell, she needed him to know everything he had done to his little girl.

The night Tate raped her, she returned to the dorm, opened her safe, found some stamps and put one on each letter. Fifteen letters were in the safe and fifteen were mailed to Joe Combs that night. Each told about her progress, about JoJo's progress, and about her mother's pure hatred for her father. She had no idea why she was telling him these things. At the time, she felt he needed these updates. And now, she felt he needed to know her.

Warm rain drizzled on her face as she walked over to the mailbox and dropped in all fifteen letters. It felt so final. For a second, she desired to immerse her hand into the darkness of the box and retrieve the letters, but the image of Tate writhing on top of her and telling her she wanted it as much as he did, obliterated the urge.

With the fifteen letters mailed, she started writing more letters. The new set reflected a brand of hate-filled language.

Briefly, she entertained thoughts of Joe writing back. But how could that happen? She never put a return address on the envelopes, and she never mentioned the college name in her letters. If he wanted to, she supposed he could find out where she was located, but she didn't care. She was like a boxer ready to stand toe to toe with her father. She could hear bone-crushing punches landing on his face. If he found her, he would end up wishing he had not.

Mimi put the most recent letter in an envelope and placed a stamp on it. She pulled on her lightweight jacket and zipped it. Although it was springtime, the nights in Ohio could get a little chilly. With the letter stuffed in her pocket, she walked out to the mailbox, which sat at the end of the street. She could have dropped the letter in the receptacle provided in the dorm, but she was using the time it took to walk to the mailbox to decide something.

By the time she dropped the letter inside the mailbox, she had made up her mind.

If getting love and affection from someone required her to open her legs, then she would be opening her legs a lot. No one would have to take it from her again. Not her father or some fake boyfriend. She wouldn't care about making friends or acquiring love interests. This was a time to be openly sexual, and she would be using the time well. Mimi wouldn't care if it seemed like brief happiness mixed with long-term loneliness. She wouldn't worry about the consequences.

She shook her head and said aloud, "It doesn't matter if I'm lonely. Nothing matters at all." Again she shook her head. Why did it sound like making the declaration itself was lonely?

"Mimi?"

She turned to see a guy from one of her classes, but she could not remember which one. Also, his name escaped her. He was short, thick, and strong. "Runt" was the first word that came to her mind when she looked at him. "Bulldog" came in a close second.

"Are you talking to yourself?" he asked.

She smiled. "No, I'm talking to you." She sauntered over to him and placed a hand delicately on his shoulder.

Chapter 31
Holding a Secret

A yellow sticky note on the door alerted her to "Call JoJo." While another note beneath it announced "Call Bizzy." The handwriting, with large loops on the letter "C" and slants in JoJo and Bizzy's name, revealed the messenger was the same person; most likely, the girl whose dorm room was next to the public telephone area. Lucky her. The room was larger, but the price of it required the occupant to answer the phone at all hours of the night just so it wasn't ringing incessantly. Every time the girl left a note, it looked as if she had written it with rage in her fingers.

Mimi ripped both notes off as she opened the door. She threw the notes in the trashcan. The Heider building was her new home for her sophomore year, and she loved it. The rooms in Heider had been designed as single units with thin walls. As long as you owned a nice set of headsets, you could live in pure peace.

Since Mimi had moved to this new dorm three months ago, JoJo, Bizzy, and/or her mother had phoned at least once or twice a month. What did they not get? The second year at Foster would run smoothly, as long as she concentrated and did her work. She did not have time to listen to someone while they "checked in" with her. Mimi was just fine. She did not need or want any "checking in."

She dropped her bag on top of her bed. The key to maintaining a room in Heider was maximizing the use of the smallest amount of space. The 8-feet by 6-inch box she called "home" instilled a bit of claustrophobia in the senses. To quell those concerns, the designers of the dorm placed a bay window about half the size of the wall as part of each room's layout. This meant that no matter where you were in Heider, you had a view of the outside. Depending on which wing a student was assigned to, the view ranged from the well-kept landscape of the quad area to the dumpster located in the rear of the dorm.

The room itself had a decorum at which a true artist or an architect would scoff. Each neutral painted wall was constructed with a grade of plaster that failed at holding nails. Picture frames and celebratory exams had to be affixed with push pins. Anything else resulted in a huge dimple. The linoleum floor boasted a pattern of three rose-colored diamonds in every square. Mimi's first action after she moved in was to cover the hideous pattern with her throw rug. On one side of the room, a white plastic desk and a wooden vanity were glued side by side, making it easy to lean over and wash the hands after eating a messy sandwich. Occupants could roll on the wheels of a muted mauve colored plastic desk chair from desk to vanity and back. On the other side, a taupe-colored twin bed was raised about four or four and a half feet off the floor, leaving a treasure of storage space beneath the bed. The final piece of furniture in the room was a mirror-less three-drawer bureau, which matched the bed frame of the twin bed. This was how all the rooms at Heider were designed. It was up to the occupant to add her own personal touches.

The most personal touch Mimi included was her safe, which was tucked under the bed at the far corner. She pulled a white envelope from her bag and bent down to open the safe. Before placing the latest Joe Combs indictment into the safe, she sat on the throw rug and crossed her legs as she pressed the letter between her hands as if saying a prayer. She rocked gently back and forth.

This letter had been written following a recent three-day binge. The first time a binge occurred, Mimi had been so afraid that she ran through a winter snowstorm to Peyton's apartment.

She, Peyton, and Billy were still study partners and occasionally they went out together. But it didn't take Mimi long to realize Billy was interested in being more than Peyton's study partner. It took Peyton a while longer to recognize the blatant signs, such as his continual staring and specific attention to her smallest needs, but once Peyton realized what was happening, she began to reciprocate. Mimi became the extra set of plates people decided against buying because they really only needed two sets. Before Peyton and Billy had to struggle with ways to exclude her, she was merciful and excluded herself.

However, the binge had terrified her, and she bolted through snowflakes, slipping and sliding down the streets and once crashing into the ground. When she reached Peyton's apartment, she was drenched with perspiration and the cold wetness of snowflakes.

"Mimi?" Peyton's surprised response when she opened the door informed Mimi of what she already knew: Billy was in the apartment, and Peyton's roommate was not at home. "Do we have a study group tonight?"

Mimi imagined her wet hair was frizzy on the top, and parts of it were clinging to her face. She had grabbed a coat but had not buttoned it, so her T-shirt clung to her body. If Peyton noticed this, she did not ask about it.

"This isn't our night?" Mimi responded. "I must be getting old. See you later, Peyton." She turned to go back down the steps without hearing Peyton say a word about the fact that she wasn't carrying her book bag.

She traced her steps back to her dorm room with a much saner pace. Upon entering her room, she found the dictionary on the desk and looked up the word "binge." With her forefinger guiding her through every word in the definition, she concluded that the second part of the definition most fit her situation. She understood she was expressing "an unrestrained and often excessive indulgence" and somehow knowing the meaning eased her mind.

There had been one other binge since the first, and the latest had caused her to write the letter she held.

The first day of the last binge was Friday. With a black sky lit by brilliant stars, she and Billy and Peyton had gone to an off campus house party. Billy asked Mimi to dance, but over his shoulder she saw the look of disappointment in Peyton's eyes. She lied, telling Billy she was a klutz and he should ask Peyton instead. Peyton's cheeks blushed as Billy led her to the center of the floor. Mimi watched as Billy gyrated in harmony with Peyton and believed she had done a good deed. Several fast dances went by, and she noticed she was giving true meaning to the word "wallflower" as she leaned against the cold, cement wall.

A churning in her soul began to speak to her, and she wondered whether she had worn the right dress or the right shoes. Was her hair laying in the right pattern? Was her lipstick smudged? Moreover, why didn't people love her?

The response to the last question was simple. *Because I'm holding a secret, a dirty secret, that people can see. Because of what I did, my family was turned upside down. Why did I tell? Why did I let it happen? My father truly loved me, didn't he?*

Just as a headache began to form in her temples, she saw his hand. The guy looked like a younger version of Billy Dee Williams. The extended hand reminded her of the scene in *Lady Sings the Blues* where Billy Dee, holding a dollar toward Diana Ross' character, asks if she wants his hand to fall off. Mimi danced several dances with the guy, and when a slower paced song played, she drew herself close to his body and let its warmth shut down the questions.

In his dorm room, she let him have what she felt unworthy of keeping. The release of pleasure had given her such a peace that the next night she went to an off campus party alone. The guy who asked her to dance had a friend who had just broken up with his girlfriend. By some record of events that she was unable to recall, she ended up in the friend's bedroom. She told herself she was comforting him, when in reality, he unknowingly was comforting her.

On Sunday, the final day of the binge, she had promised Bryan Fontaine, a struggling ball player, that she would show him a technique for memorizing dates in their History of the World class. Bryan was a simpleton, who was no match for Mimi's powers of persuasion. Before he realized it, she was on his bed, and he was doing something he knew he should not be doing. Afterward, Bryan cried and begged Mimi not to tell his girlfriend. She promised and left his room without showing him the memorization technique.

Back in her own room, she vomited three times into the washbowl of the vanity. Sex with three different guys, three days in a row, and she had not used protection. Thoughts of pregnancy and disease weighed on her, and she vowed it was the last time. The next time she would see the binge coming. That next time she would run from the opportunities that became more prevalent during a binge.

The pledge drove her to the desk to write the letter she now held in her hands.

December 1, 1992

Dear Daddy,

The other day I was thinking about the time we went to see the Phillies play ball. Do you remember, Daddy?

The trip was more for JoJo than for me, but since it was your weekend to have us visit, I had to tag along. I don't remember much about the game except I ate my first snow cone there. My lips were blue-black and you and JoJo kidded that I should not kiss you on the cheeks because it might turn you into frozen snowmen.

I also remember needing to go to the bathroom during the seventh inning because snow cones are just frozen water. I'm smiling now because I remember you holding my hand as we walked, and I kept looking at the ground. And you stopped walking and bent down to scoop my chin in your hand. Do you remember what you said, Daddy? I do. You told me to always walk with my head held high because it showed I was confident and proud of myself.

A week later, my neck was sore because I had spent the week with my head held so high that my chin was practically pointing upward. (Smile)

I remember that after the game, JoJo needed to go home to work on something for school, but I begged Mommy to let me finish the weekend at your apartment. As we climbed the stairway, because that stupid elevator was broke—again—you told me I was doing a good job holding my head high, and then you took me inside the apartment and touched me until you had your own personal orgasm. I don't' think you even noticed that at that moment my head was so low that I felt everything but confident and proud.

Did you notice, Daddy? Did you care?

I think now that I should have killed you back then. In your sleep I should have done it.

Love,

Mimi

Sitting on the rug and gently rocking back and forth, she halted. Removing the letter from the envelope, she rewrote the entire letter without the last two sentences. She placed it in a new envelope, sealed it, and put it in the safe until she could mail it the next day.

As she closed the safe door, the click of the lock sealing the letter inside was like the ending of the binge, which sealed everything she knew, real and unreal, inside of her.

Chapter 32
What Are You Doing Here?

She asked him again, believing he hadn't heard her the first time.

"What are you doing here?"

"Well, my dear, hello to you." He smiled.

She frowned in return. "Answer me."

He flustered an explanation. "Man, did you get up on the wrong side of the bed this morning. Look, I'm on a break from my studies, but that doesn't mean I have to leave campus. I still live in the neighborhood, ya know." He tried to smile again, but faltered when he looked in her eyes.

Mimi had not seen Tate since the end of her freshman year. After the rape, she refused to open the door if he knocked. If she saw him in a hallway, she passed without looking or speaking to him.

After a week of trying to communicate with her, he passed her in the stairwell of the dorm and whispered, "Crazy girl." In the cavern of the stairwell, the insult echoed a little. Then Tate left Mimi alone.

Standing in front of her now, he looked almost the same. Except his face appeared a bit fuller, showing he was probably eating too much and exercising too little. She understood. Her life now included a bit more eating and a few more pounds.

"I'm just so glad to see you. How have you been?" Tate asked.

"I'm fine." The grocery bags seemed much heavier than before, but she refused to put them on the ground. She refused to give Tate any hope that she might converse with him.

"You're right. You do look fine. You look real good. Have you lost some weight?"

She rolled her eyes and pushed past him. "I need to go."

"Mimi." He grabbed her arm. She jerked away. "Can I talk to you? Just for a minute. Please, baby."

She wanted to bash Tate's head in with one of the bags, but neither carried anything that would do much damage. "What do you want? You have one minute. And don't you dare call me *baby* again."

"Okay. Okay. Look, ba—I mean, look . . . I miss you. Can I take you out sometime? Maybe we can pick up where we left off."

Again, Mimi tasted her breakfast on her tongue, and fought the urge to vomit on Tate's coat. She put both bags in one hand, and with the other, stuck a finger in Tate's face. "Where . . . we . . . left . . . off? Do you even remember where we left off? Do you remember raping me? Do you remember me telling you to stop?"

"Whoa!" He stepped back and quickly scanned the area before he spoke. On a cold winter day, they were the only people on the street. "What the hell are you talking about? You wanted it. You came to that apartment for it."

"I came to that apartment because I called myself loving you."

He laughed. "Come on, ba—, I mean, Mimi. You were too young to know what love was. But I'm sure you knew what sex was, and that's why you came over, right?"

She took a deep breath and returned one of the bags to her free hand. "Bye, Tate."

As she stomped away, he called after her. "I don't know what the big deal is. Seems like you giving it away freely to more than just me these days. I just want another cut."

Mimi stopped, and a bitter wind whipped around her legs and pushed the bags out, then it moved on. Her first thought was to walk back and slap Tate, or spit on him, but those actions would not hurt him enough. So she turned and said what she knew would mortally wound his feelings.

"If I'm giving it away, I'm giving it away to men not *boys*. You will never get another cut." She turned again, and with her back to him said, "Bye, Tate."

As he hollered obscenities in response, she walked up the street with her head held high.

Part 5

Dear King...Am I Broken?

Chapter 33
Here Comes Xavier

May 21, 1993

Dear Daddy,

Great news!

I slept with some guy I met in a movie theater. Are you proud of your little girl? This is what I've been reduced to. This is what I've become. No one loves me. No one is in love with me. I'm invisible. Someone who's there and not there at the same time. People don't think of me. People don't applaud me. They don't praise me. Mommy doesn't love me. She stopped loving me the minute you touched me. She loves JoJo. He is the child of her life because you didn't taint him. You didn't spoil him. You didn't make it so it's hard for her to look at him.

Let me tell you about the guy. I go to the movies by myself because when my roommates need private time, and I'm all studied out, it's the only place to go. The only place where I can be alone and no one will notice that I'm alone. I sit in the dark and sometimes tears roll down my cheeks. No one sees them in the dark. I've been to hundreds of movies, and I can only tell you what half of them are about. The rest I cried during the entire movie.

When I went to this particular movie, I stood in line for popcorn because sometimes food brings me relief. I've gained twenty more pounds. I'm well on my way from plump to fat. I was ordering the popcorn when I noticed a guy looking at me from the next line over. I immediately thought he was staring at me in disgust, but then he winked. Why did he do that? All a guy has to do these days is show me a small amount of interest, and I'm smiling at him and letting him have what he doesn't deserve. I also become this other person. Someone brave, saucy, and brazen. The next thing I know, we're exchanging phone numbers. His name doesn't matter. He came to visit me at the apartment, we had sex, and after he left I misplaced his number. He never called again and I never tried to reach out to him.

Why did I do it? I don't know. I'm disgusted with myself, but I also feel better when someone holds me and tells me they think I'm beautiful. But it has to be someone my own age. Someone who isn't my own blood. Someone who is not my own father.

You ought to be ashamed of yourself. Are you ashamed? Don't you care what you did? How could you do it? Why did you do it? You called me Nugget. It made me feel special. Now when I hear the word "nugget" I feel dirty. Was that your intent, Daddy? Did you care about your own needs more than mine?

I'm going to go because I can't stand writing to you any longer.

I hate you with such a passion,

Mimi

Trudging home, she took in the sights of the small town in which Foster College resided.

The bakery was closed, but light emanating from a back room in the store was an indicator that they were prepping tomorrow's delicacies. The smell of warm donuts invaded her thoughts. She knew the bakery owners wouldn't be baking anything until the early hours of the next day, but when they did, those donuts were the best in the world. Her mouth watered. A few more steps and she saw the display of mannequins wearing baby doll dresses or polo shirts atop cargo pants in Truman's clothing store. Truman's could have passed for fashionable if the mannequins were not yellowing with missing pieces like the tip of a nose or an index finger. The store had to be over 100 years old.

Mimi continued on in a slow, heavy pace while making more observations. She was tired. Having a part time job was easy in the beginning. She only worked four hours a day, three times a week and every other Saturday. The owner of the closest copy store to the college campus was sympathetic to students and probably had a bigger staff than he needed, but Mimi was grateful for the job.

She was in her third year at Foster, and shared a three-bedroom apartment with Peyton and Billy. The part time job helped with some of her share of the rent, but her mother supplemented the rest. Mimi believed it was actually her brother who was helping. A while ago she suspected this was JoJo's way of asking for forgiveness for what he had said and how he had treated her. Too bad for him; she was not in the mood to give forgiveness.

As she climbed the steps to the apartment, she rubbed the strain of looking down at a copier for hours from the back of her neck. When she entered, the first sound she heard was Peyton's sing-song voice calling, "Mi-mi, dinner."

Living with people who had become her only friends in college was working well. They all had a full load and were rarely home. They took turns cooking and cleaning, and so far had not had any issues paying bills, but she wasn't kidding herself about the arrangement. They were not living together because they were the best of friends, or because it was convenient. Peyton could excuse their living arrangement to her parents as not living with a man but as living with her friends. She still had not told her parents she was dating Billy.

As Mimi walked into the kitchen, the savory aroma of dinner made her mouth water and her stomach growl. Even though Peyton's major was in engineering, she was in training to be a homemaker. While she was getting D's in the subject matter, she was getting A's in making home perfect for Billy and Mimi. She cooked delicious meals and decorated their apartment on a meager budget. Her layouts and designs for their living room, bathroom, and kitchen could have been in any magazine.

Billy was sitting at the kitchen table, which had been set with white plates, silver utensils, and beige cloth napkins. Peyton had purchased all of these at a discount store. In the center of the table, she arranged a small bouquet of fresh flowers in a crystal vase. For dinner, she had prepared a baked ziti dish with a salad. These little nice touches made Mimi pretend she was another person who was part of a special family that loved her very much.

On nights when they could share a meal together, Peyton dressed for the occasion and for Billy. Today she pulled her hair back in a bun, and it rested on the nape of her neck. She wore a cotton short-sleeved button up blouse and a red pencil skirt that stopped just above her knees. Red colored studs in her ears brightened the tone of her skin. Obviously, Billy was dumbstruck by his girlfriend and kept stealing glances at her through bites.

"So, how was your day?" Mimi said, trying to break the loving couple moment. This was the biggest challenge in living with two people who cared for each other as much as Peyton and Billy did. Often, she found herself trying to fit into what they already had going on, like a puzzle piece that just did not belong.

Peyton turned toward her and said, "Fine. I finally made a decision about my Thermodynamics class?"

"And what are you going to do?"

"I'm not going to take it. Let's face it, engineering isn't my thing."

"Don't you need the class to graduate?"

"Yes, I do, but I'm holding it off until the last possible moment. Maybe by then they'll change the rules. You never know what might happen."

Sometimes Peyton irritated Mimi. She always looked for a silver lining, that bright side, and the possibility of hope. Apparently, Billy knew about her decision already because he continued eating without saying a word. His eyes were glued to Peyton's face. Billy's major was architectural design. School had been easy for him, and he was carrying a current grade point average of 3.7. Dropping classes or rearranging his schedule was absent from his vocabulary. He simply followed the program and expected to graduate and move on to an architectural firm. Watching him, Mimi always felt like his life was set, already planned from the day he was born.

"Do we have any rolls?" he asked.

"Oh, I'm so sorry. I completely forgot." Peyton stood. "Let me get the basket."

The basket Peyton used for her rolls also doubled as a centerpiece on the living room coffee table. When she left to retrieve it, Billy leaned over and whispered, "I want to have a romantic evening with Peyton. You think you can go to a movie, or go over to a friend's house for a while?"

A revelation formed in her mind. Billy had no concept of what her life was like. Didn't he notice that she did not go anywhere but to work and school? Didn't he notice that she never invited people over to the apartment? Apparently, with Peyton on his mind, he hadn't noticed anyone else. Now he was asking her to leave their apartment and go to a non-existent friend's house.

Peyton was back before Mimi could answer. "Here we go." She dropped the basket on the center of the table and went to the oven to retrieve the dinner rolls.

Mimi glanced at Billy. "Hey, I'm stuffed. I have to run somewhere. I should be back home by about 11:30." She looked at Billy to see if this was enough time. He shook his head slightly. "I mean midnight." Billy smiled. "Okay. Don't wait up for me, kids."

As she grabbed her backpack, she could not imagine what she would do until midnight. It was only 7:00 p.m. The best she could come up with was to study at the library.

To her surprise, the college library was crowded with students huddled over books and furiously scribbling on paper. She found an empty table near a window and sat down to unpack her books.

"Mimi?" The sound of a familiar voice came from behind her. She turned and almost said "damn" out loud when she saw his face.

"Mimi?" he said again. "What are you doing here?"

"Xavier?" The tall young man in front of her had Xavier Wright's face, but elongated with a small patch of hair draped above his upper lip. She had not seen Xavier since graduation day of high school. It took her two years to get up enough courage to approach him after their friendship ended with her blundered confession of affection.

At the graduation, she had walked up to him and said, "Congratulations. I wish you the best in life." Then, she left without giving him a chance to return the sentiment. At the time, her hope was that she would never have to hear Xavier's voice or see his face again. Her hope just got obliterated.

"I can't believe it!" he said, grabbing a nearby chair and pulling it alongside hers. He smelled spicy with a hint of peppermint. As he dropped his bag to the floor, she noticed the bulge of lean muscle beneath the sleeve of his T-shirt. Xavier had been working out. "What are you doing here?"

"I go to this school. What are you doing here?"

"My girlfriend goes here. I just came up to spend the weekend with her. But I have a major exam on Monday and thought I'd better act like I want a good grade. I can't believe it's you."

Mimi hesitated in answering. Her mind was still stuck on the words "my girlfriend." "Who's your girlfriend?" she managed to ask.

"Maybe you know her. Desiree Distill. Some people call her Dezzy. She's in the architecture program here at the school."

Of course, she did not know her. She didn't have any friends besides Peyton and Billy. "My roommate's in that program. I'll ask him if he knows her." She was lying. She wasn't going to ask Billy anything, fearing too much of a connection between her world of high school and her world of college.

"Well, what are you studying here?"

"I finally decided to do journalism. I'm thinking of working for a newspaper or magazine."

"Cool. I used to like reading your work."

This came as a surprise to her. She had only given him one or two pieces, and that was just before she told him how she felt.

"What about you?"

"You know how much I like the animals. I'm studying veterinary medicine."

"That's good." Mimi looked down at her books, not certain what to ask him next. She did not like sitting this close to him. It brought back memories of standing next to him on the doorstep of her home.

"Look, I don't want to interrupt your studying, but I would like to hook up. Maybe you, me, and Dezzy could get together."

Every inch of her wanted to say no. To tell him she just wanted to be left alone, but something or someone else told Xavier, "Sure, when do you want to get together?"

"Tomorrow. We can meet somewhere for lunch."

"There's a restaurant off-campus that everybody goes to. We can meet there. It's a Mexican restaurant. I think you used to like Mexican, right? I'm sure Dezzy will know it." Mimi couldn't believe how this other person was digging her into this commitment.

"Good, good. How about 11:30? Can you do that?"

"That works."

"Good. Well, I'm off." He stood and placed the chair back in its spot under the table. "Mimi . . . wow . . . I can't believe I saw you. I'm looking forward to catching up tomorrow."

"So am I."

"I'll see ya then."

"See ya then." Good gracious! She sounded like a parrot.

She turned away as if dismissing him, but bent her head slightly so he could get a full view of her neck. She recalled he had once told her that she had a long, graceful neck like a model. He paused then walked away. When he was out of sight, she threw her pen against the table. What the heck was she doing? This other person was trying to impress and entice Xavier. She couldn't understand why. This other person had agreed to lunch so she could meet Xavier's girlfriend. Now this, she did understand. The other person wanted to see what Xavier's girlfriend looked like. Was she light skinned or dark skinned? Was her hair long or short? Were her eyes colored or basic brown? Did she have a long neck? Was she short and fat or tall and thin? Was she smart or ditzy? Did she deserve him?

She closed her book and spent the next hour staring out the window at the traffic and students coming and going. At one point, she saw Xavier leave the library. He looked over to where she still sat and he waved. She pretended not to notice him.

Chapter 34
How Bizzy Did It

Thick. Solid. Fast. Free.

Each of these words summed up three year old Barbie.

Mimi, on all fours on the floor of Barbie's bedroom, was panting. She and Barbie had been playing a familiar game, which, for lack of a formal name, Mimi simply labeled it Up and Down. The game started with Barbie begging Mimi to pick her up. When Mimi did, she squirmed to be put down. When Mimi obliged and Barbie was on the floor, the little girl would beg to be picked up again. Over and over this went until Mimi collapsed to the floor in exhaustion, and Barbie, standing next to her in some sort of toddler euphoria, burst into hysterical and high-pitched laughter and jumped on Mimi's back. Surely this child knew exactly what she was doing.

"What are you feeding her?" Mimi wheezed to Bizzy.

"You're the crazy one. I stop after three times."

"It's not that easy. Look at those cheeks. How can you say no?" She sat on the floor and pulled Barbie into her lap for a good tickle, which led to a screaming laugh.

"Mimi, why would you do that?" asked Bizzy.

Ignoring the question, she lifted Barbie in the air and buried her head in the toddler's stomach. Barbie squealed. For Mimi, the best part about coming home for break was Barbie.

Visiting with Bizzy was a nice. Her friend was a good person. She called Mimi consistently to see how she was doing. Honestly, Mimi wondered why Bizzy had not given up on her, but she knew the answer. Bizzy was not the giving-up kind. So while Bizzy made Mimi open doors and look at parts of her life she would rather leave in the dark, Barbie allowed her to close those doors and forget. Oh, how much she adored this little girl.

She slowly lowered Barbie to the floor. "Bizzy, it's no big deal. I didn't go all the way. I stopped in time."

"You shouldn't have been there at all. Are you trying to get yourself killed?"

Bizzy snatched Barbie from Mimi's arms. She placed the little girl on the changing table and kissed her face and neck. Barbie squealed again.

"You don't know who the guy was," Bizzy said while changing Barbie's shirt.

"Yes, I do. He was an old friend of Billy's, in town for the weekend."

"That doesn't mean he was safe."

"It means Billy and Peyton knew who I was with."

Bizzy shook her head. Mimi had just told her about a friend of Billy's who came to visit the three of them. Well, really he came to see Billy and Billy's girlfriend and Billy's roommate, Mimi, just happened to be home. Billy's friend, Mike something-or-another, was short but handsome, and he came with a nice motorcycle. He spent most of his visit throwing side glances at Mimi while catching up with Billy and getting to know Peyton. When he mentioned his motorcycle, it was the right opportunity for Mimi to join the conversation.

"How long have you had it?"

"About a year?"

"It looks nice."

"Ever rode on one?"

"No. I haven't."

And that was all it took.

Billy pulled her into the bathroom while she was putting on her jacket. Mike something-or-another had told her the ride might be a little chilly.

"Mimi," Billy whispered, "watch out for Mike. He's got a reputation for hitting it and quitting it." She gazed into Billy's face. He really did not know her. She liked those kind of people. The ones who provided a type of closeness and afterward left. Like a pill for a headache. A bandage for a cut.

Mike something-or-another drove her to a remote spot in the park where she let him unzip her jeans and have sex with her. She told Bizzy they just had foreplay. Mimi was not exactly proud of how far she had gone, but she did not care anymore. Being intimate with any guy sometimes, although temporarily, took the hurt away. It was what she suspected most guys wanted from her anyway.

Bizzy dressed Barbie in a new outfit. She placed the little girl on the floor. "I don't care that they knew him. I care that what you did isn't like you. Lately, you've been taking these risks that don't make sense. You know what you did wasn't right. Do you want a life like mine? I love Barbie. I really do, but being a mom, and a single mom at that, is hard work. I can do it, but if I had a choice, I would have chosen a different scenario." Bizzy paused. She took a deep breath. "Tell me, Mimi, what's wrong?"

Mimi looked into Bizzy's eyes. They glistened with concern. Mimi looked away. "Nothing's wrong, Bizzy. I was just having fun."

"This isn't fun. This is destroying you."

"You're getting all worked up for nothing. I'm not destroying myself."

"Mimi, do you remember when I came back home from down south?" Mimi shook her head. She knew where this was going, and she hated that it was going there again. Every time they had this conversation, she thought she owed it to Bizzy to at least listen, even if sometimes it went in one ear and out the other. "You remember that I told you I was saved?"

"I remember." Exasperation.

"Before then I was a wreck. Here I was, nearly eighteen, pregnant, jobless, and a bit homeless. Or, let's just say, I wasn't in my own home. I was scared, and I felt like no one could understand and no one could walk with me or help me. I remember sitting in church with my grandmother, listening to the minister talk about how Jesus loved me so much that he died for me, and he died so that I could have a relationship with God that would save me from the destruction I was heading for. The minister said all I had to do was accept Christ's act of love. That's all I had to do. And it would begin to open my heart, so that God could give me the love he desired to give me."

Mimi shifted. The talk about God always made her think of her grandmother, and that made her uncomfortable.

"All I'm saying is I'm concerned for you, and the only one who can help you through this is the Lord Jesus. He wants you to have a relationship with his Father that will change your life and help you . . ." Bizzy never paused when she shared like this. Usually, her bubbly, non-stop voice ran on until she was done.

"Help me what?" Mimi demanded.

"Help you love yourself," Bizzy said after taking another deep breath.

Mimi was sitting on the floor with Barbie, who was picking up colored blocks and handing them to her. After each one, she shouted the color of the block at Mimi as if Mimi may not know what it was. Mimi took a block from Barbie and said, "I love myself. I love myself a lot. Why would you think I don't love myself?"

"Mimi, I just don't think a person who loves herself does destructive things like sleeping with men they don't know. What about disease or pregnancy?"

Okay, so she knows that I did do more than foreplay with the motorcycle guy. Mimi confessed, "I used protection. What's the big deal, Bizzy?" Mimi frowned.

"I'm just concerned."

"No, you're just judging."

"How can you say that? I'm not judging you. I love you, and I'm looking out for what's best for you."

"You love me? Cut it out, Bizzy. You don't love me." Mimi stood. "You know what? I have to go home. My mother is having my brother and his wife over for dinner. I promised I'd be there."

"O-kay." Bizzy's face was colorless, and her lips were turned down a little at the corners. Her voice cracked. Mimi felt guilty.

"Look. I understand. I know you care about me. Thanks for doing so."

She kissed Barbie on the forehead. The little girl said something about the blue block in her hand and shoved it into Mimi's face. Mimi smiled as she took the block, placed it on the floor, and gave Barbie one more kiss.

As she walked out the door, Bizzy said, "Please stop hurting yourself."

Mimi closed the door gently behind her.

Chapter 35
Tomas is What?

Tomas was genuinely a nice person, and Mimi hated her.

This little princess with a good heart had come through the door with gifts and intentions on helping wherever needed. At their wedding, Mimi was sure the smile Tomas wore became exaggerated each time Faye came near; like Tomas was clenching her teeth to prevent saying something she might regret. But this version of Tomas wore a warm and wide smile that made her cheeks plump whenever she put it on. She spent time in the kitchen talking to Faye and time in Mimi's bedroom picking her brain about her college experience while sharing her own.

In addition, Tomas was a pretty woman. She had perfect hair, which seemed to shine even in dim light. She had perfect eyes, perfect lips, and a perfect nose. She accented every facial feature with just a touch of makeup that made her look like a petite-sized model. Her voice was soft and light like a love song melody. She sat next to JoJo and occasionally rested her hand on his arm or on top of his hand. Yes, this version of Tomas was different from the version she saw years ago in the picture on JoJo's mirror. This Tomas had changed. Perhaps it was marriage that did it.

So when summed up, this version of Tomas was one more person who would draw attention in this family and further solidify Mimi's invisibility.

Tomas and JoJo had come to visit while Mimi was home for the summer. Mimi would be moving on to her last year at Foster, so she suspected her mother had orchestrated this event to sort of celebrate the occasion. However, she didn't understand why. It was not as if they were a close knit family. Mimi barely spoke with Tomas or JoJo, and had limited communication with her mother as well.

They were all sitting in the kitchen eating one of her mother's big family meals. In reality, JoJo, Tomas, and her mother ate and chatted while she observed like a judge at a competition. Tomas was sharing a story about a charity event she and JoJo had attended. As Mimi watched her, she speculated that this woman may have been encouraging JoJo to subsidize her college living arrangements. Tomas had such a big heart for giving to others, so it would make sense if she was responsible for the furniture in Mimi's dorm room during freshman year. If she did not pay for anything, she had at least influenced her husband to make those decisions. She had a hold on JoJo that was either obsession or true love.

Her mother was saying, "When are you two going to give me some grandchildren?"

It was the typical conversation. Her mother always embarked on this road of questioning eventually. Whenever, Mimi was home and could hear her mother talking to JoJo on the phone, the question would surface, sometimes from nowhere. They would be talking about anything but children, and her mother would pop out the question.

"Well, actually . . ." Tomas hugged JoJo's arm. "We do have some news."

Her mother's mouth flew open, and she covered it with her hand. "No! Yes! Yes!" She flew from her chair and gathered them both up in one huge hug. She was crying and saying "yes" at the same time. She stepped back from them and put her hands on her cheeks. "I'm so happy . . . so happy for you both. Oh, I have so much to do. When are you due?"

"I'm three months now."

"Stand up, stand up. Let me look at you." She ripped Tomas from her seat, twirled her around like a ballerina and then touched her stomach. "I know it's too early, but I'm sure he can hear all the commotion. You're on your way, little man."

"How can you be so sure it's a boy, Mom?" JoJo asked.

She answered him absently while examining Tomas' face and her stomach. "I don't know," she said. "I've always just felt like your first child would be a boy."

Had her mother had thoughts about Mimi's first child? She guided Tomas back to the chair as if she wore a "handle with care" label on her chest. JoJo grinned.

"I've got so much to do. When I get to church, I'm going to ask them to put you on the prayer list. We need to start praying now for my grandson and for a healthy pregnancy."

Mimi's mouth fell open. "Church?"

"Yes. I'm attending the Westville Community Church. It's about a half hour drive from here. I'm hoping we can all go this Sunday."

"Since when did you start going to church?"

"I've been going for about a year and a half now. I thought I told you."

"No, you did not tell me." Mimi turned to JoJo. "Did you know?"

He had been smiling at Tomas. "What?"

"Did you know she was attending church?"

"Well, ah, yeah. She told me."

Mimi turned to Tomas. Her words were like a cat pouncing on a piece of string. "Did you know?"

Tomas had been gleaming at being able to let out news of a baby on the way, but her face flipped now to what Mimi recognized as her stressed look. Her eyes became slits and her mouth pursed. She blinked quickly as she answered, "Well, yes, I did too."

"Did she tell you, or did JoJo tell you?"

Tomas looked at JoJo then at Faye, then back to JoJo. Each of them looked confused. Mimi knew she had startled them with her tone of questioning.

"Um . . . Faye told me."

"So, my mother talks directly to you about her life?"

"I'm not sure what you mean. We talk about her life. Yes, we do."

Mimi stood up. She threw her napkin on the table. "Mom, you would rather talk to a stranger about things in your life than your own daughter."

"Wait a minute, Mimi. Tomas isn't a stranger." JoJo was on his feet.

"Mimi-bear—" began her mother.

"You don't get it. I'm *tired*. This family is about you, JoJo, and whatever surrounds you both." She turned to JoJo. "Your wife gets attention. You get attention, but Mimi . . . well, she's like somebody we adopted and are now obligated to, but we don't have to like it, do we?" She couldn't stop herself. So much was coming out. Mimi turned to Tomas, wanting everyone to get a piece of this action. "You think this family is so perfect, huh? Tomas, has he told you our little family secret?"

"Mimi—" her mother tried again, her voice filled with warning.

"No, I guess he hasn't. Ask them where our father is. Ask them, Tomas."

Her mother, who had moved away from the table to the refrigerator, fell against the door as if she depended on it to hold her up.

JoJo glared at Mimi.

"Ask them what our father is in jail for." She glared back at JoJo. "You know I write him letters."

JoJo stepped back now and crashed into his chair. It slammed against the floor.

"I write letters to a man I hate because I hate the people who are supposed to love me even more." This was not true, but again, she couldn't stop. She saw that what she said was hurting them. A small wave of satisfaction filled her. This must have been what it felt like to get marijuana high. She headed out of the kitchen but stopped at the doorway.

"Congratulations, Tomas. But I do feel sorry for your baby. Coming into this family can be deadly."

And this must be what if felt like when you came down off that marijuana high. She was never doing drugs. She had gone to Bizzy's house. It was late, and in her haste to leave her family behind, she did not call, but she knew Bizzy would be awake. Since Barbie's birth, Bizzy had developed strange sleeping patterns that at times had her up at one in the morning doing laundry.

Sitting at the kitchen table, Mimi wept bitterly while Bizzy patted her back. She unloaded a partially true story, leaving out the pieces about her father being in jail. She wasn't ready to tell Bizzy this. But as she repeated the events of her night, some of it did not sound right. It made her look like an idiot. Bizzy was quiet. The only sounds mixing together were Mimi's sniffling, the hum of the refrigerator, and Bizzy's hand rubbing across the back of Mimi's shirt. Finally, Mimi took a gulp of air and released it. She didn't like this quiet. She wanted to hear Bizzy's voice.

"Do you want to sleep in my bed tonight?" Bizzy asked.

Mimi nodded. She was overcome with a weariness she had never experienced before. All -night study sessions were nothing compared to the exhaustion she felt now. Bizzy helped her up from the table.

"Go lie in the bed."

Bizzy's voice reminded her of a peaceful lake, and Mimi followed her as she led her to the bedroom, where Mimi dropped across the bed with all her clothes on. Bizzy left and returned with a glass of water. She made Mimi sit up and drink the liquid, which felt soothing as it slid down the back of her throat. She had no idea how dry she had become inside. Bizzy made her undress and put on a nightgown she had pulled from the top drawer.

Once Mimi settled under the covers, Bizzy shut off the light. "You'll feel better after you get some sleep." She pulled the door closed as she left the room.

Go to sleep? Impossible. Staring at the ceiling, her eyes felt raw. Images of the production she had just given for her family filled her soul. She wanted to weep again, and she slowly closed her eyes.

When she opened them, her foot was sticking out from under the blankets and hanging over the edge of the bed. The sun was up, and the room was entirely lit. Mimi glanced around and saw the pictures of Barbie on the bureaus, the nightstands, the window sills and the walls. She surveyed the room, which was cluttered but not messy. Folded clothes sat in an armchair. Bizzy's medical assistant uniform hung on the knob of her closet door. Her bureau held an array of perfumes, lotions, and beauty products from several manufacturers. On the nightstand lay a worn copy of the Bible. Bizzy had slips of paper sticking out from various sections in the book. A cloth covered notebook with a network of flowers and vines and the words "My Journal" in printed script, lay on top of the Bible.

Muffled voices floated from the kitchen and up through the floor. The clanging of pots signaled someone was about to prepare a meal. She heard a soft knock, and the door opened.

"Mimi," called Bizzy, but Barbie pushed past her mother's leg and ran into the room. She grabbed Mimi's exposed foot.

"Auntie Mee Mee. Auntie Mee Mee." Mimi liked the feel of the soft, fat fingers pulling at her foot. Her body tingled from the touch. She pretended not to hear the little girl. "Wake up, Auntie Mee Mee. Wake up. Time for brek fust."

Mimi turned and stretched. She pulled her feet in and Barbie fell toward the bed. "Who's that?" she asked.

"It's me. Barbee."

"Who?"

"It's me. Barbee."

"Who?"

"Bar*bee*."

"Who?"

"Bar*bee!*"

"Is that you, Barbie?"

"Yes, Auntie Mee Mee."

"I can't see you. Come closer."

Trusting Barbie crawled into the bed, and Mimi said, "Gotcha!" She started tickling Barbie, whose laughing screams were probably heard a block away.

"Don't get her started," said Bizzy.

She sat on the edge of the bed. Mimi sat up and placed Barbie on her lap. The little girl started picking at the watch on Mimi's arm. "Why don't you take a shower? Breakfast should be ready in twenty minutes. I washed and dried your clothes. I'll bring them up in a minute." Bizzy stood and hoisted Barbie into the air, then settled her on her hip. "Everything's in the bathroom for you." She turned to go, then stopped. "Your mother called. She sounded very worried. I told her you were fine and would be back home today."

Hearing that her mother called made Mimi's heart skip a beat. A lump formed in her throat, and she was sad and weary all over again.

"I told your mother you'd be home this morning. I'm not kicking you out, but we all have to go to work and Barbie to day care. And, I think you need to talk to your mother. We can talk later if you want."

Bizzy sat Barbie on the floor, but snugly held the child's hand in her own when Barbie tried to run back to the bed. "You know, Mimi, I hope you know that I love you."

Mimi looked out the window. Quiet. Bizzy left the room. Why was she being so unyielding? She knew Bizzy loved her. She even knew JoJo and her mother and even Tomas loved her. But for some reason, it was not enough. She hadn't found the love that would make the hurt go away. She needed that love.

She gazed at Bizzy's journal again. A desire to see what Bizzy wrote in the book overcame her. She glanced at the closed door then picked up the journal. She turned to the last entry and read a few lines.

I wish Mimi knew about God's love. I wish she knew how much he could help her through his Son. Mimi is trying to destroy herself. I've been there. The only way out was Christ. I don't know what to do anymore. I've talked and talked, but Mimi just shakes her head in agreement then goes out and does the same thing again. I don't have any choice but to keep praying now and keep reminding her how much I love her. I truly do. I love Mimi. She's a sister to me.

The entry was dated yesterday, before Mimi came knocking on the door in the middle of the night. A pot banged as it hit the floor. Startled, Mimi dropped the book to the floor. She snatched it up and quickly put it back on top of the Bible. A piece of pink paper sticking out from the side of the Bible caught her eye. She lifted the Bible and turned to the page where the pink paper lay. On the paper, scribbled in Bizzy's handwriting were the words, "Favorite Scripture." Beneath it was written, "Psalm 121:1." Mimi looked at the citation on the open page. At the top was Psalm 121. She went to the first verse and read, "I will lift up mine eyes unto the hills. My help comes from the Lord."

She closed the Bible and returned it to the spot on the table, placing the journal back on top. Bizzy's love appeared to go deep, but so had Joe Combs' love. Someone told you

they loved you and then they did something to prove they
didn't love you.

*I appreciate what you've done, Bizzy. I really do, but...will you also
take something from me?*

That afternoon, Mimi apologized to everyone, but the
mood of the house was uncomfortable. She had thrown a
bomb into the party. She didn't expect everyone to move
about as if cake was not smeared on the walls and the
ceilings.

To relieve the tension, she decided to go back to school
early to prepare for her next semester. JoJo volunteered to
drive her to the train stop. The entire ride was made mostly
in silence. Once JoJo turned on the radio, but every station
provided a song whose lightheartedness did not match the
atmosphere of the car. Eventually, he gave up and turned the
radio off.

At the train station, she repeatedly told him that he did not
need to wait with her, but he answered, "I don't mind."

In more silence, they stood next to each other as the sun
beat on their heads and people passed by engaged deeply in
conversation. When the train finally arrived, he helped her
hoist her bag up the stairs of a train car.

She said, "Thanks. And again, I'm sorry. Please tell Tomas
I know all she's done for me, and I truly appreciate it. Tell
her I know I wouldn't be able to live in my apartment if it
wasn't for her influence."

JoJo blinked before he said anything. For a second, Mimi
thought he was clearing tears from his eyes. "Tomas didn't
do it. She doesn't even know what I'm doing for you. I know

I don't deserve it, but . . . can you stop hating me for one second?"

The train whistle blew, and the conductor appeared. "Miss, you have to go inside."

"Okay," she said to the man. Mimi stepped inside the train and tugged the bag into an open seat near a window. She looked back at JoJo, who stood on the platform with his hands in his pockets, watching her.

Chapter 36
The Life of the Sea Urchin

Professor Towns was notorious for introducing topic tangents. He'd provide information which students dutifully followed down a path, assuming some nugget for a test or morsel for their life would be found. Sometimes, all they got was Professor Towns sharing a bit of knowledge he couldn't contain. Trouble was, students never knew when there was a reward, or when there was an empty purse and thus, had to follow him each time.

He had shown the class a picture of a sea urchin and announced, "I don't know much about marine life, but from what I've read… the sea urchin is a *fascinating* creature." Towns had a tendency of pausing where there was no comma. On the words "fascinating creature," he snapped his fingers.

Really! Mimi sensed a tangent opening up. She almost groaned loudly, but stifled it by placing her hand over her mouth.

Professor Towns continued, "Shaped like a globe and masked in a shell covered with varying lengths of what looks like pine needles…most sea urchins rest on the sandy carpets of ocean floors. Occasionally, they make their homes among the rocky cliffs…of shallow waters." He was theatrical and probably participated in an improv group, or did some acting as a side hobby.

"The most common sea urchin is about four and a half inches in size. Uncommon ones...have been found to be as large as fourteen inches."

His eyes wide with the look of one who believes he has revealed something the listener is unaware of. As if plotting some secret plan, he lowered his voice and said, "And do you know how sea urchins mate?"

No, but I bet you are gonna tell me.

"When sea urchins mate, they do it openly with the female releasing eggs...into the murky water and the male sprinkling his sperm...among those eggs."

Yuck. She was beginning to drift into a daydream, certain that the sea urchin tale had nothing to do with World Literature, when Professor Towns tugged on his salt and pepper beard and wiped his baldhead with a handkerchief.

"And I bet you have no idea... how the urchin protects itself. Glad you asked." He grinned at his own joke. "While the prickly needles protruding from its body should be enough to scare off any predator, the urchin digs holes in the sea's bottom...or in the rocks and buries itself.. until danger passes by." He crossed his arms; a satisfactory smile danced on his lips.

The girl next to her giggled. But for Mimi, this last point resonated. As the reality of broken family relationships with her brother and her mother, a squandered friendship with Bizzy, and masquerades of love and closeness with strangers swelled upon her, Mimi needed relief. As the shame and guilt of being touched by her father assaulted her, she wanted nothing more than freedom.

The tragic journeys of writers and journalists before her now made sense. She understood why some of them took their own lives. She understood why the weight of living became too difficult to bear. She understood that her thoughts were becoming borderline dangerous.

And like the sea urchin, Mimi dug a hole in work and school and buried herself there, waiting for the danger to pass her by.

The fall semester of senior year had begun with the speed and fury of a jet plane charging through the skies. She had no time for anyone or anything. And she liked the distraction. She rarely saw Peyton or Billy and doubted if they even saw each other. The classes were more demanding, and everyone was somewhere studying. Even Peyton, with a renewed, although belated, interest in engineering, was suddenly consumed with trying to bring her GPA higher.

With her head so far in the hole, it had taken Mimi a few days to notice a note, written in Billy's script, sitting on the table beside the phone. There was a message on the answering machine for her from Xavier Wright. Her lips became instantly dry, and she licked them softly while pressing the button to play the message.

She had avoided lunch with Xavier and Dezzy. When he called, she conveniently was nowhere near home and remained away for the entire day. Her desire to see what Dezzy looked like was crushed by her suspicion that the girl was probably beautiful and thus, probably deserved Xavier.

The message was the last one on the machine, and his voice had an essence that captured well on tape. "Hello, this message is for Mimi Combs. Mimi, it's Xavier. I'll be back in town this weekend. I was hoping we could have lunch or dinner together. Please call me, and let me know if it works for you. I hope to hear from you. My number is . . ."

While he rattled the digits, she scrambled to find a pen and had to replay the message to hear his phone number again.

She glanced at the calendar. It was Friday. He was already on his way to the campus. She could call his dorm and leave a message. This would at least acknowledge receipt of his own message, without having to talk directly to him. All that was left was to make sure she did not answer the phone throughout the weekend. Playing this game was childish. She knew that. But it was safe and a perfect way to keep her head in the hole.

She dialed his number. The phone rang twice while she riffled through the refrigerator for a dinner of leftover takeout meals.

"Hello?"

She stood up and bumped her head against the freezer door. "Oww!" she screamed.

"Hello?" he said again.

"I'm sorry," she said, rubbing the back of her head. "I'm calling for Xavier."

"It's me, Mimi." It was him. The richness in his voice made her forget the bump on her head temporarily. "Are you okay?"

"Yes, I just banged my head just as you were answering the phone."

"Oh, I'm sorry. You okay?"

"I'm fine. I got your message. I'm sorry I'm late. I just saw the note from my roommate."

"No problem."

Xavier explained that he had changed his plans because he had not heard from her. He would be up the following weekend if she was available. She was trapped and had to agree to lunch. They set a time, and Xavier told her he could pick her up.

She sat heavily on the chair at the kitchen table as she prepared to tackle the part of the conversation she had spent the last few minutes dancing around.

"So. I'll see you and Dezzy at noon. I'm looking forward to it."

"No. Just me. Dezzy is studying, but she said maybe she'll catch up with us later."

Later? What did he mean? Mimi was terrified, confused, and delighted; it was a cocktail of feelings she was having trouble digesting. Xavier explained that Dezzy was embroiled in her senior project, and it demanded all of her time. She probably would not be able to join them.

How in the world could this woman trust her man with a woman she had never met before? The essence of the act said lunch with an old friend was no real concern of hers, even if that friend was female. Confident girl. A man with Xavier's good looks was always approached by women. But Mimi suspected that he had not shared with Dezzy how Mimi felt about him in high school.

Xavier told Dezzy he would spend the afternoon with Mimi and would call her to let her know what they were doing, in case she wanted to join them. So much ran through Mimi's head as he spoke. It was pleasingly disconcerting that he assumed she would have a whole afternoon to give him. To imagine what the afternoon might be like without a third party to steer the conversation from past hurts was nerve-wracking. She sat at the kitchen table for thirty minutes after she said good-bye to him.

Over the next few days, she masterminded ways to cancel, and by the following Saturday, she still had no solution that would not sound like she was making excuses not to see him. When he arrived, he told her about a place he found in a small community about a sixty minute drive north of the college campus. Yep, a sixty minute drive. She should have been a bit ticked off with this assumption she'd have all this time for him. Instead, her heart leapt.

"Sometimes if Dezzy is busy I have to keep myself preoccupied, so I explore. This little community is for the affluent." He smiled and added, "In other words, the filthy rich. The mainline road has tons of specialty restaurants. I know you like Mexican, so this little spot is something I think you'll enjoy."

And she did. The food was great, but his company was even better. They talked about high school, family, and friends. Xavier had tons more friends than she did. While she spoke only of Peyton, Billy, and Bizzy, Xavier shared the names and current lives of many people she knew from high school. As they broached various subjects, they skirted the topic of what broke up their friendship.

Mimi had such a good time that she readily agreed to window shopping up and down the streets of the neighborhood. She enjoyed this type of shopping because it gave her ideas without spending the actual money, which she did not have. At some point, Xavier called Dezzy, but the girl reassured him there was no way she could stop her project. Mimi could hear her voice through the phone, though Xavier had it pressed to his ear.

She felt like she was eavesdropping and contemplated walking away when she heard Dezzy say, "Just have a good time, babe. Tell Mimi hi. Gotta go."

The long buzz of the dial tone replaced her presence just as Xavier was saying, "Good-bye." He hung up the phone, turned to Mimi, and murmured, "She's pretty busy." He tucked the phone in his pocket and put an arm on Mimi's shoulder. "Let's keep going, okay?" Lightness replaced the sullenness of his previous murmur.

They continued their foray, walking into shops which varied widely in their product. One store boasted a walk back into history amidst its antique wares. Another offered the finest in vinyl music records. They stopped at an ice cream shop and split a hot fudge sundae while they laughed and joked as if they had only been apart a day and not several years.

At a small candy store, they each bought tiny glass figurines shaped like animals. When held against a light, the figurines put a colorful pattern on the wall. She brought a bear pawing at the sky and a cat sleeping with its tail wrapped around its head. She thought about putting them in her bedroom window. Xavier bought a lion with its head held high and a monkey dancing to a silent song.

As the shop owner chatted with them and wrapped the figurines, Mimi asked Xavier, "You think Dezzy will like them?"

He took the bag with his figurines from the owner, thanked her, and handed the bag to Mimi. "They're for you."

"What?" Confusion then revelation. "No. You don't have to do that."

"I want to do something for you."

"No, Really. Keep your money in your pocket. You're a struggling college student just like me."

"Please. I want to do this for you."

She opened her mouth to balk again, but nothing came out. She knew she *shouldn't* take this gift. She knew he *shouldn't* be giving her a gift, even if the cost was only ten dollars. That sixth sense she sometimes got that warned her about a direction, came over her as if she was pulling on an overcoat. Finally, with the shop owner broadcasting a sweet, smug, matchmaker smile, Mimi took the bag and said, "Thank you. You didn't have to do this."

"I wanted to." He took her hand and squeezed it briefly, then let it drop.

She looked down at her hand, then back into his face and wanted to kiss him. Instead she inwardly slapped herself and looked down while asking, "Do you want to start the trip back?"

"Sure."

As they pulled onto the highway, he said, "I have one more place to show you. I found this while exploring one day too."

Xavier drove for a bit, then turned off the highway at an exit with a sign marked "Hill Top High." They followed a curvaceous road to a clearing where other parked cars faced a wooden fence which lined a cliff's edge. The cliff overlooked the town. As the sun began to dim, red, white, and green lights slowly came on among the town's windows and the place sparkled like a Christmas tree.

"Beautiful," she whispered. From the cliff's top, the sky dazzled with stars and the scent of clean air filled her nostrils.

They stepped out of the car, and Xavier rummaged in the trunk for something while Mimi stood by the fence. Amazed at the sight of the sky, she wondered if it was always like this, and she never noticed because she was so far in the hole.

"Here we go." Xavier spread a blanket on the hood of his car. He sat on top of it.

"Won't that damage your hood?"

"Naw, it'll be okay." He reached out for her hand. Doubtful, she let him pull her up to the hood.

They watched the stars for an hour, and their occasional comments about the bright lights in the sky filled their conversation. Xavier saw the known constellations clearly, but Mimi struggled.

"I always have a hard time with the Big Dipper and Little Dipper." She squinted. "Do you see them?"

"Mimi . . . about high school."

Strange way to answer a question. The air left her body. For a second she refused to inhale. They had been avoiding this conversation. She was certain it would ruin the day. Xavier had sat next to her contemplating how to begin, and he chose this way and this moment.

"You never gave me a chance to explain myself," he said.

"I'm not sure what there was to explain, Xay." The nickname from high school fell from her lips with such a familiarity. "You said you liked me as a friend. End of that story."

She pulled at the edge of her blue plaid skirt that stopped just above her knees. Mimi had worn an off white, mock turtleneck, short sleeve sweater and blue tights to complete the ensemble. She had pulled her hair back into a small ponytail and smoothed her edges with cream. As simple as it sounded, it took her three hours to come up with this outfit and the hairstyle. The skirt was the only nice piece of clothing she had that curved in the right places, accentuating her rear and her hips without announcing her stomach mound. The sweater was a bit tight and made her breasts appear bigger and rounder. As she sat on the hood, she realized her skirt hiked another inch higher, revealing more thigh. Even covered by tights it was repulsive to her.

"No, it's not the end of that story. Mimi. I was scared. I didn't want to change our friendship. You were the only girl in school who didn't get stupid when you saw me. We had good conversations. Real good ones, and I really enjoyed being with you." He rubbed his eyes then turned toward her. "I thought if *I* told you how *I* felt, it would change some of that for us . . . For me . . ." He laughed. "Seems like there was no way to go with that, huh? What I said changed everything."

She looked at him, wanting to hear more. She wanted to hear what she longed to hear that day in McDonald's when a dried ketchup stain on the table said more to her than he did.

"How did you feel?" she asked.

He returned her gaze. "I loved you." Xavier paused. The words took their time connecting with her eardrums and finding their way to her heart. Xavier was giving her the time she needed. A minute later, he continued, "But . . ." A deep breath. ". . . I was a high school boy. A high school boy with friends who sometimes laughed at the quiet girl with the big, beautiful eyes, the round, perfect face, the long, slender neck and the gentle laugh from her non-judging soul." He shifted his position, pulling one knee toward his body and wrapping his arms around it. "I was afraid of what they might say if suddenly we were a couple." He laughed again, but she could tell he was nervous. "Here I was. I didn't care what people thought, but for some reason I cared what they thought about you. It drove me crazy thinking about why they didn't see what I saw in you." He took a second deep breath. "So I chickened out. It was easier to lie to you. Easier not to explain that I was a bit shallow and had no guts."

She studied her fingernails. The deep red polish she had asked Peyton to paint for her shined back. Bits and pieces of her time in high school reflected in the gloss of the nails. She remembered the pain of loneliness and the choice of invisibility. The revelation was clear. Even when you were invisible, people saw you.

He continued. "I thought that if I said all that, it would hurt you. I loved you so much; I didn't want to hurt you. I really just wanted to fix me. Ya know . . . I wanted to find a way not to care what they said about you." He leaned back on the car window, his hand rubbing his forehead.

Her thoughts drifted to a movie about a boy who loved a girl that others tormented. Mimi saw the movie years after its release, and she could not stop crying. The boy's initial goal was to have sex with the girl because the rumors indicated she was that kind of girl. As he spent time with her, his fondness for her blossomed. He saw the depths of what others never took the time to search. In the end of *Buster and Billie*, ignorance, hate, and jealously led to the girl's death. In the final scene of the movie, the boy collects almost every flower in their small town and takes it to the girl's grave.

Xavier had said, "I didn't want to hurt you." *Was there a risk in caring for someone others hate?*

She turned to him and asked, "How do you feel now? Tell me right now. Don't think about it. Tell me how you feel now." Her heart was racing. Her voice was cracking as she struggled to fight tears.

He turned toward her. He appeared to be studying every part of her face, then he let his eyes meet hers. He said, "I still love you."

Time has its moments when people stop to think before they act. This was not one of those moments for Mimi. She leaned forward and kissed him. He kissed her back soft and slowly, and ended the kiss with a gentle peck on her lips. Xavier wrapped his arms around her. As they leaned against the window shield, Mimi came out of the hole.

Chapter 37
I'm Dezzy

Guilt, coupled with a slightly nasty message from her mother made her drop a thank you card in the mail to JoJo. He had called and left several messages, but she had not spoken to him since he took her the train station. At that time, he had confessed to being her benefactor. She had to admit her response had been empty of gratitude and a bit on the rude side. Yet, with her own brother she was uncomfortable with direct contact just to say "thank you" and chose to purchase a card instead. She didn't feel moved enough to resolve any issues with him. She didn't want to talk to JoJo.

In fact, she had no desire to talk with anyone except Xavier. Messages from Bizzy, her mother, and JoJo were left unattended. Messages from Xavier received her immediate attention.

He contacted her two or three times a week, using almost every mode of communication from phone to e-mail. Sometimes they had a brief chat just to say hello; other times it was a detailed conversation that ended with one or both of them having to stay up longer through the night to meet some assignment deadline.

One day Xavier phoned and asked if he could stop by the apartment. Mimi was wrapping up her work shift and happily told him she would meet him there. The sound of his voice, the image of his face, and the proximity of his presence in a room delighted her; she was trying to stop herself, but she was losing. She was falling for Xavier Wright—again.

Sitting on their worn, black leather sofa, wearing a red cotton button up shirt and jeans, he resembled a beacon on a black sea. She followed his lips as he expressed a conversation he had with Dezzy. Something about a minor argument over the amount of time Xavier and Dezzy were spending together. Mimi didn't understand or care about the argument.

In the middle of a sentence, he asked if she wanted to get dinner. "I'm bending your ear over this. I'm sorry," he said. A hint of frustration covered his face.

She reached over and tried to smooth it away. "It's okay," she said.

Dinner was take-out Chinese food from a store a few blocks away. While they chatted about matters other than Dezzy, Billy and Peyton joined them. Immediately, Billy developed a kinship with Xavier as they glided from conversations on sports to cars to politics. But Peyton spent the meal with a wrinkle in her forehead and her lips poked out.

When Xavier left she asked, "Doesn't this man have a girlfriend?"

Mimi nearly dropped the plate she was carrying. She did not think Peyton or Billy knew anything about her life. "Weeelll, yes . . . yes."

"So why is he spending so much time with you?"

"We're friends, Peyton."

"Mimi, trust me. This isn't cool."

She waved Peyton away with a grin and rushed to her bedroom. What Peyton said rang of sensibility and truth. Her own gut told her they were getting too close to be just friends. Her heart told her to ignore her gut.

The first invitation from Xavier to return to the Mexican restaurant in the small town north of the college was a turning point. It moved them from friends to more than friends, from "hanging out" to "dating."

They travelled to the town on several occasions. Mimi used the hour long drive to the distant town as a time to study, talk with Xavier, or both. Occasionally, she looked for the signal that they were close to the town. A ragged and bare tree bending on the side of a hill as if it were walking up meant they were only five minutes from the restaurant. The sight of the tree always struck her with the idea of struggle. She silently rooted for the lifeless form to make it up that hill, to overcome everything that kept it back and held it down, to live and love again in spite of pain. When she saw the tree, she would pack away her books and enjoy the comfortable silence that filled the car.

On their third out of town visit to the restaurant, two things happened. First, Mimi discovered that it was possible to grow tired of Mexican food. She shared her thoughts with Xavier, and he began a search for a variety of places to eat. Second, she realized that she wasn't the only one struggling with their relationship.

They had not put a definition to what they were doing. She refused to label it "cheating." Something seemed ugly about the word. In the three short months she had been reconnecting with Xavier, she had gone from hating herself to liking herself, from fear to courage, from shame to blissful forgetfulness. She was even approaching her schoolwork with a new found gusto. Everything was better now that she was with Xavier. The word "cheating" obliterated her progress.

A conversation initiated by Xavier, after they saw the struggling tree, told her he was also having difficulty with how their relationship was proceeding.

"Mee," he called her name with such a softness she had to lean closer. He held the steering wheel with one hand, while the other rested against his thigh. He lifted this hand and placed it on top of hers.

"Yeah." She was watching his hand and feeling its warmth and its strength.

"I need to say something to Dezz." She almost pulled her hand away. He sensed it and gently applied more pressure. "Listen to me. I need to stop dating Dezz and officially start dating you. Don't you think that's right?"

Parts of her longed to leap at him. First her heart, next her hands, her arms, her body, lastly her soul. She wanted all of him. She spent the rest of the ride trying to control her thoughts. She hadn't served herself to him on a plate—yet. Besides the one kiss, they had done nothing more, but this man and what he was saying was weakening her. She was dying to give him what she thought he deserved. What she thought would make him stay with her, love her.

Shortly after this conversation, Xavier called on a day when the ice covered the apartment windows and the heater struggled to keep the place warm. He asked if she wanted to take a drive to the town on the weekend. He had a surprise for her. She was elated. Perhaps he had spoken to Dezzy and wanted to share that they could make their dating official. In that case, she planned to make the weekend a celebration, and she used her little savings to locate a motel and a pale orange, transparent negligee.

Warnings come in all forms, but the most basic is the warning that begins at the base of the neck and crawls down the spine. It travels back up and flares into the shoulders while making a straight path to the head, where it sits announcing there is something wrong. When she heard the knock at the door, she felt the warning. It was Saturday, and Xavier had said he would pick her up at eleven a.m., so she rushed to the door without bothering to check the peephole.

On the other side, a slender girl with a round face, heavily lashed eyes and a petite mouth stared back at Mimi. Her eyes were puffy, their whites streaked with red lines.

"May I help you?" Mimi asked.

"Yes, you can help me, you whore. I'm Dezzy." At that announcement, the girl raised her hand and slapped Mimi so hard that Mimi fell back into the apartment and onto the floor. She lay there holding her cheek. Dezzy was breathing hard. One tear rolled down her face. Another quickly followed it. She wiped them away.

"Did you think I wouldn't find out? There's a saying about six degrees of separation, *slut.* Do you know what that means?" Mimi assumed she was not supposed to answer. "It means that it will take about six tries before you find someone you have in common with another person. That's what happened for you and Xavier and the waiter in the restaurant you like to visit."

Mimi struggled to get to her feet.

"Stay down, you trash. This is the way it should be . . . Trash on the ground. That's what you are."

Mimi dutifully fell back to the floor.

Dezzy looked wild. Fire replaced the tears in her eyes. Her hair, which was tied neatly with a ribbon, had become undone and now hung with parts on her shoulders and parts still held in place by the ribbon.

"The waiter knew someone who knew someone and so on, and before I know it, someone in my International Business class is telling me about a restaurant they thought they saw my boyfriend in." She stepped into the apartment.

"Now, Xavier is a good man, so all I have to do is confront him. I know the restaurant because he told me about it the first time. But the way this friend talks, it sounds like you and Xavier are regulars."

Mimi could feel the ground spinning beneath her. Now she was the one breathing hard.

"I ask Xavier and he tells me the truth, and he tells me how it happened. Basically, I'm too busy. You're too available." She pointed her finger at Mimi. "But then I do some research on you. You got a little reputation. I sit by a guy in my IB class who tasted you."

Briefly, Dezzy looked as if she was considering spitting on Mimi. She relaxed her puckered lips and continued. "He called you a *nice lay*, an *easy chick*." She laughed. "I don't have a thing to worry about. I'm keeping my man."

Peyton and Billy appeared in the doorway behind Dezzy.

Mimi's head hurt now. Who had she slept with who took an International Business class? But more importantly, had Dezzy told Xavier what the guy said?

As if on cue, Dezzy added, "And I told him what this guy said and what they say about you around campus. And you know what? You know what?" She put her hands on her hips and growled at Mimi. "His face changed, like he was disappointed. Really? Disappointed by a whore." She laughed again.

Mimi felt something slam inside her.

"I was glad when he reassured me he hadn't dirtied himself by having sex with you. I don't want nothing nasty on Xavier, you stinking, dirty whore." Dezzy kneeled beside Mimi. "You sad excuse for a woman. You're like a free prostitute. Anybody can get it, and they don't have to pay a dime." She leaned closer. "Get your pathetic life together, and stay away from my man. It's over." She stood up and stormed out the door, pushing Peyton and Billy aside.

"Oh!" She turned back. "And if you need some loving, I got the number of a strip joint. You can go there and put your dirty stuff out to anybody. Hell, there's a bum on the corner out here. I'm sure he wants a taste of what everyone else had." Dezzy threw a balled up piece of paper at Mimi.

She ducked as it whizzed by her head.

Part 6

Dear King...Am I Healed?

Chapter 38
A Free Prostitute

Where was she supposed to go and what was she supposed to do? Xavier refused to return her phone calls. She couldn't go home. She couldn't call anyone and tell them what happened. So, she chose to spend the beginning of winter break by herself, locked away in the apartment.

She sat on her bed and crafted a letter to her father.

December 17, 1994

Dear Joe Combs,

You sorry excuse for a human being. I'm dead inside, and you killed me. I have no idea of how to love, and that is all your fault.

I hate you.

Mimi

Those three sentences were all she put on the paper before she started crying into her pillow. When the pillow was drenched, she mailed the letter, then returned home and crawled into bed. She didn't eat for two days, and on the third day she traveled to the pharmacy to get something to help her sleep. The over-the-counter product warned about taking too much over a certain time period. She read the warning carefully, assuring she knew exactly how to execute it. While filling and draining a glass of juice, she kept reading and rereading.

On the fourth day, she heard the click of the front lock as someone inserted a key and turned it. The door opened, and she heard Bizzy's voice. "Mimi?"

She called from her bedroom, "Bizzy? What are you doing here?"

Bizzy appeared in the doorway and behind her was JoJo. They both looked exhausted. With weary expressions on their faces, they surveyed her bedroom.

Clothes were strewn all over the room. Mimi had knocked over a lamp and didn't bother picking it up. Dresser drawers had been pulled out, and clothing dangled from some of them. Her bed was a tangled mess of sheets and blankets. And on the window sill, the glass animal figurines were broken into pieces. Briefly, she considered that the room might smell musty because she had not showered.

She pulled herself up and sat on the bed's edge.

"Don't you ever, *ever* talk about my room." Bizzy began picking up clothes from a chair in the corner. Once she cleaned the chair off, she dragged it next to Mimi's bed.

"Your roommate called me."

"Billy? Billy called you?"

"Nope. Peyton. Peyton called me." Dark circles rested underneath Bizzy's eyes. She licked the dryness away from her lips. "She called me, and I called your brother to drive me here."

Mimi looked at JoJo. "You flew home to drive Bizzy seven hours?"

"No. I was hoping you'd be home for the winter break, so I came down. Tomas couldn't fly, but she told me to tell you hi."

Bizzy picked up the sleeping medicine and turned over the package. Mimi had already unpacked the container and laid all the pills on top of her nightstand. "Want to talk about it?" Bizzy said, reading the package.

"Talk about what? If Peyton called you, she probably told you everything."

"No. Not everything. She said there was a bad scene at the apartment over Xavier. Imagine my surprise. I don't even know who Xavier is. And I thought you told me about the big things in your life."

JoJo was leaning against her bedroom doorframe. His hair had only been partially combed, and his face matched Bizzy's worried look. He coughed then, and Bizzy sat up straight as if she was just remembering he'd brought her. She asked, "JoJo can you make us some tea?"

"Sure." He started to say something else, but glanced at Mimi, then went away.

As Bizzy continued, Mimi wondered if she and JoJo had decided in the car which of them would do all the talking, and Bizzy had won.

"Peyton said you really needed to be with someone who cared about you. And here we are. My dad is hot with you though. He wanted to have a special picture done for me and Barbie, but, oh well, it's not every day you get to be a real friend to someone, is it?"

"I'm okay, Bizzy. Just go back home. Both of you should go home."

"Really? You're okay?" She waved the box in the air.

"I wasn't going to take any pills, or do anything stupid like that." As soon as she said the sentence, she knew she was lying. She continued, her voice quivering, " I just feel like—like . . . Oh, what's the use? No one would care if I was gone, and all this would stop, wouldn't it? I wouldn't be trying so hard to find someone to . . . love me."

Bizzy moved to the edge of the bed and put her arms around Mimi. The touch was electric, and Mimi began to weep. Bizzy's voice was soothing as she whispered in Mimi's ear that everything would be all right. It was the voice Bizzy used to calm Barbie.

"You're looking in the wrong place. Someone is waiting to love you. He'll always love you. Just reach out to him. Let him love you."

Bizzy was not talking about a man. She was talking about God. Mimi cried loud and hard into Bizzy's chest. She cried until her eyes burned with dryness. She cried so much that when she pulled back, she saw a cup of steaming tea beside her bed. JoJo was gone.

"Drink some tea," coaxed Bizzy, handing Mimi the cup. "Why don't you come home with us? You can stay with me and Barbie."

Mimi shook her head in agreement. The mention of Barbie's name slightly cheering her broken heart. As she and Bizzy packed her bag, JoJo secured the apartment, locking windows and unplugging appliances. She sat in the back of the car and said very little during the ride home. As she watched the passing sky grow dark, and the stars began to peek out, she thought of Xavier, and her heart ached.

Winter break had been therapeutic. Unconditional love from Barbie and Bizzy, her mother and JoJo, pulling her into every conversation and activity, and one or two "just because" conversations with Tomas had temporarily lightened her heart of its heavy load. Everyone asked if she needed to talk. No one forced her to talk. Her shattered pieces were gradually being pulled back together, but the adhesive was only tape. She needed a permanent fix, a permanent bonding agent to help her.

She shared some of her feelings with Bizzy as they watched Barbie crawl through a giant pool of red, yellow, and green plastic balls. Bizzy had invited Mimi to the local Chuck E. Cheese with her father and Barbie. Having passed many Chuck E. Cheese signs in her lifetime, Mimi was curious. Now she had a valid reason to go into the place and that reason was Barbie.

The symphony of children screaming, game bells dinging, and high-pitched singing amazed Mimi. While it was an assault on adult ears, Barbie sank right into the activity. Her grandfather monitored her progress as she slipped down slides and climbed up ladders, and Mimi and Bizzy watched and enjoyed the scene.

In the midst of this never ending party, Bizzy asked a question that seemed to lower the volume on the noise, leaving only the two of them in the room. "Are you still in love with him?"

Mimi slowly shook her head up and down. She had no more tears left.

"Why?"

Mimi paused. The question was not harsh. It did not have an air of accusation. Bizzy wasn't judging her. It was a simple inquiry that Mimi had to think about. She finally said,

"Because he was kind and good to me. Because we got along well, and he liked being around me."

Bizzy gently pushed for more. "Anything else?"

Mimi had to search her brain. She was missing something important. The reasons she had just explained could apply to anyone on the street.

Barbie let out a loud yelp and waved to them from the netted cage that surrounded one of the play areas. She bolted through a tunnel, and her grandfather moved with her from the outside. He was doing his best not to lose sight of her.

Mimi watched the scene of grandfather and granddaughter interacting and said, "Because he loved me back. And, he wanted to take care of me. He wanted to protect me. I think he was a champion for me. I know that he would have done anything in the world for me."

"And now?"

"Now what?" Mimi looked at Bizzy.

"Now, how do you think he feels about you?"

She didn't know how he felt, and she had a hard time understanding how, when someone loved you that much, they could hurt you. How could they think to do anything that would hurt you? Xavier had hurt her indeed. He had not let her explain. He seemed to just walk away from her—again.

She said, "I don't think he loves me anymore." She saw Barbie step from the play area carrying a bright blue plastic ball. She handed it to her grandfather, who picked up Barbie instead, and taking the ball from her, tossed it back into a box. They both headed to a concession stand with matching rosy cheeks. Mimi said, "But after what I did. After what I've done. I don't deserve to be loved."

Bizzy put a hand on Mimi's arm. "That's not true at all."

"Yes it is."

Mimi began to tell Bizzy the whole ordeal, starting with her relationship with a man who already had a girlfriend. Bizzy's eyes widened a little, and she took a deep breath but remained silent. "But that's not the worst thing I've done." Mimi told Bizzy about her father. Bizzy sat still, clasped her hands together in a small ball and brought them to her lips. Mimi told her about the touching, the intercourse, the fear of pregnancy, the court. She was talking so fast and robotically, that she barely noticed the single tear that escaped Bizzy's left eye and rolled down to the end of her cheek. Mimi barely noticed the slight nod Bizzy gave her father as he was returning with Barbie and pretzels and soda back to the table. She barely noticed the detour Bizzy's father took as he headed over to the play area.

Suddenly, Mimi heard only her own voice. She heard herself say, "I don't know how anybody could love a person who did that with her own father. Who let her own father touch her like that."

Bizzy pulled Mimi's hands into her own, and she began to pray. The sound of the words "Dear God" shocked Mimi at first. They were sitting in a public place. She was confused as to whether she should jerk her hands away, or sit perfectly still. Bizzy's prayer was about healing, and release and love. She was asking God to do these things for Mimi.

Why on earth would he do this for me?

About two minutes had passed before Bizzy finally said, "Amen." She let go of Mimi's hands. They fell back to the table like heavy stones.

"Mimi, you deserve to be loved by someone who will not take anything from you. Especially something you do not want to give away. You were born to be loved. From day one that has been part of your purpose. And God, my friend, is waiting to fulfill that purpose for you. He's waiting for you to let him love you."

Mimi studied her hands. She could actually see the heaviness in them. "Bizzy, please don't tell anyone," she begged.

Bizzy hugged her. "It's not my story to tell to people. I can only pray for you to realize who you are in Christ. Your worth."

When Mimi returned to school for her last semester, she found a church nearby and absorbed her life in school, work, and church. She had to find out more about this love Bizzy had said she was worthy of, and her best option was a church since this seemed to be where Bizzy discovered this love.

Her first week back in school was filled with Billy and Peyton tiptoeing through the apartment and asking her questions as if she was on her deathbed. She finally had to tell them she was okay, and she only wanted to get on with life, leaving Xavier behind her.

Peyton thought it was the best idea she had heard in a long while.

The three of them fell into an unwritten contractual agreement to never mention the episode again. Although the subject was dead in their apartment, Mimi continued to wonder if Xavier had been able to easily move on with his life and leave her behind. It seemed she and Xavier would have some sort of drama always and should leave each other alone.

Dezzy's words were constant unwanted visitors in her mind. "Slut" and "whore" popped up without warning.

Once, she dreamed she was on the floor, and Dezzy stood over her beating her with a bat that had the insults written all over it. She felt like Dezzy described. The more she learned about the love Bizzy spoke of, the more she felt unworthy of it.

One Sunday, she sat on the hard wooden seat in the third row from the back of the church and let her own conflicting thoughts mix with the pastor's preaching. He was teaching about a woman who was a prostitute in the Bible. He taught about how prostitution worked in Biblical times and the reason the woman turned to prostitution was probably some of the same reasons which exist today. As he spoke, Mimi clearly heard Dezzy say "free prostitute." The accusation faded into the background as the pastor continued. Although he had no proof of why she chose prostitution, he imagined what it made her feel like.

"She may have hated herself," he was saying. "She may have felt unclean, felt unworthy of love."

Mimi sat taller in her seat. It creaked under the shift of weight, but no one noticed the sound. All eyes were on the pastor. Mimi knew he had just described her own struggle. He continued with an intensity that pulled a listener to his side.

"Her pain must have been great. Great enough to drive her to Jesus' feet, where she used her own tears to wash his feet and her own hair to dry them. This was the depth of her sorrow."

Faces throughout the congregation, including Mimi's, must have contorted in disgust because the pastor said, "I know. I know. I know what you're thinking. And yes, Jesus' feet were dirty. During that time, they wore sandals and travelled dusty roads all the time. Normally when you came to somebody's house, one of the first things the host did was give you water to wash your feet." He stuck one finger in the air and paused. "This was a measurement of her pain and her cry for help. She knew she needed to wash the feet of the one who loved her unconditionally."

He stressed that before Jesus, the feelings the woman experienced, only helped her to remain in prostitution instead of getting out.

"She was in a cyclical downward spiral." He took his index finger and began to make circular movements slowly downward as he spoke. "Over and over. Down and down. The more she felt unworthy, the more she practiced unworthy activity. But then Jesus . . ." He stopped and wiped the imaginary spiral away. "Jesus made her feel worthy and deserving of something other than the rewards of the prostitute's life."

He moved from the pulpit and walked closer to the congregation. He often did this as a way of getting close to the people, closer to their needs. Sometimes, he would sit next to someone and talk directly to them. At first, Mimi worried about this kind of exposure, but later relaxed. She felt confident she had chosen a seat too far in the back for him to travel the distance.

However, today as he spoke, he moved further and further up the aisle toward the back of the church.

"I imagine Jesus showed her something new about herself. Something she probably never realized before." Soon the pastor would be only two rows away from where Mimi sat. "I want you all to turn to something. Turn to Psalm 139. I believe Jesus reminded her about something that our Maker, our God, did for all of us."

The sound of people turning the pages of their Bibles filled the room. The pastor paused briefly, then tapped the

shoulder of a young woman who sat on the end of the row
he was standing near. The row was just one step from the
row in which Mimi sat.

The pastor asked the young woman to read verses one
through fourteen. She stood, but her shoulders slumped as if
she dreaded being seen and heard. Mimi sympathized with
her. The pastor placed a hand on her shoulder as if
reassuring her, and he asked her again to read the verses.

As the young woman began with the first verse, the sound
and strength of her voice grew. Her shoulders began to rise
and her chest protruded. Her lips slowly formed a smile as
the words spilled from her mouth:

1. *You have searched me, Lord, and you know me.*

2. *You know when I sit and when I rise; you perceive my thoughts
   from afar.*

3. *You discern my going out and my lying down; you are familiar
   with all my ways.*

4. *Before a word is on my tongue, you, Lord, know it completely.*

5. *You hem me in behind and before, and you lay your hand upon
   me.*

6. *Such knowledge is too wonderful for me, too lofty for me to
   attain.*

7. *Where can I go from your Spirit? Where can I flee from your
   presence?*

8. *If I go up to the heavens, you are there; if I make my bed in the
   depths, you are there.*

9. *If I rise on the wings of the dawn, if I settle on the far side of the
   sea,*

10. *Even there your hand will guide me, your right hand will hold me fast.*

11. *If I say, "Surely the darkness will hide me and the night become light around me,"*

12. *Even the darkness will not be dark to you; the night will shine like the day, for darkness is as light to you.*

13. *For you created my inmost being; you knit me together in my mother's womb.*

14. *I praise you because I am fearfully and wonderfully made; your works are wonderful, I know that full well.*

On the final words, the woman looked around the room. Pride exuded from her. Mimi, whose posture had also changed with each word, now sat straighter in her seat, her own chest extended, and she recognized a familiar sign in the woman's eyes. She saw it because she felt it as well. It was the sign of relief.

"Thank you," the pastor said. As the young woman sat down, he continued. "Jesus loved this woman, this prostitute, in a way that reminded her about her worth. His love reminded her that she was wonderfully and fearfully made by a loving God. His love reminded her that she was worthy of being loved by the Father."

He looked directly at Mimi. "I can see Jesus' love saying to her, 'My father made you in a wonderful way. He made you in a high, respectful way. Why are you spitting on what he made?' That's what he's saying. Why are *you* spitting on what he made?"

The pastor looked around the room and spread his arms out to everyone. "My friends, perhaps something happened in your life that was like the cycle of prostitution for this woman. The more that something reminded her of what she perceived as ineptness, the more she practiced that ineptness. But Christ wants to remind you that you are not inept. You are God's child, and he wants to love you. Let him love you. Let Christ build the way to our loving God."

The pastor walked back to the front of the church, and as he wrapped up his sermon, Mimi thought about the scripture. She was fearfully and wonderfully made. So why was she letting her father's choice of incest make her think any less of herself? Why was she feeling unworthy of being loved? And being loved in the right way?

The pastor asked, "Does anyone want to embrace Christ's love today? Are you ready to embrace the love you deserve?"

So many times in her life she found herself doing something for which she had no explanation. On this day, she found herself standing and moving down the aisle because she wanted that love. Something was pushing on her front trying to take her back to her seat, but a force on her back was pushing even harder, guiding her to the waiting minister.

That day she learned that because she believed Christ died for her and that he was raised from the dead for her and because she confessed she was something called a sinner and only Christ's love could remove that label, she was now saved from the destruction she put on herself.

She remembered when Bizzy first met her for lunch and had used the word "saved." Mimi wanted to read all about this being saved, and she knew the person who could help her was Bizzy. She called her friend as soon as she was at home. Bizzy told her to read the book of John in the Bible and gave her scriptures. Then she asked, "How do you feel, Mimi?"

"I feel . . ." Mimi was lost for the words which described the euphoria of relief on her. When having sex with strangers, she temporarily released the weight, but it did not match the inner peace she now had. Even the love she still carried for Xavier had not given her such contentment. She started again, "I feel like I'm home."

"I'm happy about that. But realize it will take time. Getting past what you've been through doesn't happen overnight for everyone."

"How long do you think it will take, Bizzy? How long before the thoughts of feeling like trash go completely away?"

"I'm not sure. It's really up to you. It's your process. And it will take as long as it takes for you to realize and accept who you truly are. It will take as long as it takes for you to embrace that you are God's gold."

She had been holding onto something ever since she went home for winter break. It was boarded up inside her, trapped behind layers of wooden planks and several "Keep Out" signs.

A tear rolled down her hand that held the receiver. Only then did she realize her eyes were wet. She had been holding on to tears; she freed them.

Chapter 39
Would You Like to Start Over?

A black balloon with silver and red stars bursting around the word "Congratulations," drifted toward the sky. Mark (JoJo and Tomas's baby boy), pointed at it and contorted his face. He was about to wail, but Bizzy quickly rushed to his side with a second balloon that she dangled in front of him. He snapped his head toward the balloon and grabbed at it while Bizzy tightly held the string. Tomas, her face freshly scrubbed and wearing an adoring smile, nodded at Bizzy and silently mouthed, "Thank you."

Mimi's family and friends had formed a semi-circle around her. Since she continued to visit the church until she completed her last semester, she even had a few members in this crowd cheering her on and proudly beaming at her. JoJo sidled next to her and gave her a bear hug that made her graduation cap slip forward. They both broke into laughter. She let the warmth of his body next to her permeate her soul with a reminder of how good it felt to have her big brother back.

Her mother approached and placed her hands on Mimi's cheeks. The touch was warm and soft. "I'm so proud of you Mimi-cake."

"Thanks, Mom." Her mother wore a beautiful yellow sundress with a white pearl necklace and matching earrings. Her hair was pulled into her signature bun at the back and a mauve colored lipstick glistened on her lips. Faye did not look anywhere near where her late fifties were taking her. She was a gorgeous woman, and Mimi was proud of her. Lovingly, she embraced her mother as Faye joined the other side and assisted JoJo in a quick Squeeze-the-Lemon game (Mimi in the middle) while Bizzy snapped photos.

One by one, family and friends hugged her, kissed her cheeks, and took endless pictures. Even Mark gave her a sloppy kiss that left spittle as its reward and smudged her blush a bit, but she didn't mind. Her family was with her and God loved her. She was ready to take on life.

As Tomas was pulling Mark's arms from around her neck, Mimi's cheek-aching smile faded. Xavier was standing behind her brother. She opened her mouth and quickly closed it, while he began to move toward her.

"Congratulations, Mimi."

She was hesitant, unsure of what would come out of her mouth if she spoke, but she found two questions: "What are you doing here? Why aren't you at your own ceremony?"

Her group of supporters looked from her to Xavier and back. "My ceremony already happened, so I wanted to come see you graduate," he responded.

JoJo, sensing a need for a big brother moment, reached his hand out to Xavier. "I'm JoJo. Mimi's brother."

Xavier took his hand and shook it. "I'm Xavier."

Besides Barbie and Mark, who were engaged in a game of Peek-a-boo, and the church members, who still wore puzzled looks because of the effect this young man was having on Mimi, everyone else inhaled deeply.

Xavier cringed. "I take it by that sound you all know who I am."

"Why would you want to see me graduate? We haven't spoken in months." Mimi was slightly annoyed. Bizzy reached out and patted Mimi's arm.

"I know. I know. I probably should have called you, but after Dezzy told me all that stuff about you and . . ." Xavier stopped. He was speaking to a whole audience, not just her. "Can I just have a second alone with you?"

Mimi sighed and handed her cap and flowers to her mother, who gave her a questioning look as if to ask if she was okay with this. She smiled as it dawned on her they all thought Xavier's presence might ignite some psychotic episode in her.

"It's okay," Mimi said aloud, trying to reassure everyone. She hoped it would calm any fears that she might buy another box of pills.

She and Xavier walked to a nearby tree.

"Look, Mee. I just felt ashamed. Ashamed of cheating on Dezzy. Ashamed for you because of what she said. And part of me didn't believe it. We'd spent so much time together. I couldn't imagine you slept around. It didn't sound like you."

"I did, Xavier. I was hurt. I was lonely. There's a lot about my past you don't know, but I thought the best way to ease that pain was to find people to love me sexually. Or to do what I thought was love. It's all behind me now. I've got the love of Jesus. I'm healing, and I'm moving on."

"I guess I let you down again." He looked into her eyes.

She returned the look. "No. I let myself down. To be honest, besides the way we did it, you were the one good thing in my life."

He smiled, and a joy she had never seen in him before filled his face. "So did I hear you right? You're saved?"

Mimi cocked her head and placed her hands on her hips. "Yes. I'm saved."

"That's good. I'm so glad to hear that."

"Why?"

"Because I'm saved too."

"Really?"

"Really."

She looked at him, and a familiar longing filled her soul. Desires she thought she had under control, bubbled to the surface. Her mind began to orchestrate a way to be with him and to love him, or at least, love him in the way she was familiar with. She looked at her waiting family and shook her head quickly to kill the thought. For Xavier, it may have looked as if she may have been saying "no" to an unasked question.

"What happened with Dezzy? I've felt so guilty. So ashamed. Once I tried to apologize, but she wasn't having it. I thought I'd stay away from her, before I found myself on my butt again."

He laughed. "She was feisty, wasn't she?"

Xavier explained that he too felt an enormous amount of guilt in what he had done to Dezzy. He had tried to rebuild their relationship. Show her that she could trust him again. But after a couple of months, he had to ask himself what made it so easy to be unfaithful to her.

He paused and looked at Mimi. "I had to ask myself why I wasn't the man I thought I was."

He told Mimi he realized he wasn't supposed to be with Dezzy. Her way of functioning in a relationship built loads of mistrust. "It was sort of self-fulfilling. You think you can't trust your man. You keep telling yourself you can't trust your man. And pow! You end up not being able to trust your man. But it's not an excuse. I knew in the beginning we shouldn't have been together. I should've been more than a coward and broke it off early."

"You need to work on that a bit, don't you?"

Open and vulnerable to her, he said, "I do, don't I? So that I can be a better man for the woman I'm supposed to be with, right?"

"Right," Mimi said.

She looked over at the party of loved ones waiting for her. Each was trying to appear nonchalant, as if they were not watching this conversation unfold. Every one of them would probably kill to be a fly on a tree next to Xavier and her.

"Well, I'm so sorry for my part in all of it. I hope someday you can forgive me," she said.

"And I hope someday you can forgive me," he returned.

"You are forgiven," Mimi told him. Her mind contained only thoughts for his good. She truly had forgiven him.

"And you are forgiven," he said, looking again in her eyes.

They let a quiet and reflective moment pass between them. The sounds of cameras clicking and the drum of multiple conversations faded into the background.

She glanced again at her family and friends, and asked, "Would you like to join us? We're going to a nearby restaurant to celebrate, then off to my new life."

"What are you doing?"

She chuckled. "Actually, I'm going to stay here a while and work for a local news station."

"Cool. I'm moving here to work for a local vet while I do my graduate work."

"Wow. I'm glad to see you're accomplishing what you wanted."

"As are you."

She clapped her hands together and bit her lip. "Xavier, would you like to start over?" she asked.

He was still looking at her as if watching every feature on her face.

"Yes, I would . . . Hi, I'm Xavier Wright." He extended his hand.

She took it and shook it. "Hi, I'm Mimi Combs."

Chapter 40
Ain't You a Christian and All?

May 5, 1997

Dear Joe,

I'm working a good job now, and I'm dating a good guy. You need to know you haven't broken me. As they say, "What you meant for evil, God meant for good." I feel better about myself, and I'm now saved. That means I've invited Christ to be a part of my life. And it's wonderful, Joe. Just wonderful. I feel sorry for you because until you change your life, nothing good will ever happen for you or to you.

Get it together.

Mimi

Licking the stamp and placing it on the envelope, she mused about what she knew about her father to date. Joe Combs had done most of his time in jail, but a good behavior program gave him a chance for early parole. He followed all the rules of his release, including seeing a parole agent faithfully. He was employed as a maintenance worker for the city government. And he lived alone in a row home in the Kensington section of Philadelphia. She sent letters to his new home address.

Mimi now lived in an apartment near the news station. It was small but worked well for someone living without roommates. She dreamed of owning a big house someday, but for the present, the apartment suited her just fine. She decorated it with theme colors of orange and red and hung pale yellow curtains on the kitchen window. A picture of Xavier hugging her close sat on her desk. She and Xavier had been talking about marriage lately, and she knew he was planning the best way to propose. The prospect of a proposal, the potential of a career she always wanted, and the taste of independence should have brought her to a place of freedom and completion. Unfortunately, she was not there.

Slowly she began gliding in the rocking chair she had purchased just for these quiet and reflective periods.

A few weeks ago, she had a long overdue family huddle with JoJo and her mother. They talked for hours about all that Mimi had gone through after the incest. They talked about the letters she mailed Joe. They talked about how JoJo blamed her for breaking up the family and how she felt like her mother shared his opinion. Her mother expressed a feeling of failure for not protecting her daughter and being paralyzed by a fear of anything else happening to Mimi. With a box of tissues and cups of tea, they talked and cried. Then they agreed to be more open about what they were thinking as a family.

"I'm so glad we got all this out," said her mother as she dabbed her eyes with a worn out piece of tissue.

"Me too," said Mimi.

"So am I," said JoJo. "I just feel like I've been punched in the stomach and dragged down a street emotionally." Mimi and her mother shook their heads in agreement. "But it was worth it. I just feel like we missed so much in each other's lives, and we have so much to catch up on." Again, a head shaking agreement from Mimi and her mother.

"And . . ." her mother started to say something but stopped.

"What? We've been sharing so much already, Mom. And we just agreed. No more secrets," said JoJo. He sat on the arm chair next to Mimi and leaned forward to hear what their mother had to say.

Her mother exhaled deeply and picked up Mimi's hand and squeezed it. "Joe wrote me. I guess he picked up your letter writing bug."

Mimi froze. Her own hands felt icy to her. Her mother probably felt the cold touch as she held them in her hands. "What did he want? I mean, what did the letter say? Did he apologize? He should have been writing me." Mimi willed herself to stop the flood of questions. It amazed her how much was still bottled up inside her when it came to her father. She had so many questions to ask him with the biggest one being "why?" She had read a number of books on incest. They all said the molester was probably abused before. This was a true testament to the adage "hurt people hurt people." Perhaps her father had been hurt and he turned it on her. She wanted to know if this was true. But she felt a little betrayed. Why write her mother? Mimi was the one he had hurt.

Faye continued to squeeze and rub Mimi's hands as if trying to warm them. "He wants to see you."

"What!" JoJo stood up. "What does he want to see her for?"

"The letter said he wanted to talk to her." Her mother went into her own bedroom and returned with a crumbled piece of paper and a battered envelope. The paper and envelope had been balled up then smoothed out again. "I'll admit I was tempted to throw it away and forget it, but I felt like that wasn't my decision to make. If you want me to, I can go throw this away, and we can forget Joe Combs ever existed." Still standing, her mother extended the letter to Mimi.

"No." Mimi took the letter and envelope from her mother. "I want to see what he said." She opened the letter and began reading aloud.

February 10, 1997

Hello Faye,

I hope you're doing well. I know that's hard to believe, but I do hope so. I know by now the State notified you I've been released from jail. I did my time and I'm now living in the Badlands. It's okay. Crime is everywhere, but as long as an old man like me keeps to himself, things are cool. I don't know if you know this, but Mimi's been sending me letters for a few years. I kept every one of them. That girl has your gift for words and jabbing a person with them at the right time. I was hoping I could see her. Could you see if she wants to see me? In one of her letters, she said she was saved. So that's nice. Ask her if she wants to see me. We can meet anytime she wants.

Sincerely,

Joe

JoJo read over her shoulder. "He sounds like he was here yesterday and nothing has really happened. This dude . . . I know he's my father, but he's sick."

"Yes, he is sick. But I think he's sick spiritually," said Mimi, repeating something she had read somewhere, but she doubted if she had embraced this knowledge as her own.

Silently, she read the letter again, while JoJo added, "Well, I think he's selfish. Mimi, you don't have to see him."

A million thoughts flew through her mind, but one suddenly locked itself inside her head, pushing all others away. She was not as complete as she thought she was. She was not as healed as she thought she was. And she was not as free as she thought she was. She needed to know something. She needed to know why. Mimi just wanted to ask him why, and if she did not do it now, she knew she would never do it. "I want to see him."

Her mother plopped on the couch with a heavy thud. "Well, let me go with you."

"I want to go too," said JoJo.

She looked at them both. "I'd like that. But I have to talk to him alone."

"That's fine," they responded in unison. They formed a group hug and tightly held on to one another. Afterward, Mimi excused herself to the bathroom.

She had put on a brave façade for their benefit. Had they seen what she truly felt, they would have surely talked her out of meeting her father. She turned both faucet handles to full blast and sank to the floor. She hugged herself to stop her body from trembling, but it wasn't working. Not only was she shaking, but her heart was pounding in her ears and her throat was burning with dryness. Was she ready to face this man, Joe Combs, her father, her daddy? She truly did not know the answer.

She would never forget the day she told Xavier about her father. They had gone to the Botanical Gardens of the Franklin Park Conservatory. She loved the place, even though at times it caused her allergies to raise their ugly heads. It was a sacrifice she was willing to make just to take in the beauty.

They were walking along a path lined with vibrant rose-colored flowers with dark white spots in the petals and sun yellow seed pods in the center. The fragrance was inviting, and she bent closer to one to inhale. Along one wall of the flowers was a wooden bench, and they sat on it to spend more time among the beauty of the flowers. She was itching to pluck one when she noticed Xavier pulling a small box from his pocket. The box was decorated with the same flowers. He took her hand.

"Mee." He kneeled before her, saying her name again. "Mee, I love you."

But before he could go on, she slid from the bench and knelt with him. She pressed her lips to his ears and whispered what she had kept from him for far too long. Passersby gave a knowing smile to the couple. Lovers always expressed their love and many proposals had been delivered in the beauty of the gardens. If any of them knew the truth she was giving this man, the level she was taking her heart to for him, they may have shrunk back, fearing a contagious disease.

Mimi sat back on her heels and searched his face. She moved back to the bench, her eyes never leaving his face. Her heart was pounding fast and hard. He closed his eyes as if he was absorbing what she had just said.

"Xay, I understand if . . ." But he put his fingers on her lips. She fell silent.

The garden path became quiet. The tweet of an overhead bird came and went, and again the quiet took its place. A light breeze twirled the scent of flowers, and she thought they were engulfed in it like a mini tornado. Xavier was holding one of her hands.

"Mee, I love you. I will do my best not to hurt you. I will do my best to keep you protected. I will be your hero. And I will always be your friend. I will be a partner through valleys and hills. This is my resume of love I give to you. I hope you accept it and let me have the perfect job of being your husband."

She said "yes" without consideration; no thinking was required. She understood if he had asked her in tenth grade when they stood on her doorstep, and he smoothed a loose strand of her hair back on her head, she would have said "yes."

Xavier had given her the gift of unconditional love that day. She knew it well. God had been giving it to her since the day she let Christ into her heart. And she was willing to give that gift back to Xavier in marriage.

True to his promise, Xavier was always protecting her. So she was not surprised by his response when she told him about meeting her father. He insisted on driving her there and standing next to her while she talked with Joe. Mimi made several attempts to convince him it was a conversation she needed to have alone, but she consented to his presence, along with her mother and JoJo's.

Up until a few minutes before they saw her father walk into the park where they agreed to meet, Mimi thought she could talk to him by herself. But her feet and her hands shook, and her heart would not stop beating rapidly. Her brain seemed to be rattling in her head. Standing beside her mother, who was idly chatting about getting Mark a classical music CD, Mimi began to hyperventilate.

"It will help him learn better and faster," her mother said. Mimi knew the intention was to get her to think of something else until her father arrived, but all she could think of was his arrival.

"Mom . . . Mom. I can't do this."

Her mother slipped an arm around Mimi's waist. "You want to leave?"

"Nnn-no. I-I just don't think I can talk to him by myself. Will you stay?"

They had worked the plan out at home and decided that Xavier and JoJo would follow in JoJo's car and would sit some distance away in the park. Faye and Mimi would drive together in Mimi's car, and when Joe Combs arrived, her mother would go to the car with JoJo and Xavier. That had been the home plan, but Mimi could not carry it out now.

Her mother dialed her son's cell phone. "Change in plans. I'm staying with Mimi."

"Good." Mimi heard JoJo's voice boom from the phone's speaker.

Flipping the phone lid closed, Faye looked across the park. Mimi followed her gaze and saw a tall, thin man lumbering toward them wearing blue khaki pants and a blue windbreaker. On top of his head, he wore a tan baseball cap pulled down low and covering his eyes. He wore a mustache dotted with gray as well. Physically, he walked stooped.

"There's Joe," she said.

He took long strides, but they lacked confidence. When he was in front of the two women, he took off his cap. His hair was gray, and his skin was darker. Mimi couldn't look into his eyes. She wouldn't look into his face. Her eyes fixed on the space behind him.

"Joe," said Faye, with her lips already poked out and a scowl across her forehead. Her arms folded tightly.

"Faye," he responded. Then he looked at Mimi. "Mimi. You've grown into a beautiful woman. I thought your handwriting indicated how pretty you'd become."

Bile rose in the back of her throat. Hearing his voice was like having him touch her again. "You asked for this meeting. What do you want, Joe?" She pushed these words past the taste of vomit on her tongue, then she crossed her arms. To him, she and her mother must look like matching stone statues.

"I just wanted to see what you looked like and hear your voice. You were always my Nugget. I missed you."

The name "Nugget" made her cringe. "Joe, are you aware that you went to jail for raping your own daughter? If you miss me, it's your own fault."

"Now here we go," he said. "I thought we'd be able to have more conversation before you went there. Look, I paid my price. Do you know how much trouble they give a guy accused of a crime like that in jail? It was rough on me too, you know." She knew enough to know that socially, her father had very few friends. Most of the time, he was alone. But she had no sympathy for him.

"Rough on you? Rough on you!"

"Look, I was hoping to put it behind us and move on. I was hoping to start seeing you again." He reached out to touch her arm. She stepped back, and her mother raised her hand in a balled up fist.

"Hold it. Hold it." I was just going to touch your arm. "Hold it, Muhammad Ali," he said to Faye.

"Let me just ask you two questions." Tears stung Mimi's eyes, and she tried to hold them back, but they resisted her efforts and poured out. Her nose began to run and her mother rummaged in her handbag for a tissue. "Why? Are you sorry? . . . Why did you do it, Daddy? And are you even sorry you did it, Daddy?"

He rubbed the top of his head with his hand, then put his cap back on. "Look, I don't know. Why do we have to go back? Ain't you a Christian and all? Just forget the past and move forward. It don't matter." Perhaps this was easy to do for a man who no longer bothered his ex-wife or his children. Joe had never even met his grandchild, although Mimi had informed him of Mark's birth. That letter included her normal venom of hate. Every letter she wrote him was an intentional effort to remind him of the life he was missing.

Mimi's mouth flew open. Words were caught in her throat. The tears stopped like someone had turned off the faucet. Slowly she said, "This was a mistake. Good-bye, Joe." She pulled the car door open and sat in the passenger side, slamming the door behind her.

Faye looked at him. "Joe, I'm also a Christian, but I'm still working on some things, so I need to tell you that I hope you burn in hell for this." She crossed to the driver's side, got in the car, and drove away.

The meeting with Joe Combs lasted five minutes. As Mimi stared out the car window, she laughed to herself at how nearly twenty years of pain could not be resolved in five minutes. Why was she thinking it could?

Chapter 41
Have You Forgiven Him?

For Mimi, married life was one hundred times better than single life; most likely because of the single life she led before giving her life to Christ. They had been married one year, and she was still saying she'd rather be married than single. Oh, how she loved this man.

Life was definitely on a much brighter side. Her job as a journalist at the station was going well. Xavier was almost done with graduate school and was seeking an internship with a local animal hospital. She spoke often to her mother, JoJo, and Tomas, and she even had conversations with the children. Mark, whose level of patience for the telephone was nil, usually talked for about three minutes before he was off to some other activity. But JoJo and Tomas' second child, Stephanie, could actually keep Mimi on the phone for a full half hour. The phone fascinated the little girl, and she loved to talk on it even if she mostly babbled strange words.

Mimi also spoke frequently with Bizzy, who was finally in a relationship that looked like it might lead to marriage. A man from church had been watching Bizzy, and he was doing some old-fashioned courting. No kissing yet, and they had already been dating for three months.

Whenever she spoke with Bizzy, she included time for a conversation with Barbie, who was growing into a beautiful child. Barbie chatted about school and friends and begged to visit her Auntie Mimi and Uncle Xavier.

Indeed, Mimi was happier than she had ever been. However, sometimes, while sitting in her rocking chair, she became overwhelmed by thoughts and feelings that her life package was still incomplete, that she was still somehow in bondage to something. At those times, only prayer eased her and gave her peace. She expressed some of this to Bizzy during a recent visit.

Bizzy and Barbie had come to Ohio during Thanksgiving break. Mimi was shocked by Barbie's growth spurt. The last time they saw each other had been at the wedding, but Barbie had grown another inch or two. Her puffy baby cheeks were beginning to thin, and she was lean and strong for a seven year old.

Once again, Mimi found herself asking, "What are you feeding her?"

Bizzy bellowed, "It's good stock. She comes from good stock." Bizzy stood and began to model her own figure which somehow had slipped back into the athletic form of her younger years.

Mimi laughed with her. "Well, as they say, you got it going on, girl."

Bizzy sat in her seat and released a contented sigh, and they fell into the comfortable silence of best friends. The apartment mirrored their mood since Xavier, who was involved with the youth in the church, had taken Barbie with him to a bowling event. On the way out the door she bombarded him with question after question about the lanes, the balls, and the teens they would meet. Xavier answered each question with such patience it made Mimi beam. She knew without a doubt he was going to be a great dad.

This thought sparked a memory of her own father at a time when he was not the molester she now knew. She hated that a good memory of Xavier was soiled by a memory of her father. She was in deep thought when Bizzy said , "I wish I knew what your father was doing to you at the time."

The concern in Bizzy's voice ripped Mimi back to the present. "What could you have done? We were only six. And it didn't really get full force until he divorced my mom and was living in his own apartment. By then, we moved to a new school district."

"Still, sometimes I wish I knew and could have done something to help you."

Mimi sat up. "You've done more to help me in these last few years than you can ever know." She leaned over and placed her hand on top of Bizzy's. "You saved my life. You led me to Christ."

Bizzy rubbed her eyes. "I'm glad you feel that way."

"I do. It's just that . . . well . . . I wish he wouldn't invade my thoughts so much. I just want to forget him."

They fell into a silence again, but it wasn't long before Bizzy said, "So can I ask you a question?"

"Sure. Go ahead."

"Have you forgiven him?"

Mimi sat back in the chair. The question hung in the air like a billboard sign. Had she forgiven him?

"No."

"Don't you think you ought to?"

"Why, Bizzy? It's not going to do anything for me, but it will surely give him some relief. I told you what happened when we met."

In fact, she came home, took the phone into the bathroom and called Bizzy. She relayed the whole story to her while Xavier sat on the floor outside the door. She knew he was there because this is what he always did when something upset her to the point of calling Bizzy.

"I agree. But not only does the Bible tell us to forgive. I truly believe God gives us this command for a reason. I think he knows if we hold on to un-forgiveness, we never start loving again. We may live our lives like everything's cool, but deep inside something is tearing at us and not allowing us to be all we can be for Him. Forgiveness is His plan for life restoration." Bizzy leaned forward. "Do you want your life restored?"

That night she lay in bed next to Xavier. His breathing was heavy, and his arm was thrown over her stomach. She thought about what Bizzy said. Wasn't her life already restored? The weight of Xavier's arm on her stomach made her think of what it would be like to carry their child. But would her child suffer if her life was not completely restored?

She knew biblically, forgiveness was the right thing to do. God said we owed it to others since He had given it to us. Jesus forgave his tormenters and killers. And God commanded that we continue to give forgiveness daily. But, even knowing this, she did not want to give Joe Combs forgiveness.

Their first, last, and only meeting after his release from prison left her thinking he was a selfish man. She believed he would never acknowledge nor feel remorse for what he did. Withholding forgiveness was probably the last thing she could hold onto. He probably wanted it, but with her holding on to it, he would never receive it. She felt forgiving him left her with none of the cards, none of the power, none of the strength. He had it all and was in control.

The sound of her grandmother's voice filled their bedroom. Mimi grinned. She had not heard her grandmother's voice in years. It melted her heart.

She remembered the day when they had been on their way home from church, and she had asked JoJo what seventy times seven was. Exasperated at being interrupted by her, he said, "Why do you want to know?"

"Because the pastor said we have to forgive people seventy times seven. I'm counting how often I have to forgive you."

They broke into arguing and a barrage name-calling, and their grandmother quickly put a stop to it. "I know I did not hear the two of you just say what you said to each other."

They lowered their heads and said in unison, "Sorry, Grandma."

JoJo was about to add that Mimi had started it and barely got out, "But she st—" when their grandmother whipped the car to the side of the road.

"I don't care who started it, but I'm ending it. You do not talk to each other like that. Do you hear me?"

Again in unison they said, "Yes, Grandma."

"Mimi, the answer is 490. Seventy times seven is 490. But although Jesus gave that number, I don't believe he meant for you to keep a record of each time you forgive."

"See," JoJo said, but he cast his eyes down when he saw his grandmother's sharp look.

"Jesus meant that you should get into a habit of forgiving, so if you have to forgive on a regular basis, you just find it easy to forgive. This comes with practice. Doing it over and over. I'm not sure the number really matters." She put the car in drive and pulled back onto the road. "And besides, when you empty your heart of un-forgiveness, you give God a chance to fill it up with more love."

In the darkness of her bedroom, Mimi spoke aloud. "My strength comes from the Lord. Giving forgiveness to Joe will only open me up to receive more from God." Xavier stirred, caught his breath, and fell back into heavy breathing. She carefully lifted his arm and slid from under the sheets.

In the kitchen, she went to her desk and pulled out a piece of paper. The letter she wrote was short and to the point. She began with "Dear Joe." Then she scratched out his name and wrote "Daddy."

July 26, 1999

Dear ~~Joe~~ Daddy,

The last time we met, you asked me a question. You said, "Aren't you a Christian?" And yes, I am. At the time, I wasn't ready to move on, to pretend this never happened or even to forget it did. But now I am. I need to move on, so that my life will be all it can be for the Lord. Unless I use my experience, I'll only be drowned by my experience. So the last part of my moving on is to let you know I forgive you. I hope you can move forward in your life. I don't know if you need my forgiveness in order to do so, but I'm giving it to you anyway.

I'll keep praying for you.

May God touch your life and deliver you to Himself,

Mimi

Chapter 42
I'm Not Qualified to Make That Decision

The phone ringing sounded loud and obnoxious. She was folding Xavier's shirt when she heard it and started to let the machine get it, but something about the ring begged her to answer. Mimi dropped the shirt and raced to the living room. She picked it up just as the answering machine clicked on.

"Hello?" she panted into the receiver. Mimi was seven months pregnant and found carrying what seemed like a basketball wasn't a whole lot of fun. Besides that, she adored feeling the baby move and seeing its heartbeat on ultrasounds. They had decided to be surprised by the sex of the baby, though every time she went to a store she had second thoughts because it would have been so much easier to buy certain things if she knew whether she was having a boy or a girl.

"Hello. May I speak with Mrs. Mimi Wright?"

She silently groaned. Telemarketer. Wearily she said, "This is Mrs. Wright."

"Mrs. Wright. I'm calling from Temple University Hospital in Philadelphia. We got your number from your father's wallet. It was written on a note labeled 'in case of emergency.' Your father has had untreated pneumonia for some time. He's now at our hospital, and I'm afraid we're not sure about his prognosis. The pneumonia has advanced

far into his lungs, and ma'am, well, you may want to come
see him."

Mimi hung up the phone after gathering all the
information. The nurse said her father was resting at the
moment but comatose. She wasn't sure if he was aware of
people's presence, but Mimi should remain hopeful. She
advised Mimi to come soon.

When Xavier came home, she told him about it.
Sometimes when they talked, he would get a pensive,
faraway look, and she would watch his features, not wanting
to interrupt his thoughts. She watched the curve of his nose,
the length of his lashes, and the fullness of his lips. She
dreamed about kissing those lips, that nose, and those eyes.
Sometimes, he would catch her staring at him and smile at
her. As she shared this news about her father, she watched
the curve of his nose as it hitched up.

"What do you want to do?" he asked.

"I want to go."

He looked at her for a moment, and he smoothed her hair
away from her face. Xavier traced her lips with his finger,
letting it linger over the scar at the corner. Rubbing her
stomach, he said, "Okay. I'll—"

"I want to go alone."

"No, Mimi. No way."

"I need to let go of this man's sin against me, and I need to
be strong enough to trust only the Lord to help me with it."

"I'm your husband. I'm supposed to help you with it."

"And you have, but before I fall into leaning on you
exclusively, I have to lean on the Father." She pointed
upward.

He rubbed his hands together and they made the sound of sandpaper. She smiled since she had to continually remind him to use moisturizer. "Okay, but at least let me drive you. You can go in and see him by yourself, but you're not travelling alone."

She stood up. Her belly was in his face. "I knew I wouldn't be."

Joe Combs was fighting for each breath. A clear tube secured with what looked like a strap around his head extended from his mouth. The tube was connected to a machine. And every time the machine took a breath, so did he. His chest rose and fell, timed to beat of the machine. A needle was taped into his arm and liquid from an IV dripped into a tube and then into his veins. His eyes were closed but moved back and forth rapidly as if he were having a dream he could not wake up from.

At the sight of him, Mimi's stomach twisted and churned. It was as if the baby could see him as well and was disturbed by the image. The nurse stood next to her and explained the situation.

"At this point, we're on a wait and see. He's not responding well to treatment. The doctor will arrive in a moment to discuss options with you."

The woman moved toward the door, but Mimi grabbed her arm. "Options?"

"Yes, ma'am. If he should stop breathing and needs assistance to be resuscitated, you'll need to think of the options. Do you want us to revive him? Would you rather not? That sort of thing."

Mimi blinked. She came to see him, not make a life decision for him. "I'm not qualified to make that type of decision. I'm his daughter, but I haven't played any role in his life."

"I'm sorry, ma'am. It's a decision that we ask his next of kin to make, and you're it." The nurse left, and the room felt eerily quiet to Mimi. Only the pumping sound of the machine and the heaving of Joe's breathing filled the room. She pulled the extra chair in his room closer to his bedside.

"Joe," she called. "Can you hear me?" His eyes continued their rapid back and forth movement.

Mimi reached into her handbag and pulled out her Bible. She placed the bag on the floor. "Well, I don't know if you can hear me, but there's something you should know. I really do forgive you. I mailed you that letter, but in case you had trouble believing it, I came in person to let you know." She stood up and bent closer to his ear. "Do you hear me, Joe? I said I really do forgive you."

She opened her Bible and began smoothing pages. For some reason, she was a little nervous and touching the pages gave her comfort.

"Do you remember what I asked you when we met?" She stopped playing with the pages of her Bible. " I asked you two questions. I asked why you did it and if you were sorry. I'm sure you recall those questions because you didn't have an answer. I did a little research. You know, putting my college degree to work and all." She didn't know why, but her voice sounded as if she was addressing a stranger. "Anyway, I found out that sometimes people who've been molested turn and molest others. I guess I'll never know if that was your story, but I highly recommend that if you've never forgiven that person who hurt you, do it now. Let go of hurt and pain by forgiving them."

The baby kicked and she smiled down at her stomach. "You can't see this now, of course, but I'm pregnant. Two more months and another grandchild will be here. You need to understand that in my forgiveness, I would have let you visit with our child, but I would have never left you alone with him or her. I don't know the baby's sex. I do know this, it's a kicker. Boy, does this baby kick." She rubbed her stomach. "I think I would have wanted my child to know the father I knew as a little girl. You were so kind and sweet, and I knew nobody in the whole world loved me like my daddy." Her voice cracked and tears filled her eyes. "Where did all that go, Daddy? That's the one lesson I'm taking from you into motherhood. I want this child to never doubt, misunderstand or misplace my love for him or her."

She sat down and raised her voice so he could hear her. "I've got to rest a little. It's tough carrying all this extra weight. I have no idea how women with many children do it over and over again. But I'm told once our child is here we'll truly understand that it's worth the sacrifice." She stared at the machine monitoring his heartbeat. It kept changing numbers, and they were rising higher and higher as she spoke.

"I guess I'm just rambling, now. I did want to share something with you. I told you I was saved now, but I didn't tell you what that meant. It means I asked Christ to be a part of my life so that I can be all the Lord wants me to be. I don't know if you believe in Christ or God. But I know Grandma did, and she was so feisty I'll bet she told you about him. Gosh, sometimes I miss her so much."

She paused as memories of her grandmother swept through her. "Well, if you'd like to invite Christ to become a part of your life you can do it now. Even with all this stuff hooked up to you, you can still accept him. He's so powerful that your being asleep is a small thing to him. If you're interested in receiving him, just repeat after me in your heart. Say 'Dear Lord Jesus, I need you. And I invite you into my heart. I believe you are the son of God. I believe you died on the cross for the wrong things I've done, and I believe you rose again to open a relationship of eternal life between me and God. I receive you now and ask that you forgive me for all the wrong things I've done in life. I invite you to walk with me now.'"

Mimi took a deep breath and closed her Bible. "If you've sincerely said those words in your heart then you are saved now as well. And as God has forgiven you, so do I." The heart rate monitor continued to climb. "I have to go now, Daddy. May God touch you now in this life and in the life after."

She rose and walked out the door. As it closed behind her, she heard the heart rate monitor buzz an incessant sound. A flurry of orchestrated activity began to take place at the nurse's station, and her father's room quickly filled with people wearing hospital scrubs. The nurse turned and called her name, but Mimi kept walking.

Chapter 43
Her Father's Eyes

Xavier Jr. was a plump little boy with enough energy for two babies. If he was not laughing, he was trying to talk. Several times, Mimi found him moving his lips and cocking his head as if he was saying something meaningful. She resorted to answering him as if she understood. He could go on for hours with her not understanding a word he said, but he seemed to understand everything she said.

Xavier Jr., XJ for short, was an exact replica of his father, except he had something Mimi recognized the first day he was born. His grandfather's eyes. The thick lashes, the hazel-colored eyes, the slightly downward slant, and the look of longing. It was the same look her father gave her at times. The eyes would brighten when she talked to XJ, or tickled him, or gave him any form of attention. Once she acknowledged him, he would dismiss her and go on his way.

She wondered if that was what her father lacked. Did he need attention? Did he need to know someone cared about him? Did he need to know someone wanted to hear what he had to say? She wasn't sure, but she promised that XJ would know the love, the untainted love her father gave her early in her childhood.

On the day he turned one year old, they threw him a big bash with his grandparents, aunts, uncles and cousins in attendance. Bizzy and Barbie also came, and Barbie was XJ's official god-sister. She felt honored to be named to the role and took her duties seriously, even down to asking, "Does this mean if you die, he gets to come live with me, and I'll get to help raise him with Mommy and Mr. Mike?"

Xavier Sr., always amazed at the wisdom Barbie showed, answered. "Well, no, but I would like to see you influence him to be as great a person as you are."

Barbie blushed but quickly said, "I can do that."

With everyone in attendance, XJ had a ball. He chased balloons, played in the moon bounce they rented, and he gave his god-sister a sloppy cake-covered kiss. Mimi snapped the shot and stared at his eyes. They revealed what her father's eyes might have looked like if they were filled with happiness.

That night when the guests were gone and the house was quiet, Mimi sat at her desk and wrote the last letter she would ever write to her father.

September 7, 2000

Dear Daddy,

I now know what you lacked in life. I hope in the last moments of your life you finally got it. Life should not be filled with just sorrow, and if one does have sorrow they have to let God give them joy. You never got to experience joy in your life. I mean, real joy, which nothing can touch. For that I'm very sorry. I think if I'd understood all that you missed out on, I may have been able to make the sorrow go out of your eyes. But I didn't and it wasn't my responsibility, but part of all I've gone through has made me a better person. I'm hoping it's making me a better wife, a better mother, a better friend, a better daughter, a better sister, a better Christian.

Love,

Mimi

She placed the letter in an envelope, sealed it, and put it between the center pages of her Bible.

Then she took out a fresh piece of paper and let her pen flow across the page. She wrote, "Released. Chapter 1."

The Beginning...

Dear Reader,

I hope the time you've spent in this book with Mimi Combs has encouraged and inspired you.

Sexual abuse in childhood can damage a life. Without healing, one's life might be wrought with pain and unanswered questions such as "Why do I do that?" or "Why do I think like that?"

For Mimi Combs, a key part of healing was giving her life to Christ. You can join Mimi and initiate your personal healing process by giving your life to Christ. It's simple and it's up to you. No forcing. No trickery. If you want to, read on and follow these three easy steps:

• Accept Jesus as the ruler of your life and one who saves you

• Believe Jesus died for you, and through his death you are saved from the devastating effects of your sexual abuse

• Confess your belief with your mouth

The last one can be accomplished through a simple prayer which you can say right now. Repeat this aloud:

Jesus I need you. What happened to me as a child hurt me. It left me with some devastating consequences which sometimes show themselves in actions that are not pleasing to God. But I believe you gave up your life for this moment in my life. Because you died for me, came back to life, and now sit in heaven with God, I don't have to live like this. I invite you into my life. I invite you to take control of my life. Through your Holy Spirit, I know my healing has begun. Thank you and Amen.

It's that simple. You've taken the first step to taking control of your healing. Your next steps include:

1. Find a good church home. This should be a place where they teach the Bible, which is your guide on how to live as a believer in Christ.

2. Read the Bible daily. Don't just take my word or the word of others. Anytime you hear something, read it for yourself. In reading on your own, start with the New Testament in the section titled "John" and keep going on from there.

3. Start talking with God daily. This is all about praying, which is talking to God about what you read in his Bible. Talk to him about what's in your heart. Talk to him about your healing. Talk to him about everything and anything. He's ready to listen and to help.

I love you, and I am praying for your healing. If you said the prayer, let us know by emailing us at:

isaidtheprayer@surrenderedpen.com

God Bless,

Andrea

The Author

Andrea Gadson is a freelance writer, blogger, publisher, and entrepreneur. Her company, SurrenderedPen, publishes life changing books in fiction and non-fiction arenas.

Her debut novel, Released – In Search of A King, and its companion workbook empowers childhood sexual abuse victims with tools to enable their healing process.

As a victim and survivor of childhood sexual abuse, Andrea is sensitive to the need for inner healing. Her writing captures a tale that relates to every victim's own personal story.

Andrea currently resides in Southern New Jersey with her husband and partner, Derik.

Made in the USA
Middletown, DE
19 April 2016